WEB OF LIES

A BROOK BROTHERS NOVEL

TRACIE DELANEY

BOOKS BY TRACIE DELANEY

The Winning Ace Series

Cash - A Winning Ace Short Story

Winning Ace

Losing Game

Grand Slam

Winning Ace Boxset

Mismatch

Break Point - A Winning Ace Novella

Stand-alone

My Gift To You

The Brook Brothers Series

The Blame Game

Against All Odds

His To Protect

Web of Lies

Irresistibly Mine Series

Tempting Christa

Avenging Christa

Full Velocity Series

Friction

Gridlock (coming soon)

Inside Track (coming soon)

CHAPTER 1

Dex held her breath as the ping from the elevator reached her, and her leg bounced so violently she banged her knee against the underside of her desk. The second Thursday of every month—i.e. today—was her favorite day of the week. She'd take extra care with her hair and makeup and be sure to wear a nice dress and heels, just in case. Not that *he* ever noticed.

It *had* to be him, although he was early today—unusually. Punctuality wasn't Nate Brook's forte, a characteristic that irritated the hell out of her boss, obnoxious Hollywood agent extraordinaire, Bernard Sullivan.

Nate didn't care, though. And Bernard couldn't do a damn thing about it because Nate was hot property. Every agent in town wanted to sign him. Dollar signs flashed in front of their eyes at the mere thought of the potential Nate brought for huge paydays, adding to their already overflowing coffers.

It had taken Nate almost five years to really make it when, two years earlier, he'd hit the jackpot, landing the lead part in a new television show. It was already on season three with at least two more seasons commissioned. Think *Walking Dead* or *Friends*, not that those two shows had anything in common with the one Nate headlined. Their similarity lay in the huge success both had achieved. The agents of those stars were still buying holiday homes in Barbados from the residuals that continued to flood in from the shows' global distribution rights.

The elevator doors opened, and Nate strode out. Dex froze. Her pulse jolted, same as always when Nate fixed his piercing blue eyes on her. Goddamn, that man was *fine*, from the jut of his jaw to the soles of his feet, and the confident way he held himself. She couldn't get enough. As he reached her, a delicious tingle crept up her spine. To Nate, though, Dex might as well be part of the furniture for all the notice he took of her whenever he came to see Bernard. His disdain wasn't a surprise. Someone like Nate, on a steep upward trajectory to superstardom, only had starlets on his arm. Girls who knew how to keep their mouths firmly shut on the red carpet—and wide open in the bedroom.

Normally Nate gave a curt nod in her direction then entered Bernard's office without knocking and, starstruck, she'd mumble a pointless, "Go right in, Mr. Brook," after him. Except today, normal service wasn't on the agenda.

She scrambled to her feet and stood in front of the door to Bernard's office. He'd given her strict instructions he didn't want to be disturbed—by anyone. And Bernard wasn't the kind of man who took kindly to being ignored. She'd survived his vicious temper for six months, significantly exceeding the tenure of her predecessors. Bernard had sacked four assistants in the last year alone, and at twenty-two Dex was by far the youngest, yet she'd outlasted them all. She'd managed this amazing feat by being polite and non-combative—in stark contrast to her true self. She really needed this job. She did *not* need to make it easy for Bernard to make her unlucky number five.

"He's got someone with him right now, Mr. Brook. If you'd like to take a seat." She haplessly waved her arm at the row of pristine leather chairs to her right. No faux leather for Bernard. His clients expected nothing less. "Can I get you a c-coffee?"

Dex's face heated. It was the most she'd ever said to him.

He turned his attention on her which set off a delicious flutter in her abdomen. Stunning was a shitty description for someone as perfect as Nate, but Dex had never been very good with fancy words. For one brief moment, she allowed herself to imagine what those full lips would feel like slanted across her own, how protected she'd feel, wrapped in Nate's muscled arms. How she'd bet he knew exactly how to wring multiple orgasms from a woman.

His eyes narrowed. "No," he snapped at her offer of refreshment. He reached around her to grab the doorknob.

Dex shifted to block him, her heartbeat thrumming in her ears. Conflict wasn't something she enjoyed at the best of times—although when necessary, she didn't shy away—but going up against the object of her obsession? One-way ticket to pukesville.

"I really am sorry, Mr. Brook, but I can't let you go in there. Mr. Sullivan won't be long."

Those captivating eyes narrowed farther. Ignoring her instruction, he made another move to get around her. She dodged, blocking him again, her face burning. Nate moved closer, his body near enough for her to feel the heat pouring off of him. Her attention dropped to his chest. Lean, hard, his black T-shirt clinging to him, not an inch of material wasted. Like most actors, Nate's body was as important to his career as a computer or pen would be to a writer. A key tool of the job. The industry expected—no, demanded—their leading men and women to take fitness seriously. There were exceptions of course, like with anything in life, but they were few and far between.

"Is that an order?" he asked softly, dipping his head, bringing those lips so near to hers. His tone held a hint of mirth, but one look in those eyes told Dex he wasn't joking. She forced a swallow down her throat, painful as barbed wire.

"No, I-I," she stammered.

"Good."

Nate's hands gripped her waist. He lifted her out of the way as if she weighed nothing more than a feather. *Actually lifted her.* His touch branded her skin, leaving a scorching burn in its wake. The majority of Dex's dreams consisted of being touched by Nate, but nothing prepared her for the reality. Her legs wobbled as her feet made contact with solid ground once more, and she put a hand on the wall to steady herself. Nate's lips twitched. Damn the man. He must know the effect he had on women, and he was reveling in it.

Before Dex could find her voice—or her legs—Nate had pushed open the door to Bernard's office.

Dex sucked in a breath, her eyes burning at the scene inside.

Nate laughed.

Dex most certainly didn't.

"Fucking hell, Bernard," he said, laughing, while Dex averted her eyes from the sight of her boss's flabby white ass as he scrambled to his feet and pulled up his pants. The girl he'd been screwing didn't even blush. She simply smoothed her skirt in place and jumped down from the desk. It didn't escape Dex's notice that the girl wasn't wearing panties.

"You kept me waiting for *this?*" Nate sauntered into her boss's office and gracefully sank into a chair, his long legs splayed wide, hands laced behind his head.

"Hey!" the blonde said, although her annoyance was as fake as her boobs.

Bernard turned his furious gaze on Dex. "I told you I didn't want to be disturbed," he snapped, his voice colder than having a bucket of ice water poured over her head.

Dex didn't get to answer. Instead, Nate interjected with, "I'll bet you did," a deep chuckle rumbling in his chest.

Bernard ushered the woman out of his office and, with another enraged glance at Dex, slammed the door in her face.

Shit.

"WHAT *WOULD* MARJORIE SAY," Nate said, unable to keep the humor out of his voice.

Bernard's wife would kill him if she found out and, as Marjorie held the purse strings, as well as Bernard's balls, he might find himself sleeping rough on Santa Monica Boulevard if she got wind of this escapade—sans his 'nads. Nate had no doubt the blonde wannabe wasn't the first starlet Bernard had buried his cock in, but she was the first Nate had caught him with. And by God, he was going to turn this situation to his advantage.

Bernard gave him a horrified look. "You won't say anything, right? I mean, she meant nothing. Another grabby little whore after representation for a talent that doesn't exist. I only did what any red-blooded male would do and took what was on offer."

Nate hid his disgust behind the hint of a smile. He loathed men like Bernard who used their power to abuse those desperate for a helping hand in an industry as corrupt as Hollywood. Still, Nate was about to deliver a valuable lesson to Bernard and his minuscule cock—one he'd do well to remember.

"Well, that depends," Nate drawled, rubbing his chin.

"On what?" Fear turned Bernard's voice thick and heavy, and a sheen of sweat broke out on his forehead, despite the super-efficient air conditioning.

Nate rose from the chair and headed over to the corner of the office. He opened the cupboard where his agent kept the good bourbon and poured himself a drink.

By the time he'd strolled back to his chair and sat back down, Bernard had schooled his expression into one of nonchalance. He didn't fool Nate, though. Bernard was the best agent in town, but he wasn't a nice man. He only did things which benefited himself, and Nate had no doubt if he hadn't already landed the lead in *The Liar*, a title that was a brilliant irony to his own sorry excuse of a life, Bernard wouldn't have wanted to know.

As it was, Bernard had approached Nate during the filming of season one and made promises about a better pay deal. He'd delivered, renegotiating Nate's salary with the studio, which resulted in a significant increase from what his agent at the time had managed. But it wasn't benevolence. Bernard had also insisted on a thirty percent cut of the higher wage which was significantly more than Nate had paid his previous representative—not to mention a shitload more than Bernard charged his more established clients.

Nate had been patient, bided his time. Life had taught him that patience usually brought rewards. And right here was his.

He sipped his drink and eyed Bernard over the rim of his glass. "Ten percent," Nate said.

"Of what?" Bernard scratched his flabby cheek, the burst blood vessels caused by years of alcohol abuse giving him a red, blotchy appearance.

"That's your new fee."

Bernard's eyes widened as he caught on. "You have got to be joking," he choked.

Nate shook his head. "Your time of bleeding me dry is up, Bernard. I want the same deal you give to every other established actor on your books."

"Without me, you'd be earning two-fifths of fuck all. I deserve my cut."

"And you've had it. For almost two years. Ten percent," Nate repeated. "Or Marjorie gets a phone call."

"You wouldn't dare."

Nate laughed, the sound hollow and without mirth. "Don't push me. It would be a mistake."

Bernard leaned back in his chair and crossed his arms, resting them on his heart-attack-waiting-to-happen stomach. "You might think you're a hotshot in this town, but I can ruin your career like that." He clicked his fingers.

Nate placed his palms on Bernard's desk and bent forward. "Try it," he said quietly. "Here's something you don't know about me, Bernard. I'm not like the majority of power-hungry people in this town. Sure, I like acting. And I like the money. But the fame? Nah, that does nothing for me. So if I don't work in this town…" Nate shrugged. "Who gives a shit? I'll go get a job on Broadway. My whole family is in New York. Maybe it's time I went home."

Not that he had any intention of doing such a thing. The less time he spent in the company of his brothers the better. Still, Bernard didn't know that.

Bernard's face turned puce. He might be a dick, but he could do the math. Thirty percent of nothing was nothing. The better deal was to take ten percent of something. Nate settled back in his chair, fully expecting Bernard to negotiate. It wouldn't do him any good. Nate wasn't bluffing. He'd already made up his mind he wouldn't sign back on after the five seasons he'd committed to wrapped. Two more years in this crazy town, and that was it. Of course, he wouldn't tell Bernard that. Let the fat bastard think he had years of screwing Nate ahead of him.

"Twenty," Bernard said.

Nate kept his face straight and shook his head. "Ten."

"Fifteen."

Nate yawned. "I don't have all day."

Bernard's chin lowered to his chest, and Nate knew he'd won.

"Fine," he spat. "Ten percent."

Nate rose from his chair and stuck out his hand. "Nice doing business with you, Bernard. Don't worry, your secret's safe with me."

Bernard shook his hand, although he looked as though he'd rather rip it off.

Nate left the office, whistling. He pulled the door shut behind him. Bernard's PA—Lex? Tex?—was sitting behind her desk, clicking away on a keyboard, her face still burning from catching her boss with his pants down. Literally. Nate gave her a wide grin.

"He might need a drink. Make it a strong one."

Heading for the elevator, he couldn't stop laughing.

CHAPTER 2

D ex took a deep breath and, on unsteady legs, got to her feet. What had gone on between Bernard and Nate? From the looks of the latter, he'd come out of the conversation on top if his broad smile and cockier-than-normal swagger was anything to go by.

She took two steps toward Bernard's office, her mind already made up that she wouldn't mention what she'd seen. It was better to ignore the situation—even if the sight of her boss's huge pumping ass and half-flaccid cock was burned onto her retinas. What she wouldn't give to be able to unsee that horrendous sight.

Before she could push open his door, however, it swung open, and Bernard stomped out. He pointed a pudgy finger in her direction.

"You're fired."

Bile rose in Dex's throat, and prickles appeared along her spine. "Bernard, please don't. I need this job. You know I do. I'm sorry. It won't happen again."

"Damn right it won't. I told you not to let anyone in, and what do you go and do? Let Nate fucking Brook barge his way past, and now, because of your *ineptitude*, I'm seriously out of pocket."

Another jab of a finger in her direction. "So *you* can go flip burgers for all I care."

"You can rely on my discretion," she said, completely breaking her own rule to never mention what she'd seen. After all, desperate times called for desperate measures.

It was a mistake.

Bernard's nostrils flared, and the noise of his breathing increased as he turned cold, flinty eyes on her. "Oh, I know that, missy," he said through clenched teeth. "My power in this town spreads far and wide. You'd do well to remember that." With every word, he bent farther over her, and it took all of Dex's willpower not to recoil from his foul-smelling breath. And then he straightened. "But I'm not mean-spirited." Dex almost choked at his barefaced lie. "I'll give you two weeks' severance." He turned away and, as he reached the door to his office, he glanced over his shoulder. "Now pack up your stuff and get out."

The door slammed shut. A sob broke from Dex's throat. Bernard was a terrible boss, but the pay was great. She couldn't afford to take a lesser paid job and maintain the payments on Mom's nursing home. Damn Nate Brook. Why couldn't he have done as he was told and waited? And now, she was unemployed, and it was all his fault.

With trembling hands, Dex packed up her desk. Her vision kept blurring as tears sprang to her eyes. What now? She couldn't afford to be out of work for a day, let alone permanently. What about Mom? Two weeks to find something else that had equivalent pay was almost impossible, especially as she'd be asked why she'd left her last job. Even if she didn't reveal she'd been fired, it wouldn't take long for them to find out. Bernard had a big mouth. Bigger than his ass, and that was saying something. She couldn't even use the fact he'd been cheating on his wife as leverage. Bernard would ruin her. He'd said he would, and she believed him.

It didn't take Dex long to get her stuff together and, with her shoulders back and head held high, she left the building, but not before she heard the two receptionists gossiping about "Yet another one Bernard has fired."

Dex put the small cardboard box containing her things in the trunk of her car and climbed inside the ancient Ford. She turned the key in the ignition, and her exhaust made a horrible rattling sound. Goddammit. The last thing she needed was a hefty auto repair bill.

As the enormity of her situation came over her, Dex slammed the palm of her hand into the steering wheel. Fuck Bernard. And fuck Nate Brook. Maybe she should give up and move back to Wisconsin. But that would mean finding another nursing home for Mom, and she was so settled at Oak Ridge.

As soon as her anger subsided, she put the car into drive and set off for her apartment. The minute she stepped through the door, her cell rang. She answered with one hand and opened a tin of cat food for Milo with the other.

"Hello."

"When were you going to tell me you've been fired?"

Dex's heart plummeted. Elva, her sister.

"How did you find out?"

"I stopped by your office to see if you wanted to go out tonight, and there was a smug little blonde who couldn't have been older than eighteen sitting at your desk."

Dex ignored the sharp pain that raced across her chest. It hadn't taken Bernard long to replace her, even temporarily.

"When I'd absorbed it enough to get my own head around the disaster that is my life."

Her sister tsked. "Don't be ridiculous. You're young, smart, pretty enough to work in Hollywood, you'll be fine."

Dex winced at Elva's backhanded compliment. "It might be a little more difficult than that. Once it gets around Bernard fired me, it won't be easy to get another well-paying job. I'm worried about how on earth I'm going to keep the payments up on Mom's home."

"We'll work it out, sis," Elva said, her tone softening. "Maybe I can put in a bit more."

"No," Dex said, her tone firm and determined. "Any spare money you have should go on the kids. I'll figure it out." *Somehow.*

"Look, why don't we go out for a drink tonight. I haven't been out in ages. Andy isn't working, so he can look after the kids, and you can tell me why Bernard fired you."

Except I can't. Dex made a mental note to come up with a plausible story. Although her sister was discreet, Dex couldn't risk Elva letting something slip to Andy who then, in turn, told his co-workers over a beer. No, better to make something up. This town thrived on gossip, and she couldn't allow his indiscretion to get around.

"Okay," she said. "Sounds good."

A few hours later, Dex met Elva at a bar on Sunset. Dex had to bite the side of her cheek to stop the tears from coming as they hugged. Elva picked a booth near the entrance where a light breeze cooled the heat inside the bar. Even though it was a Tuesday night, the place was still busy, although not nearly as packed as a Friday or Saturday night.

After ordering their drinks, Elva took Dex's hands in hers. "I know you're worried, sis, but it will all work out. Things always do."

"I hope so," Dex said, forcing an external positivity she most certainly wasn't feeling internally.

"So…" Elva tilted her head to one side as she asked, "What happened?"

"Oh, it was nothing really," Dex said, feigning nonchalance. "Bernard's a bastard."

"We know *that*." Elva grinned. "But that doesn't give him the right to fire you for nothing. There's such a thing as worker's rights."

Dex bit her lip in what she hoped would look coy. "Okay, it wasn't nothing exactly. I was rude to a client who got a bit over-friendly, if you know what I mean. I should have just brushed it off."

"Why should you?" Elva said, outraged on Dex's behalf. "You're not a piece of meat that can be mauled. This town pisses me off. Its attitude is still unbelievably outdated, despite the #metoo campaign."

Dex shrugged. "It doesn't matter anyway. What's done is done. I'll pick myself up and start looking for another job in the morning."

Elva's cocked eyebrow gave Dex a clear message that said, "This isn't over", but at least her sister let it drop for now.

Dex drank three Long Island Iced Teas that she really couldn't afford, but the alcohol did cool the fire brewing inside. Calling it a night, she and Elva wandered outside. Once Dex had settled Elva in a taxi—her sister was traveling in the opposite direction to Dex—she glanced left and right, hoping to spot another soon. While she waited, her gaze caught a familiar figure on the other side of the street. Someone she'd recognize in a heartbeat, considering she spent far too much time studying him. Every. Single. Thing.

Nate Brook.

He was sporting a baseball cap pulled low over his eyes in an attempt at a disguise, but she'd know that over-confident strut anywhere. He was with a couple of friends. They were laughing as they walked down the street, without a care in the world.

He clearly hadn't given her, or the trouble he'd gotten her into, a second thought. Burning rage hissed through her, demanding release. Her hands formed into fists. What a bastard! Gorgeous, yes. Her secret obsession, absolutely, but still a bastard. How *dare* *he* be out enjoying himself when he'd gotten her fired. He needed a lesson, and she was going to give it to him—with both barrels. What else did she have to lose? If she hadn't been on the wrong side of sober, she'd never pluck up the courage to tackle him, but the alcohol had emboldened her.

She started across the road. "Hey, you," she yelled as he and his friends were about to enter a club.

A car came out of nowhere, blaring its horn at the crazy woman in the middle of the street. Dex flipped up her middle finger as the car swerved around her. The driver's arm came out of the window, and he returned the favor.

Nate and his two friends turned around. Nate gave her an arrogant stare followed by a good old-fashioned eye sweep. When he didn't see anything that caught his interest, he shoved one of his friends on the shoulder, encouraging him inside.

"Nate Brook, stop right there."

Nate paused, turning his attention to her. "Sorry, sweetheart, no autographs tonight."

His friends sniggered and stepped inside. Nate followed. Dex put her hands on her hips. Fine. If he wanted his humiliation to be public, she was happy to oblige.

She sprinted the rest of the way across the street and stormed into the club after them. She hadn't gotten very far when a huge guy put his arm out, stopping her from going any farther.

"Can I help you, miss?"

Dex set her shoulders. If she didn't act quick, she'd lose her chance. So she went for it.

"Nate Brook, you complete bastard," she yelled at his retreating back. "You fucking got me fired today."

Nate froze, one foot in front of the other. He slowly turned around, recognition sparking in those magnetic eyes of his.

"You're Bernard's PA," he said.

Dex's anger scored a fiery trail through her veins. She was going to kill him. "Not anymore, thanks to you," she hissed.

Nate frowned and stroked his chin. Then he gestured to the bouncer to let her through. She stepped over the threshold and found her elbow in a firm grip as Nate Brook propelled her into the club.

CHAPTER 3

N ate towed Bernard's pint-sized PA—he still couldn't remember her fucking name—toward the VIP area. Velvet ropes were pulled back as he approached and then were immediately dropped back in place. He gave his friends the nod that he wanted a few minutes alone to find out what the hell was going on. Two bouncers stood in front of the rope. No one was getting through them unless Nate gave the go-ahead.

He let go of... of... *oh for fuck's sake.* "What's your name?"

She looked at him with utter loathing and planted her hands on her hips. "I've worked for Bernard Sullivan for six months, during which time you must have been to the office on more than ten occasions, and you don't know my *goddamn name.*"

Nate theatrically clamped his hands over his ears as she screamed the last part. "All right, sweetheart, no need to pierce an eardrum."

She jabbed a finger in his face. "My name is Dex, you complete and total ass. And you got me fired from my job. A job I *need!*"

Nate took a step back and made a calming motion with his hands. "One thing at a time, sweetheart. Firstly, what kind of a name is Dex for a girl?"

Her eyes widened. "Are you trying to be rude on purpose, or does it just come naturally?"

Nate's lips twitched. This one was a little fireball. It had been a while—too long—since he'd been called out on his shit. Apart from his brothers, obviously. One of the reasons he kept his distance. Not the main reason, of course. Regardless, he was definitely enjoying the experience.

"If you think that was rude, you must have led a very sheltered life."

She kicked her chin up and drew herself up to her full height, which must have been all of five-foot one if she was lucky.

"What's the point," she said. "The great Nate Brook is hardly likely to give a shit about a nobody like me."

She went to brush past him.

Nate stuck out his arm. "Whoa there, Titch. Where d'you think you're going?"

She crossed her arms over her chest. "Titch? What the hell does that mean? Some stupid Hollywood 'in joke' I presume."

Nate sniggered. It was a word he'd picked up at school in London. It meant a small person. Suited Dex perfectly, in height if not in personality. When he didn't answer her question, she huffed.

"I'm going home," she spat. "To search for a job."

She tried to leave once more. Nate grabbed her around the waist and lifted her in the air. She weighed next to nothing, but what she lacked in physical stature, she made up for in one hell of a pair of lungs, evidenced by the loud squeal she made when he picked her up and plunked her on the navy leather couch at the back of the VIP area.

He stood in front of her, barring her way. "You'll leave when I say you can leave. And can you drop the decibel level? I can barely hear myself think."

Her mouth dropped open in astonishment at his sheer gall. "You can't keep me here against my will. And I am *not* loud."

He grinned. "I can do anything I want to, sweetheart. Fancy your chances getting past me, and then past them two?" He jerked his head back, indicating the bouncers standing guard. "And believe me, loud is a polite term. Fucking deafening would be more accurate."

Her lips pressed together in a fierce grimace as she glared at him, fire pouring from navy-blue eyes that had him staring longer than he should have. He could almost see her mind ticking over, weighing up her options. And then her shoulders bowed in defeat.

"If you must know, my dad named me after Soren Dexter, the pro-footballer who played defense for the Green Bay Packers. Dad was a huge fan. It didn't occur to him that Dexter wasn't the most suitable name for a girl. I use Dex because... well, just because."

"At least you weren't named after Dexter Morgan." Dex gave him a confused head-tilt—which was fucking adorable by the way —and he grinned. "TV show. The male lead, Dexter, was a serial killer. It's a great show. You should get it on Netflix."

"Oh, nice." Dex's tone dripped sarcasm. "Although I'd like to kill you for getting me fired today."

Nate took a seat beside her, his arm stretched along the back of the couch. He didn't miss the burn creeping up Dex's neck, and the quiet sigh she let out as his thigh pressed against hers. Looked like Little Miss Dex had a crush on him. Except unlike the other starlet sycophants who constantly pawed and begged for attention, Dex wasn't going to let the small matter of physical attraction detract from the actual bodily harm she wanted to dole out.

"Yes, let's get to that. So are you gonna tell me what happened?"

Her eyes flashed all kinds of hatred his way. "I wasn't supposed to let anyone into Bernard's office."

Nate chuckled. "And we all know why, don't we?"

Dex's lips twitched, despite her predicament. Maybe she was

starting to thaw out. Good. He wanted to see whether he still found her interesting when she wasn't breathing fire.

"And because you ignored my instruction, Bernard fired me."

Nate's temper rose on her behalf, even though before tonight, he'd barely noticed she existed. Bernard Sullivan was a fuckwit and a bully. To blame a woman who didn't stand a chance of stopping Nate, even if she'd been several inches taller, was unacceptable.

As an idea took hold, Nate got to his feet and held out his hand.

"Okay, Titch, let's go."

Dex frowned. "Where to? And stop calling me Titch."

Nate flashed her the kind of grin he knew from experience girls found hard to resist. Dex was no exception. Without question, she took his hand, the resultant blush confirming his earlier assertion. The thought brought a smile to his lips. He liked this little dynamo, and he wasn't going to stand for Bernard Sullivan thinking he could get away with what he'd done to her.

Not if Nate had anything to do with it.

DEX SAT QUIETLY beside Nate as he drove east. Her senses were on high alert sitting so close to him. She breathed deeply through her nose. His cologne tickled her nostrils, the scent extremely pleasant. She'd even go so far as to say sensual. Oh, who was she kidding? The masculine smell of him, his close proximity, the way he'd held her hand as they'd left the bar—yeah, she was warm from the inside out.

All those months she'd fantasized about what she'd say to Nate Brook if she got the chance, but those practiced conversations had been moot when he'd never so much as glanced her way. Yet today, he'd touched her not once, but three times. At the office earlier and then twice in the club. And now she had the chance to say everything she'd ever wanted, the proverbial cat had gotten her damn tongue.

"How did a girl like you end up working for Bernard Sullivan anyway?" Nate asked.

Dex bristled—and her tongue untwisted itself. "What do you mean, 'a girl like me'? One who doesn't think fame and fortune is everything, one who isn't pretty enough, or one that won't let a disgusting fat bastard like Bernard stick it in me in the hope he'll get me a walk-on part in the latest sitcom to hit Hollywood Boulevard?"

Nate briefly took his hands off the steering wheel to hold them in the air. "Whoa, mama. That's a fucking big chip you've got there. Must be weighing you down. Is that why you're so small?"

It was a good job Nate's lips twitched, because if she hadn't figured he was teasing her, she'd have slammed her elbow into his gonads.

"I'm small in stature. Big in personality."

Nate threw back his head and laughed, two rarely seen dimples briefly softening the brooding features he was known for. "You're not kidding."

Dex couldn't help herself. He might be an arrogant ass who was far too attractive for his own good, but she found his humor infectious. She started laughing along with him.

"I don't think you understand how tough it is for someone like me. I'm not interested in being an actress, a producer, anything to do with the film industry. I want to do an honest day's work for an honest day's pay."

"If you're not interested in movies, why are you living in Los Angeles?"

Dex grazed her bottom lip with her teeth. Nate wouldn't care that Mom's nursing home sucked every spare penny from Dex. He'd hardly be interested in the fact she worked most weekends on the checkout at her local supermarket because as well-paid as the job with Bernard was—had been—it wasn't nearly enough to pay the bills that kept rolling in. He wouldn't give a shit that she lived on packs of ramen noodles that were filling and damned cheap.

Instead she settled for, "My sister lives close by."

"Is she in the business?"

"No, but her husband is. He's a cameraman."

"Ah, I see."

No, you don't.

Nate turned into a tree-lined street with grass edges so perfect, they had to have been styled by a hairdresser. Not a blade of grass was out of place. They must be in Beverly Hills. Nowhere else in the greater Los Angeles area smelled of so much money. Dex guessed where they were going, and she stiffened in her seat.

"Tell me we're not going to Bernard's house."

Nate gave her a sideways glance. "I could. But I'd be lying."

Dex covered her face with her hands and groaned out an, "Oh, Christ, no."

"Relax," Nate said. "I'll do all the talking. In five minutes, you'll have your job back."

Dex wanted to scream at him, "What if I don't want my job back?" It wouldn't be a complete lie. She *didn't* want her job back. Especially after Bernard had been so foul to her, let alone the fact she'd never be able to forget the image of his ass pumping up and down as he'd heaved over that girl.

Yep, she definitely didn't want her job back—but she *needed it.*

Dex expelled a resigned sigh. Reading people was a specialty. She'd known Bernard was a sleaze at her interview, but she'd been confident she could handle him. And she had. Even when he'd propositioned her within her first week on the job. She'd politely but firmly turned him down while pandering to his ego. She made it all about her *professionalism.* Of course Bernard was attractive… she'd lied. Of course she'd be interested if they weren't working together, but she made a point of never dating people she worked with. He'd lapped it up and the wet kiss he'd planted on her cheek had been the last time he'd touched her. She'd scrubbed her entire body that night, rubbing her skin raw.

Nate, though, was an interesting character. He was a man who did precisely as he pleased. If he'd decided they were visiting Bernard at midnight, then his course was set. There would be no diverting him from that. But Nate only cared about number one. So, the fact he'd decided to treat her like some sort of charity case had her confused. What was his game? He wasn't interested in her sexually, she was sure of that. But Nate would demand payment of some sort, the form it took being something she'd have to wait for, on tenterhooks.

Nate pulled up outside a mansion: wrought-iron gates topped with the initials BS—which of course stood for Bernard Sullivan, but she thought Bull Shit worked much better—protected a house so large, her apartment would fit inside the garage. A paved driveway with lawn either side led up to the columned front door. Window boxes housed a spray of colorful flowers and, if Dex craned her neck, she could make out a balcony which wrapped around the sides and, potentially, the rear of the property. A pretentious house for a pretentious man.

"Ready?" Nate asked as he wound down the driver's-side window.

Dex shook her head. "Not in the slightest."

Nate ignored her reticence and pressed the buzzer. Five seconds later, it was answered.

"Sullivan residence. Whom may I say is calling?"

Dex held back a nervous giggle at the formal greeting and the absence in mentioning the late hour. Maybe visitors at any time of the day and night wasn't unusual for Bernard.

"It's Nate Brook. I need to see Mr. Sullivan urgently."

"One moment, sir."

Nate flashed a grin at Dex who'd decided chewing on her nails might quell the violent churning in her stomach.

Within thirty seconds, the wrought-iron gates eased open.

Nate drove up the driveway. He parked directly outside Bernard's front door and climbed out. When Dex remained frozen in place, he dipped his tall frame and looked inside the car.

"Coming?"

"Do I have a choice?" Dex grumbled.

Nate chuckled. "You're welcome," he said, slamming the car door behind him.

On heavy legs, Dex got out of the car and trudged after him. By the time she caught up, the front door was open, a uniformed maid waiting to greet them.

"Mr. Brook. Mr. Sullivan is in his study. Follow me please."

Dex waited for her to ask who Nate's companion was, but she simply waved them both inside and clicked the door shut behind them. Maybe this wasn't the first time Nate had visited Bernard late at night with a girl in tow. Jealousy nipped at her insides, which she immediately quashed.

The interior of Bernard's home was as opulent as the exterior. Highly polished marble floors led to a carpeted staircase, with the fanciest balustrade Dex had ever seen. In the center of the hall-way, an oversized vase was filled with enough flowers to stock a florist's, and above, a sumptuous chandelier hung from an ornate ceiling.

The maid's soft-soled shoes didn't make a sound as she led them to the other side of the hallway. Dex kept her head facing forward, even though she was dying to have a good look around. The maid drew to a halt in front of a thick, oak door. Nate's fingers touched hers, sending a shockwave of electricity shooting up her arm.

"Say nothing. Let me lead," he whispered as they were ushered inside.

Bernard was sitting behind an enormous desk—also oak—with a green lamp providing additional lighting. His head came up when they walked inside. He spotted Nate first, and his eyes narrowed. And then his gaze fell on Dex.

"What the hell is going on?" he said, getting up from behind his desk. Unlike in the office where he wore suits, Bernard's casual attire clung to his larger-than-was-healthy frame. His stomach protruded over the top of a pair of jeans. Really, a man with Bernard's physique should not wear denim.

"I need a quick word, Bernard," Nate said, casually strolling over to a couch and folding himself onto it with a gracefulness that took Dex's breath away. He really was beautiful. She should have taken the opportunity to study him up close on the drive over, but she'd been too nervous. Still was. Butterflies—and not the good kind—swarmed her stomach, and she surreptitiously wiped clammy hands on her jacket.

"What the fuck is this bimbo doing here?"

Dex locked her spine, crossing her arms over her chest. She clamped her jaw shut—with great difficulty.

"She's with me," Nate said, his tone dripping ice.

His fingers curled around her forearm, and he tugged her down beside him. His words, as well as his touch, sent a delicious tingle spreading through Dex's chest, and goosebumps sprang up everywhere. Even though it meant nothing, she'd file that statement away for later and use it in another fantasy about Nate while she lay alone in the dark, her fingers inching inside her panties.

"And you'd do well to mind your language and your fucking tone," he added.

Bernard's face reddened. "If you're here for another conversation about my cut, you've wasted your time."

Nate laughed. "No, I think a sixty-six percent reduction in your cut is enough for one day."

Dex withheld a gasp. So *that* was what had put Bernard in such a foul mood.

"Then what the hell *do* you want, because I wasn't bluffing, Nate. You can only push me so far, and you've hit the limit."

Nate rubbed his chin thoughtfully as he scrutinized Bernard's face. Dex found her eyes drawn to his long, slender fingers. She'd bet they were skilled hands. What a shame she'd never get to find out the amount of pleasure they could give.

"Dex tells me you fired her today."

"So what?" Bernard spat. "She couldn't follow a simple fucking order."

Nate slowly rose from the couch. In three long strides he'd reached Bernard. The men weren't too different in height, but something about the way Nate held himself made him the more threatening figure, despite Bernard's considerable bulk. Dex shivered. She hoped she'd never be on the other end of Nate Brook looking at her with such menace.

"She followed the order just fine. *I* ignored it."

"Her bad."

"No." Nate poked Bernard in the chest. "Your bad. And my bad. She did nothing wrong, so here's what's going to happen. Either you give Dex her job back, or I'm going to have a quick chat with Marjorie."

Bernard's eyes widened. "We had a deal," he said, spittle forming in the corners of his mouth. "A reduction in my fee for your silence."

Nate nodded. "That was before I heard what happened to Dex. I'm revising our deal."

Bernard's fists shook, and he gave Nate an intense, fevered stare. Nate didn't budge an inch. He looked almost bored. Dex half-expected him to yawn and check his watch.

"I'll ruin you."

Nate barked out a mirthless laugh. "Oh, Bernard, don't you remember anything from our conversation earlier? Let me remind you. I. Don't. Care. I don't need millions in the bank, or adoring fans knocking down my door, or my face on the front of GQ to define who I am. I act because I *like* acting. If it isn't in TV shows and movies, it'll be Broadway, or London's West End. Or a local fucking theater that seats twenty." He tapped his temple.

"Get it into your thick skull. You have zero leverage over me. Zero."

Whatever Dex had thought about Nate Brook prior to that moment disappeared as fast as the morning mist was burned away by the sun. She'd completely misjudged the guy. She'd fallen for the oldest trick in the book and allowed herself to be swayed by the public image, mistaking it for reality.

A vein throbbed in Bernard's forehead. He flashed a hate-filled glare at Dex then turned back to Nate. "Fine. She can have her job back. Now leave my house."

Nate shook his head. "Two things. First, you will apologize to Dex for the way you treated her."

"Over my dead body," Bernard said.

Nate looked him up and down. "The way you're living, Bernard, that won't be too far away. Now apologize."

Dex held her breath, wondering what Nate's next move would be if Bernard refused again.

"Fine. I apologize," Bernard said, the cold glance in her direction telling Dex he would make her pay.

She'd witnessed Bernard in not one, but two, humiliating circumstances, and a man like him wanted to present a very different public image. She held back a shudder and lifted her chin.

"I accept," she said, the first words she'd uttered since arriving at Bernard's home.

"Excellent," Nate said, giving her a quick wink. "Secondly, see Dex here has a very difficult job working for you. She has to deal with arrogant pricks like me on a daily basis, not to mention having to look at your ugly mug every day. So, I think a pay rise is in order."

Dex's gasp was drowned out by Bernard's, "Fuck off."

Nate shrugged. "Fine. If that's the way you want it." He cocked his head at Dex and wandered over to the door. She followed. "It's been ages since I saw Marjorie. You really should take her out more, Bernard."

For a big man, Bernard moved fast. Nate had only opened the door a couple of inches when Bernard slammed his large hand against it. "Okay, okay. Five percent."

"Fifteen," Nate hit back.

Dex's heart thundered, the soft muscle pounding against her ribcage. She leaned close to Nate, her elbow digging into his ribs. "Don't push it. I need this job," she muttered out of the side of her mouth.

Nate ignored her as Bernard countered. "Ten."

Nate laughed. "This isn't a negotiation, Bernard. Fifteen percent. Backdated to the start of the month."

After a few seconds, Bernard's shoulders actually sagged in defeat, and he nodded curtly. "Deal," he said through a clenched jaw.

Jesus, Nate Brook was something else. Bernard was feared and revered in this town, and yet Nate had stood his ground and won —for the second time that day.

He turned cold eyes on Dex. "You start at eight in the morning. And your first job is to fire the stupid blonde temp and sort out the fucking mess she's made of my calendar."

"Yes, Bernard," Dex said, purposely keeping her voice measured, with a hint of obedience. The latter only because deference would soothe Bernard's shattered ego and make her life a touch easier.

Nate opened the door. "Nice doing business with you, Bernard. Say hi to Marjorie for me." He stepped through and then hesitated. "Behave, Bernard. Dex has my number. If I hear you're bullying or mistreating her in any way, the deal is off."

And with that, he took hold of her hand—yes, *her hand*—and they left.

Once inside the car, Dex took a deep breath and let it out slowly. After witnessing such a stressful altercation, her lungs needed the oxygen she'd starved them of while inside. As Nate drove through the gates and back onto the road, Dex turned to him.

"Thank you."

Nate's lips curved into a brief smile. "You're welcome."

"You renegotiated his fee?" Dex said.

Nate nodded. "He's been fleecing me for too long. I've been waiting for an opportunity to get one over on Bernard, and you, my dear Dex, provided me with not one but two. It's me who should be thanking you."

Dex laughed. "Poor Bernard."

Nate snorted. "Don't feel too sorry for him. He'll hardly be searching in dumpsters for food—unless Marjorie finds out about his predilection for starlets with big tits."

He waggled his eyebrows. Dex laughed again.

She gave him directions to her apartment, using the thirty minutes to take a mental picture of everything about Nate—the cut of his shirt clinging to his muscular chest, the way his biceps bunched every time he lifted his arm, the angle of his strong jaw, those sexy hands that gripped the steering wheel, how he smelled. *Especially* how he smelled. Yep, she locked away every single thing in a file in her mind. When she was alone, she'd open it and let her imagination run wild.

"Thanks for the lift," she said as he pulled up outside her apartment, her hand on the door handle.

"Wait." Nate took out his wallet, and for a horrible moment, Dex thought he was going to offer her money, like an escort or a call girl. Instead, he held out a business card. "If Bernard gives you any trouble, if he even looks at you the wrong way, or says one sharp word, you call me."

With trembling fingers, Dex accepted the card. Oh, this night got better and better. Nate Brook had voluntarily given her his contact details. She tucked it in her pocket, vowing to get it laminated the following day in case she ripped it by mistake.

"I will, although after what you did back there, I think he'll be watching his mouth for a while yet."

Nate grinned. "Maybe, but remember, animals are at their most dangerous when injured. I fully expect Bernard to come out fighting at some point."

"Aren't you worried?"

"Nah."

Her eyes flickered over his face for signs he was lying, but his expression was smooth and worry free.

"Well, thanks again." She hesitated for the briefest of moments, restless with the urge to climb onto Nate's lap and put her mouth on his. To rub herself on his crotch as his heavy, thick erection rocked against her center.

"Do you need a hand?"

She twisted her head. "With what?" she asked, wondering if he could read minds.

Nate pointed his chin at the door. *Oh. Dumbass.* Heat flooded her face. She dragged her mind back to the present and away from Nate's erection potential.

"No, I can manage." She hid her blush as she climbed out and shut the door. From the safety of the sidewalk, she waved as Nate drove away. His hand came up inside the car, and he waved back.

For a few seconds, Dex stared at the business card he'd given her, then hugged herself and went inside.

CHAPTER 4

Nate's alarm went off at four a.m. He groaned and fumbled for his phone, swiping across the screen to shut the damn thing up. It would buy him five minutes snooze time. He'd only gotten in at one in the morning and he needed the extra sleep. He shouldn't have gone out the previous evening, especially knowing he had to get to the studio for an early morning shoot. He'd have regretted it if the evening had only consisted of a couple of drinks at a boring club, but the unusual turn of events had definitely been worth the heavy eyelids and lethargy he'd spend the rest of the day struggling to shake off.

He showered, dressed, grabbed an apple from the fruit bowl, and headed out. His driver was waiting curbside, a perk provided by the studio, although Nate usually preferred to drive himself. Still sometimes being indulged had its benefits. He'd be able to nap on the way in.

After being lulled to sleep by the moving vehicle, the quick jerk to a stop woke him. Feeling worse than if he hadn't napped, he rubbed his eyes and then scrubbed his face. His car door was opened and, greeting Nate with a grin far too bright at such an early hour, was his director.

"Morning. You made it."

Nate swung his legs out and, making sure he didn't bang his head, unfolded his large frame and clapped Mike on the shoulder.

"Did you doubt me?"

"Yep. Especially when I had a report that said you headed off with a petite redhead at about eleven-thirty last night."

Nate raised an eyebrow. "Is nothing sacred in this town?"

"Nope." Mike laughed. "I hope you've got plenty of energy left. Gonna be a long day."

"Yep, all good. I was in bed by one. Alone."

Mike's forehead creased. "She blow you off, or just blow you?" He cackled at his own joke.

"Neither," Nate said curtly, the disparaging dismissal of women in Hollywood grating on his few remaining nerves. "Not that it's any of your business."

Mike frowned. "Who's bitten your ass this morning?"

Nate didn't answer.

Mike huffed, muttered "Goddamn actors" under his breath, and disappeared into the studio. Nate headed toward makeup where he'd spend the next ninety minutes being turned into his character.

"Morning, Shirl," Nate said to the lead makeup artist on set, a formidable woman in her early fifties. "I need to grab a quick sandwich before we start. I've only had an apple."

Shirl shook her head and patted the seat. "Sit. I'll get one of the girls to fetch you something."

Nate did as he was told. No one messed with Shirl. Not if you wanted to keep your balls.

Mike hadn't been joking about the long day, and by the time Nate climbed into the back of his car later that evening, he could barely keep his eyes open. Now he was alone, though, his thoughts turned to Dex. He wondered how her first day back working for Bernard had gone, whether she'd had any trouble with the fat fuck. When Nate had given her his contact details the previous night, her surprise had been evident in the way her brow crinkled and her fingers trembled as she'd taken the rectangular card from him. What she didn't know was how surprised he'd been that he'd offered it. His cell phone number was a closely guarded secret. The only people who had it were his brothers, a couple of close friends, his agent, and whatever director and producer he happened to be working with.

And now Dex had it. Could be dangerous. She could sell it, tell all her friends, drunk dial him at three in the morning. It wouldn't be a disaster. He'd only have to change his number, but it'd be a pain in the ass.

Except he didn't think she'd do any of those things. Something about her screamed integrity, a word most people in this town ignored. A word *he* ignored when it suited.

His driver dropped him off outside his house, and Nate headed straight inside, thankful there were no paps with their goddamn cameras hanging around. His sudden fame two years earlier—and the resulting interest of the press and fans alike—was something Nate still hadn't gotten used to. He loved the process of making films and TV, adored the acting side of the business, but hated the surrounding bullshit. The shallowness of the industry and everyone in it was something Nate put up with, but he refused to let it touch him. He was known for being standoffish, never one to mix with other actors or any of the crew. He had a few friends, none of whom worked in the same field as him, but they didn't truly know him. No one did. Not even his three brothers.

And for good reason.

If his brothers found out what Nate had uncovered, it would blow his family apart.

Hell, it had blown him apart when he'd discovered the letter on a return trip home for Thanksgiving. In an instant, everything he understood to be true incinerated on a bonfire not of his making.

Seven years on, and the feelings reading those words had

ignited still scored his insides. Before then, Nate had been happy, excited about the future, enjoying his time in London studying at RADA, loving the independence being in another country had afforded him. And then boom! His life had blown up. He still couldn't eat turkey. Every time he tried, it stuck in his throat.

But the faded black ink on yellowing paper had explained a lot. A whole damn lot. And he'd made a vow, right then and there, that he'd keep the details of the explosive letter to himself. That he'd shoulder the secret, bury the devastating news deep down inside where he hoped, over time, his pain would recede. The problem was, though, that keeping the details close had created a distance between him and his brothers that he didn't know how to fix. But he couldn't tell them. He couldn't do that to their memory of Mom and Dad. Jax wasn't the only one who put family first.

Nate opened the fridge and lifted out a chicken pasta salad. He ate the solitary meal for one, then stripped down to his boxers and flopped onto the bed. Another early start in the morning, so he'd better get some rest. But despite the lethargy in his body and the heaviness of his lids, he couldn't get to sleep, his mind, instead, full of a certain pint-sized redhead with curls that cascaded down her back, plump, rosy lips he wanted to kiss, slate-gray soulful eyes he could drown in, and a temper fiery enough to singe flesh. He could only imagine how such intense passion would manifest itself in the bedroom.

Except imagining such things was a stupid fucking idea, because now he had a raging hard-on to contend with as well as an overactive imagination.

He launched off the bed, his erection tenting his boxers as he stomped into the bathroom and flicked on the shower. His first thought was to turn it ice cold, but then a second thought crept in, one much more appealing. Dex was all wrong. Too young, too innocent. But that didn't mean he couldn't use her image for a little self-administration. She might not have registered on his radar until she'd accosted him outside the club, but now she was inside his head—and goddammit, he couldn't get her out.

With steam filling the bathroom, he shucked his underwear and stepped into the shower. Bending his head, he gripped his dick with one hand and braced the palm of his other hand against the tiled wall. With the image of Dex firmly fixed in his mind, hip cocked out to one side as she flayed him with her eyes and lashed him with her tongue, it took less than a minute for him to climax. He groaned loudly, his body trembling as pulse after pulse of cum spurted onto his hand, immediately washed away by the torrent of water.

He switched off the shower and cursed. Instead of feeling sleepy, he was amped, horny. He toweled off and walked naked back into the bedroom, forcing himself between the sheets when what he really wanted was to drive over to Dex's apartment building, knock on every door until he found the right one, and fuck her until his dick fell off.

But he wouldn't do that—because he actually liked her. Not only for the soft place between her legs that his cock would like to get intimately acquainted with, but *her*. The woman. The last thing she needed was a man like him in her life. She deserved so much better. For once, he'd do the selfless thing and leave her alone.

Fuck, doing the right thing sucked.

On Saturday evening, Nate's driver dropped him off at home. It had been a long, exhausting week, and his body ached from the action scenes he'd filmed that day. Yet, as tired as he felt, the thought of another night spent alone didn't appeal. Then again, neither had the offers to go for a drink with the crew. His friends would be up for a heavy drinking session. He wasn't shooting the next day, so it wouldn't matter if he spent the entire time in bed with a hangover,

TRACIE DELANEY

but he didn't have the energy to put on a show tonight, to pretend he had the perfect life so everyone else could ratify their jealousy.

The door to his house closed behind him with a hollow thud, and he headed straight for the kitchen, his stomach growling with hunger. It had been too busy today to even fit in lunch. He opened the fridge. Damn. Nothing in. Pizza didn't appeal, nor did takeout. With a curse, Nate grabbed his keys and set off for the nearest grocery store.

He drove into a parking space as far away from the store as possible and grabbed a baseball cap from the glove compartment. He pulled it low over his eyes and added sunglasses, even though dusk had already fallen. In LA, people wore sunglasses *everywhere,* so he'd hardly stick out.

Turning the collar up on his jacket, he kept his head down and wandered into the store. Harassed moms dragged screaming children by the hands as they dashed down aisles, stuffing their carts with chips and chocolate and ice cream, no doubt staving off the guilt of feeding their kids such unhealthy food by telling themselves their offspring deserved a *treat.* After all, it was the weekend. Didn't everyone treat themselves at the weekend?

Nate didn't linger. He went straight to the meat counter at the back of the store. Steak, salad, maybe some mango sorbet or his favorite—frozen yogurt. With his arms piled high, he headed for the fast lane at the checkout. The guy in front had twelve items, which pissed Nate off. Couldn't the fucker read? Ten items. Ten fucking items. He let out a heavy sigh but resisted the urge to call him on it. Bringing attention to himself was the last thing he wanted. In, out, fast as possible, and then get the hell outta there.

Nate kept his head bowed as the guy in front packed up tonight's dinner, but when his own items remained stationary on the belt, he lifted his head, expecting to see the cashier tapping on her cell or picking her teeth, anything other than what she was meant to be doing—serving him.

34

Instead, his gaze met an elfin face, high cheekbones, soft gray eyes surrounded by dark lashes, and that mouth he'd fantasized about fucking while he'd gotten himself off last night.

Dex.

She stared at him, those plump, rosy lips falling open. Color flooded her cheeks, and she wrinkled her forehead, following her confusion up with a slight shake of her head.

"Would you like me to pack for you, sir?" she said, clearly deciding to ignore the fact they knew each other.

Nate glanced over his shoulder. There were no customers waiting behind him.

"What the hell are you doing here?" he asked. "Has Bernard fired you again?"

If he had, Nate was going to rip him a new asshole.

She shook her head and began scanning his items and placing them with infinite care into a plastic bag.

"Then what's going on?"

She scanned the last item. "That'll be nineteen thirty-six, sir." She avoided eye contact, her gaze fixed somewhere around his navel.

Irritated, Nate leaned in. "The only time I like sir as a form of address is in the bedroom. So call me *sir* again, and I'll expect a different kind of service."

Dex's head snapped up, and the look on her face, a hint of delight tinged with anxiety, triggered something in him. Time to stop lying to himself. He wanted her, this girl he didn't know and hadn't given a shit about until a few days ago. Yet now, with the image of her sprawled naked on his bed, his to tease, to tantalize, to play with as he saw fit, his dick hardened.

"What are *you* doing here?" she seethed.

He gave her one of his best "what the fuck?" stares. He cocked his head at the bag she'd packed for him. "Shopping. The reason you're here, though, is much more interesting."

She shrugged. "We're not all mega-rich stars with houses in Malibu and infinity pools overlooking the ocean."

Nate barked a laugh. He wasn't exactly eating beans to stay alive, but he had a ways to go before he hit the rich list. "Correct. We're not."

She narrowed her eyes, but when he stared her down, she relented. "I need the extra money."

"Why?"

He'd seen her apartment building. It wasn't in the best part of town, but not the worst either. She should be able to more than afford the rent on what Bernard was paying her *before* the raise Nate had forced him into. So why the need to take an extra job? She must be exhausted.

She handed him his shopping bag. "Card or cash?"

Clearly she'd chosen to ignore him. He smirked and handed over his credit card. "What time do you get off?"

Dex wrinkled her nose and gave him one of those fucking adorable head tilts. "Why?"

He leaned in close. Her pupils dilated, and she breathed him in. Now *that* was fucking sexy. "Because I want to get off. With you."

Her cheeks tinged with pink. She glanced around and then shushed him. "Stop it. I'm at work. The last thing I need is you getting me fired from yet another job."

He licked his lips, drawing her gaze to his mouth. "Then tell me what time you'll be finished here, and I'll go."

"Fine," she said with an annoyed huff. "Eight." She swiped his card and handed it back to him. "Will you go now?"

Nate checked his watch. He could amuse himself for a half hour. "I'll be waiting outside."

Her spine straightened, adding a couple of much-needed inches to her diminutive stature, and her eyes sparked with annoyance, but behind those sharp, slate-gray irises was definite attraction. Pleasure rushed through his veins. He might annoy the hell out of her, but she fucking wanted him—as much as he wanted her. Hollywood had taught Nate a lot about reading body language, and Dex's was sending all the right messages.

"And I'll be going home. I'm tired and irritable. I want to take a shower, then go to bed."

Nate tongued his top teeth, his eyes locking onto hers. "Sounds good to me, Titch."

He walked away, leaving Dex slack-jawed. It was a great look on her—and he knew exactly how to fill that delicious mouth of hers.

CHAPTER 5

Dex barely had time to process what had happened before a line formed at her checkout. Whatever the fates had planned for her, they clearly wanted to make her suffer in the process. Of all the supermarkets in LA, he'd walked into hers. And now, like a lion toying with its prey before ripping out the poor, unfortunate animal's throat, Nate Brook had decided it was playtime.

In a daze, she served her customers, making small talk and sharing the odd smile, but it was like her brain had been set to autopilot. All she could think about was whether Nate really would be waiting outside, and what he'd meant by his last throwaway comment.

He'd been a part of her dreams—and her deepest, darkest fantasies—for months, but now he'd finally noticed her, she wasn't sure whether to leap for joy or run and hide. At twenty-two, six years younger than Nate, she was wholly unequipped to deal with a man like him. A worldly-wise, experienced man who rubbed shoulders with the rich and famous, who probably consumed champagne and strawberries for breakfast, whereas she'd only recently stopped buying Lucky Charms and upgraded to muesli.

"Shift's over, darlin'. Time to go home."

Dex glanced up at Eric, one of the night crew, and the nicest man anyone could hope to know. She grinned and pushed back her chair. "Don't know how you stay awake through the night."

He shrugged one shoulder. "Works for me. Means I can be there to take my little ones to school and pick them up at the end of the day."

"True." She signed out of the checkout so Eric would be able to log in, and gave the waiting customer an apologetic smile. "You have a good night, Eric."

"I will. Stay safe."

She patted his arm and headed to the staff area for her coat and purse. As the exit doors opened, her heart thudded against her ribcage. She stepped outside and looked around. No sign of Nate. She lowered her head and hunched her shoulders. She should have known he was toying with her for his own amusement. Reaching into her purse for her keys, she walked over to her car. She unlocked it and opened the door, but as she went to climb inside, a hand reached around her and pushed the door closed.

"You're coming with me," Nate whispered in her ear, his breath warm, his throaty voice sinfully wicked, yet full of promise. The promise of what she wasn't quite sure.

Dex froze on the spot. So he hadn't left after all. "But my car…"

"Will be perfectly safe here overnight. I'll bring you back in the morning."

Her belly did a double backflip. *The morning.* Did that mean Nate Brook intended to stay the night with her? Every drop of saliva decided now was a good time to exit stage left. Her mouth was so dry, she couldn't even swallow, and her sharp tongue deserted her at the very moment she needed it the most.

"Turn around, Dex."

On stiff legs, she obeyed him. He was so tall—and she most definitely wasn't—that Dex had to crane her neck to meet his gaze. He was no longer wearing the baseball cap or the shades. His lips were pulled to the side in a crooked grin, his arms folded across his taut chest, sleeves rolled up to the elbows, revealing strong, muscular forearms.

All the air rushed out of her lungs, making it almost impossible to breathe, and as he stood there, quietly assessing her, she blinked. Once, twice, a third time, her heart pounding while she waited for him to make a move.

His arms fell to his sides, and he cocked his head. "Coming?"

Time to make a decision, Dex.

If she went, her life would never been the same again. Nate Brook would chew her up and toss her aside like trash as soon as he was done with her. But the devil on her shoulder couldn't help interjecting that one night with Nate was worth a thousand nights with anyone else. And if she took this chance, this risk, at least she'd have a fabulous anecdote to tell her grandkids. The one time in her life that she'd grabbed something for her—and got down and dirty with a famous Hollywood actor.

Nate didn't even wait to see if she'd follow. Instead, he strolled across the car lot, hands buried deep in the pockets of his jeans. He walked with supreme confidence, broad shoulders pushed back, spine erect, the hint of a swagger. Dex's breathing became erratic, and her pulse jolted the closer she got to Nate's car. He went around to the passenger door and opened it, the silent invitation roaring inside her head.

"Get in."

There was no "please", no "only if you're sure". Nate ordered—and expected—compliance. She almost told him to go screw himself, but the words stuck in her throat. The thing was, she wanted him. And he knew it.

With her knees virtually knocking together, Dex found herself standing in front of Nate. He stepped back to allow her room to slip inside his car, but as she went to get in, he stopped her. His hand curved around her neck, his thumb caressing her earlobe. A quiver rushed through her. Christ. Barely a touch and already she was a hot mess. She kept her gaze fixed on the ground. Her usual smart mouth had deserted her. Not too surprising really—she'd challenge anyone to hold it together around him.

"Look at me, Dex."

She inched her head upward until their eyes met. Even in the dim light of the car lot, his glacier-blue irises were beyond beautiful. Enchanting. Captivating. She was so fucked. She'd do anything he asked. Anything. As long as he kept looking at her as though she was the most fascinating thing he'd ever seen.

His thumb brushed over her lips. On a reflex, she parted them. Time stood still. She could swear the birds stopped tweeting, and the wind dropped, silencing the rustling leaves of the nearby sycamore trees.

"I'm not sure whether I prefer quiet Dex or loud and obnoxious Dex."

"Why are you doing this?"

A brief frown drew his brows low. "Doing what?"

She swung her hand between them. "This."

His lips twitched, and he lowered his head several inches until his mouth was tantalizingly close to hers. "I haven't *done* anything, or rather done *anyone* yet."

She blushed—again. Elva might have nicknamed her Mouth Almighty when they were kids, but when it came to men, Dex's experience was limited. Especially with men like Nate.

"And I haven't agreed to anything either."

Nate nodded. "True." He slipped one warm hand around the back of her neck and settled the other one in the small of her back. A thrilling shiver coursed through her as she found herself pressed up tight to his lithe body. She opened her mouth to ask him what he was playing at—and that's when he kissed her.

Actually, that was wrong. He didn't just kiss her. As his lips moved slowly over hers, and his tongue explored her mouth, he ruined her for any other man. One kiss from Nate Brook awoke a desperate need within her that only he could quench. She didn't need heaps of experience to know she was well and truly screwed.

A soft moan leaked from the back of her throat and, of their own volition, her arms snaked around his neck. Nate responded by tightening his grip and kissing her harder. A thrill sped through her veins as his erection nudged against her stomach, hard and thick and full of promise.

Then, without warning, he released her. Dex tried to catch her breath, her chest rising and falling at a rapid rate. Nate's hooded eyes stared down at her, his face a mixture of wonder and puzzlement.

"Well, that was unexpected," he murmured, more to himself than her. Then louder, "Has that persuaded you, Titch?"

Without waiting for her answer, he left the passenger door wide open and sauntered around the hood, his trademark swagger in full swing. He got in the driver's side and fired up the engine.

On legs that felt as if they belonged to someone else, Dex climbed into the car and fastened her seat belt. She risked a glance at Nate out of the corner of her eye. He wore a victorious smile that should have annoyed her. Instead, she found her own lips curving upward. Her chest burned with utter joy, and tingles spread through her hands.

"You're a cocky bastard."

Nate laughed. "If that's your way of saying I knew I'd win, then yes, I'm a cocky bastard."

"Do you always get your own way?"

Nate shifted the stick into drive. "Always," he said, the confirmation accompanied by a wink.

He pressed the gas pedal, and the car shot forward with a throaty growl. Dex wasn't sure whether the churning in her stomach was due to Nate's response or the powerful engine beneath the hood, but it felt like she'd just ridden the first dip on a roller coaster.

They traveled in silence, but when Nate missed the turning that would lead to Dex's apartment, she frowned.

"You're going in the wrong direction."

"Depends on the destination," he answered cryptically.

"But my apartment—"

"Isn't where we're headed."

Dex swallowed. That could only mean one thing. "We're going to your place?"

He nodded. "It's closer, and I'm not sure I can wait the thirty minutes it'll take to drive to your place to be inside you."

Dex bit down on her lip and closed her eyes, excitement and adrenaline curling her toes. Her heart thumped against her ribcage. Nate Brook, *the Nate Brook* was taking her to his home, and he couldn't wait to get her into bed.

But niggling at the back of her mind, through the misty haze of desire, was one question: what had changed? For six months he'd barely given her a second glance, and yet one screaming banshee moment from her—and a desire to get one over on Bernard from him—and he was hounding her like a dog chasing a bitch in heat.

It didn't matter what Nate said to the contrary. His determination to get her job back had *nothing* to do with benevolence and *everything* to do with gaining superiority in an unbalanced relationship with his agent.

So where did that leave her? She couldn't allow this to continue. Not until she had some answers.

"Can you stop the car?"

"It's not much farther."

"Nate, stop the car."

He gave her a quick side-eye. "You sick?"

She shook her head, even though he'd already turned his attention back to the road and wouldn't see her. "I need a minute."

Still the car ate up the miles, the powerful engine making it easy for Nate to weave in and out of the busy Los Angeles traffic.

"A minute for what? I can't pull over here, Titch."

"Stop the fucking car!"

That got his attention, although his compliance was accompanied by a heavy, irritated sigh and an exasperated twist to his lips.

"Okay, okay. Hang on."

He checked the right-hand mirror, maneuvered to the inside lane, and then took the next exit off the highway. He turned left at the traffic signal and then right, pulling in front of a liquor store. How apt. She could do with a shot of liquor, because now he'd done as she'd asked, she didn't know what to say. God, he'd think she was such a child, an innocent, or worse, a cock tease.

He cut the engine and twisted in his seat, his arm resting across the back of hers, close enough that if she moved her head back a couple of inches, she'd be resting on his forearm.

"Floor's yours, Dexter."

The full use of her name wasn't lost on her. He was making his point with a giant sledgehammer slammed into her skull.

"I-I just need a minute. You're going too fast. I want…" Her face burned. "I mean… I don't get it."

Nate scratched his cheek, his confusion evident. "Get what?"

She let out a quiet sigh. "Why you're interested in me all of a sudden. All those months you came to see Bernard, showing off your cocky swagger as you sauntered down the hallway. You barely even looked at me. I might as well have been a desk, or a chair, or a picture hanging on the wall for all the notice you took. Yet now… now you want to take me back to your apartment and… and…"

"Fuck you," Nate helpfully interjected. "That's what I want to do, Dex. Fuck you until you can't see straight. Until I'm etched on your body, so no matter who else comes afterward, you'll never forget the feel of my cock in your pussy."

No one had ever spoken to her so crudely, yet instead of being appalled, a flood of heat shot to her core, and... oh God, her panties were wet. She squirmed in her seat, a movement not lost on the much more experienced man sitting beside her.

"Don't over think it, Titch. We're both consenting adults. Both over twenty-one." He paused, a brief frown flickering across his face as though he hadn't thought about her age before that moment. "Yes?"

"I'm twenty-two," she said, her hoarse voice barely recognizable to her own ears.

He gave her a crooked smile, his eyes soft and filled with an emotion she couldn't read. It made him look younger, somehow. Less brittle and hardened by the Hollywood life.

He tucked a lock of hair behind her ear. "I will accept a no, Dex, but you'll have to convince me you really mean it. And I don't think you do. I think you want me as much as I want you. I don't know why I barely noticed you all these months. Probably because I'm a self-absorbed prick who's selfish through and through. But here's a few facts. One, you've been on my mind far too often these last few days. Two, I can't remember the last time I woke up thinking about a woman and went to sleep thinking about the same one. And three, the other night I jacked off in the shower with your image firmly planted in my mind."

Dex widened her eyes and forced a swallow past a throat that had decided it might be fun to severely restrict her breathing. But Nate hadn't finished.

"Sex comes easy in this town, Dex. I've lost count of the amount of pussy I can help myself to any time I choose. But like most things in life, if you don't have to work for it, then boredom kicks in pretty damn fast. It's been a long time since I wanted someone as much as I want you. You're... different."

Dex suppressed a wince at how many women Nate must have taken back to his home. How many lovers he must have had. Instead, she went with a teasing grin and a light, "Good, different?"

He unclipped his belt and shuffled closer. His hand, with those slender fingers she desperately wanted to suck, curved around the back of her neck. She held her breath, anticipating his kiss. He didn't disappoint. His lips, warm, firm, demanding, closed over hers. Dex knitted her hands into his thick hair, a sound easing from the back of her throat, a raw, hoarse sound full of longing.

Nate drew back, his chest swelling as he breathed heavily. "Jesus Christ. Yes, good fucking different. Can we go now, please?"

An awareness of the power she wielded over this man, this superstar that girls would sell their firstborn to spend an hour with, rushed through her. All of her doubts faded away. She might only get to spend one night in the bed of the man who'd filled her dreams for months on end, ever since she'd started working for Bernard, but she also knew if she walked away right that second, he would curse the missed opportunity as much as she would.

She'd barely moved her head in assent before he'd fired up the engine. Within two minutes, they were back on the highway. Except this time, he drove with one hand on the wheel and one hand on her thigh, his thumb brushing back and forth, the action both soothing and hot as all hell.

He'd been telling the truth earlier when he'd said it wasn't far to his place, because no sooner had they rejoined the highway, Nate was pulling off once more. He drove down a couple of streets, eventually turning into a driveway in front of a cute one-story property with a neatly tended front lawn, colorful flowers in the borders, and a wind chime hanging from a hook over the garage. If she'd had to guess where he lived, she'd have plumped for a sleek, contemporary apartment in a gated community, all steel and glass and hard marble flooring. Definitely not this family-type neighborhood where the house across the street had an abandoned bike with training wheels and a skateboard on the front lawn.

Nate took her hand and opened the front door. Dex found herself in an open-plan living, dining, and kitchen area, modern but homely at the same time. Dominating the room was a huge corner sofa with cushions mimicking the colors of fall, and behind that, an enormous painting of Santa Monica pier. Nate Brook was full of surprises tonight.

"Drink?" he asked, opening the large fridge and shoving his shopping bag inside.

"Whatever you're having is fine," Dex said, hoping he produced some form of alcohol. She desperately needed the calming buzz she'd get from it. "Aren't you going to eat?"

He gave her a lecherous smile. "I sure hope so, sweetheart."

Her cheeks burned for the gazillionth time that evening. If she continued blushing at such a rate, she'd faint from lack of blood to the rest of her body. Nate was expert at bringing the wrong type of color to her face.

"I-I meant the steak," she stammered.

Nate unscrewed the top off a couple of beers and handed her one. She took a grateful sip, desperate for something to soothe her dry throat and mouth.

"I'm not hungry for food right now." He reached for her hand once more. "Let's go to bed."

Her whole body shuddered with nerves, excitement, a tinge of fear, or maybe apprehension. She meekly followed him into his bedroom. The room was sparsely furnished. Pushed underneath the window was a king-size bed with dark-blue sheets and a mountain of pillows, bookended with a couple of nightstands. Opposite the bed was a five-drawer mahogany dresser with brushed steel handles, three large drawers and then two smaller ones at the top. A couple of closed doors led off the bedroom. One, she guessed, was a closet, the other a bathroom.

Nate let go of her hand. He wandered over to the window and closed the blinds. Light from the streetlamps outside Nate's house disappeared, casting the room into darkness. Dex hovered by the door, chewing on a thumbnail as she waited for her eyes to adjust to the lack of light. She blinked when Nate flicked on a lamp beside the bed. His gaze fell on her, and he crooked a finger, beckoning her. She moved toward him. He met her halfway.

"Don't be nervous," he said, as if he could read her mind.

He gently lifted her hair away from her neck, easing her head to one side to give him unfettered access. He pressed an open-mouthed kiss to her skin, and then sucked, hard. It almost felt like a branding, and Dex groaned loudly, clasping his biceps for support, her breasts pushed flat to his firm chest as he moved into her. The man was hard *everywhere*, nowhere more so than the thick rope of his erection flush against her belly.

He grasped her waist and lifted her, settling her ass on top of his dresser. Now, she was the one looking down on him, his eyes hooded, those ice-blue irises almost eclipsed by his enlarged pupils, full of lust, and want, and need.

They surely mirrored her own.

Nate slipped off her teal flats and dropped them on the floor. His hand slipped around the back of her calf, and he slowly massaged the muscle. His fingertips felt like silk on her skin, his touch soft, almost ticklish. He moved upwards and caressed the back of her knee. Then, without warning, he pushed her legs apart. Her skirt rose, mid-thigh level. She suppressed the urge to smooth it back down, to cover her knees, to give herself a few more seconds to prepare for the invasion of Nate's hot gaze.

His hands traveled up her legs, bunching her skirt around her hips. His gaze fell to the part where her legs met. She cursed her practical underwear, wishing, for the first time ever, that she was one of those girls who never left the house without wearing coordinating undergarments. A lacy bra and matching thong in a dusky pink or vibrant blue would do a lot more for her confidence than white cotton panties and a black T-shirt bra. Then again, she'd hardly known when she set off for work twelve hours ago that her night would end like this, legs spread, her most private parts almost on display for one of Hollywood's hottest properties. Things like that didn't happen to girls like her.

Nate nudged her legs together and opened the top two drawers. He then carefully wrapped his fingers around her ankles and placed each of her feet into one of the drawers, sole down. The position left her laid bare and vulnerable, and she automatically tried to cover herself with her skirt.

Nate stopped her and, with a cautionary shake of his head, bunched up her skirt once more. Dex found herself panting—her lungs expanding and contracting at such a rate as to leave her breathless—and the man had barely touched her.

He stood back, as though examining his handiwork and, with a nod of satisfaction, met her wide-eyed gaze.

"Do you feel exposed, Dex?"

She answered instantly. "Yes."

He tongued his top teeth. "When you lie in bed at night, do you think of me? Do you touch yourself?"

Holy shit. How did he know? Her chin dropped to her chest. This time the words wouldn't come. She hadn't expected him to… talk. She'd envisaged him undressing her quickly and then himself, and for the act itself to be over rather quickly. And even if it hadn't been, she'd assumed they'd be writhing on his bed right this second, their sweaty bodies colliding, twisting around one another, the sheets becoming damp beneath them as they fucked.

"Pull your panties to the side. I want to see."

She snapped her head up. "Wh-what?"

"Your panties. Pull them to the side, Dex."

She shook her head. This wasn't her. If Nate Brook was into some weird voyeuristic shit, then she wasn't the girl for him. Not even for one night.

"I-I can't."

A frown flickered across his face. "Why not?"

Her face burned with embarrassment. "I just can't. It's not… it doesn't feel right."

His confusion deepened, and then his eyebrows rose in query. "Please tell me you're not a virgin."

"No, I'm not," she snapped. Something about his attitude toward innocence irked her, spiking her anger, bringing *her* back for a moment. Just a moment. "What's wrong with virgins anyway?"

He ignored her question. "How many sexual partners have you had, Dex?"

She went to jump down from the dresser. He stopped her, holding her knees in that wide-open stance, pushing down on them so her feet remained inside the drawers.

"What business is that of yours?"

"Because if you were more experienced, me asking to see your pussy wouldn't have garnered this reaction."

When she chewed on her lip instead of responding to him, he let out a soft sigh. In an instant, she found herself standing on the floor in front of him. He brushed his thumb over her lips and then pushed the digit into her mouth. The unexpected invasion should have shocked her. Instead, she sucked, drawing a deep groan from Nate. It thrilled her, but at the same time, she had a horrible feeling she'd fucked up her one chance. A man like Nate wouldn't want a woman who balked at the idea of him looking at her most intimate parts.

But how did she explain to him the bone-crushing tiredness of trying to keep up with her schoolwork while she worked two jobs after her father died, leaving her mother penniless? How did she tell him that boys had been the very last thing on her agenda? How did she share that since coming to Los Angeles, her every waking thought had been consumed with earning enough money to keep her mother in a nursing home where she had a chance of living out her last days in comfort? The idea of having a man in her life was a luxury she couldn't afford. That was what was so perfect about this thing with Nate. She could have this one night, a night for her and her alone. Something to keep her warm as she lay alone in the dark, trying to swallow her panic because another bill had arrived that she couldn't pay.

He removed his thumb. "How many?"

She made a growl at the back of her throat, drawing a bark of laughter from him. "Good to see my Dex is still in there somewhere."

My Dex? Oh. My. God.

"Twice," she mumbled. "I've had sex twice. A guy in high school. It wasn't memorable."

His forehead creased. "Only twice?" He chuckled, and whereas she usually found the rare appearance of his dimples cute, this time, she wanted to punch him.

"Can you take me back to my car?" she said, determined to leave with at least a shred of her dignity intact.

Nate's smile fell, and he scratched his cheek, his short, neat fingernails grazing against his stubble. "No."

"Excuse me?"

"Stay."

Her pulse jolted at that one word. He still wanted her.

"Why? I can't do what you want me to. That. I can't do… that." She ducked her head, but he wasn't letting her off that easy. His palm skimmed along her jaw, and then he eased her chin up, his lips twisted into a crooked smile.

"I am going to look at your pussy, Dex. In fact, I can't wait to see it, to taste it. To taste *you*. And trust me, you'll want me to. You'll beg me to." He lowered his lips to hers in an all-too-brief kiss. "But don't worry. We'll work up to *that* as you so eloquently put it. Tonight, I'll show you that sex can be memorable, and great sex is unforgettable."

She tried to take in his words because it sounded awfully like he was intimating this wouldn't be their only encounter. Surely not? She'd never keep a man like Nate interested for long.

She shoved away those negative thoughts. There was no place for them here, tonight. She wanted this. Deserved this. Nate wanted to give it to her, and she was going to take it.

"Turn around."

Nate's quiet instruction brought her mind back to the present. Without question, she did as he'd asked. The button on her skirt popped, followed by the telltale sound of a zipper. Her skirt fell in a heap at her feet. Nate's fingers, firm yet light, fluttered over her hips as he gripped the hem of her top. He lifted it over her head. She stood there in her mismatched bra and panties, her body trembling, mind racing with what his next move would be. *Thank God I trimmed this morning.*

She jumped when he kissed the back of her thigh at the crease where it met her ass.

"Easy," he murmured.

She glanced over her shoulder. Nate was on his knees, his eyes roving over her body, his cheeks tinged with a hint of redness. He was staring at her as though she was the most delicious thing he'd ever seen, and it was *intoxicating.*

His thumbs hooked into her panties. He peeled them down her legs, an unmistakable sigh of appreciation tumbling from his lips as her bare ass was revealed to him.

"That's a mighty fine ass, little Dex," he said. And then he bit down on her left buttock.

Dex yelped, pain mingling with pleasure turning her thigh muscles to Jell-O, her legs quivering with the effort of holding her up.

"Put your hands on the dresser. It'll help support you."

He must have noticed her trembling limbs, hence his suggestion. She did as he'd instructed, and when he bit her other butt cheek, her head fell forward, a moan spilling from her lips. His hand slipped between her thighs, and then he pushed a finger inside her. Then a second finger followed.

"Jesus, you feel good, Titch." He tapped her on the ankle. "Spread your legs. Wider. Yeah, that's it."

He removed his fingers, then lapped her folds with the flat of his tongue.

A strangled sounding "Oh," fell from her lips, a weird noise because she uttered it on an inhale.

"Okay?" Nate asked, his voice rough and husky.

She inclined her head—and then he was inside her. His *tongue* was inside her, sliding back and forth, slick and hot and wet, and just when she thought the waves of pleasure couldn't get any bigger, he reached between her legs and took her clit with his thumb and forefinger. One hard pinch, and she was coming, coming, so goddamn hard, flashes of white and gold and silver blurring her vision. She closed her eyes and leaned over the dresser, the top half of her body sprawled across the cool wood as Nate's velvet tongue and talented fingers continued to prolong an orgasm that was nothing like she'd ever managed at her own hands. So quick. She'd climaxed in less than a minute. He was going to think she was so *lame.*

"Jesus Christ, so responsive," he muttered in her ear.

Her bra snapped open, and he eased the straps down her arms. His hands cupped her breasts, and she arched her back, pushing forward into his hands as he played with her nipples. They hardened and elongated underneath his touch.

He spun her in his arms, and then his mouth was on hers, their tongues coming together. He tasted sweet, but also slightly musky, and then she realized the flavor was her. The decadence and depravity of it should have grossed her out, but instead, she shivered with desire. She couldn't get enough of his touch, his body, his mouth. She slid her hands over his chest, down his muscled biceps and tight forearms where they held her so closely.

He lifted her, so effortlessly, laying her down on the bed. She blinked up at him, watching him strip off his shirt and jeans. He carelessly tossed them into the corner of the room.

Oh. My. God. I think my eyes just had an orgasm.

The outline of his erection was visible through his boxers, and he was so hard, the tip had broken free of the waistband. God, he was *huge.* She might not be a virgin in the technical sense of the word, but the two times she'd had sex hadn't exactly prepared her for someone of Nate's size.

He lay down beside her, his body so lean and tall sprawling out next to her. He explored her naked flesh with his fingertips. Goosebumps sprang up everywhere, pebbling her body.

He took hold of her hand and placed it over his erection, a low moan falling from his lips as he encouraged her to grip him. With Nate guiding the pace and pressure, she rubbed him through his underwear, but it wasn't enough. She wanted to feel him, bare and oh-so-male.

She turned onto her side and with her free hand, tugged down his boxers. She took him in her hand, flying solo this time. Nate's head fell against the pillows, his eyes rolling back, his mouth falling open.

"Yeah, oh yeah. Harder, Titch. Grip me harder."

She followed his instructions, but when she looked down at that blunt head, the skin pulled tight, his slit weeping with evidence of his arousal, she was hit with an overwhelming urge to taste him. She'd never gone down on a guy, but after Nate's gift to her, she wanted to return the favor.

She bent her head and, flattening her tongue, licked the tip of his cock. It jerked in response, and Nate rewarded her with a loud hiss, followed by, "Holy fucking shit."

And then she pulled him inside her mouth, sucking hard. She couldn't take him all, but to Nate, it didn't seem to matter. He threaded his hands through her hair, holding her steady, controlling the angle and the pace but, she noticed, careful not to push her harder than she was ready for.

His grunts and groans became louder, his breaths shorter, his body slick with sweat as he moved his hips, writhing against her willing mouth. Her excitement increased. What would it taste like when he came in her mouth? She'd already had a brief taste of his weeping tip, but she wanted more. Craved more.

And then she found herself beneath him, his knees easing her thighs apart, his enormous erection jutting from between his hips. He reached into the nightstand drawer and took out a condom, the rubber stretching as he rolled it down his length.

"This might sting a bit, Titch," he said, guiding his tip to her entrance. "Try to relax for me."

And then he pushed inside. Not gently. Forcefully. His lean hips thrust once until he was all the way in. Dex's breath left her lungs on a gasp, and her inner muscles automatically clenched to relieve the burning sensation of Nate's cock inside her.

"You weren't fucking kidding," she said.

He chuckled and rested his forearms either side of her head. "Wrap your legs around my waist, Titch. I'm gonna move."

And move he did. He fucked the pain and discomfort right out of her until all she could feel was intense pleasure, and the beginnings of a deep ache in her core that was as addictive as any drug. Nate looked down at her, his face flushed, dark eyelashes gracing his cheeks every time he blinked, momentarily hiding those stunning blue irises. Her stomach clenched. Dear God, the man was so beautiful that for a moment, the sight of him brought a rush of hot tears to her eyes.

He reached between their damp bodies and thrummed her clit as he continued to pummel her insides. The tip of his cock and the tilt of his hips made sure he was on target to hit that deep spot within her every single time. She got no warning of her impending orgasm, shattering, her insides undulating and twisting, her clit burning as Nate pinched the knot of nerves tightly between his thumb and finger.

His head fell to her shoulder and, after a couple more thrusts, he stilled, mumbling words into her neck, incoherent, yet raw-sounding and urgent.

He rolled off her, panting. Dex squeezed her eyes closed. She didn't know why her emotions were so close to the surface, but having sex with Nate had wrung her out, gnarled and tangled her insides as if he'd torn her apart and then put her back together all wrong.

He sat up and took off the condom. He tied a knot in the end and dropped it beside the bed. For some reason, it had her chuckling. When Nate frowned, she laughed even harder. She felt free, as if someone had lifted a great weight from her shoulders.

"What's so funny, Titch?" he asked, his lips curving upward even though confusion reigned in his eyes.

"Aren't you going to put that somewhere more suitable?" she said, still giggling like a thirteen-year-old watching her first porn movie with her friends and knowing she was doing something bad. "And are you ever going to tell me why you call me 'Titch'?"

Nate snuggled her into his side, pulling a throw over their naked bodies. "'Titch' is British slang for someone small in stature. Fits you perfectly."

Oh. My. God. Nate Brook has given me a nickname.

"And," he continued, "as there'll be a few more condoms joining that one tonight, I'll clear up when we're finished."

His meaning wasn't lost on her. She tilted her head back and looked at him with wide eyes and a slack mouth. Nate grinned down at her, then dropped a quick kiss on her forehead.

"I wouldn't keep that gorgeous mouth of yours hanging open too long, Titch, otherwise I'll be tempted to put something in it."

His crudeness stunned her into silence, but as her gaze met his twinkling eyes, she began to laugh, until Nate silenced her with a toe-curling kiss.

It was going to be a long night—and quite possibly, the most exciting one of her life.

CHAPTER 6

Nate slowly eased back the covers. He placed his feet flat on the floor and glanced back at Dex. Her red hair was fanned out over the pillow, both hands clasped beneath her head in mock prayer. Despite the deep ache in his body, not to mention his cock, the damn thing jerked to life just watching her sleep.

Christ, he couldn't remember the last time he'd fucked a woman through the night. How many times had he plunged inside her? Four? Five? They'd all blended into one another because no sooner had he come than his cock had stood to attention once more, like a starving dog begging for scraps.

A few strands of her hair had caught in the corner of her mouth, wafting in the air each time she breathed out. Nate carefully disentangled them, tucking them safely behind her ear. She stirred. He withdrew his hand. Not that he would mind if she woke and then reached for him, but she needed to sleep. He wasn't being benevolent. He wanted Dex well rested because he planned to keep her right where she was for at least the next few hours. Despite his bruised and tender cock, he hadn't nearly drunk his fill of her yet.

He tugged on his discarded boxers and padded into the

kitchen. Filling a glass from the faucet, he drank it down in one go and then refilled it. He wandered over to the window. The breeze had picked up, confirming the weather reports of an oncoming storm. Another reason to stay in bed and wait for the bad weather to pass. He couldn't think of a better way to spend a Sunday than buried inside Dex, with her warm, pliant body moving against his as she made those delicious sounds while he pounded into her.

Dex… what a fucking surprise she'd turned out to be. For a brief moment last night, he'd thought she was going to run. And he'd have had no choice but to stop her, because there was something different about this pint-sized little fireball that set his insides ablaze. He wasn't about to let someone go who could make him *feel*. Nate had stopped allowing himself to feel seven years ago. Some things were too painful to keep poking at with a rusty blade.

He was about to go back to bed when his phone buzzed. Irritated, he snatched it off the kitchen counter, but when he saw the sender of the text, his heart made a dash for his feet. He didn't need to swipe the screen to know what the message would say.

Four weeks, Nate. And don't even think about bailing.

Yep. As suspected. Every week the text came, like a fucking countdown clock. Ever since Jax had phoned him a few months earlier with the news that he and Indie were finally getting hitched, and Nate's response had been less than enthusiastic, the weekly texts had started. Now, don't get him wrong, he was happy for his brother. Fucking ecstatic, truth be told. Jax was one of the good guys. He deserved happiness. But Nate *hated* returning to New York. Everything that had been good about his childhood, despite the gruesome death of his parents when he was twelve, had turned to shit with the discovery of that letter.

But the cross was his to bear. His, and his alone. He had a lot of faults, a whole damned lot, but to destroy his brothers the way he'd been destroyed… not even self-absorbed Nate Brook would be *that* cruel.

It was followed up by another text. *It wouldn't be the same without you.*

Goddamn Jax and his fucking emotional blackmail. Jax was the one brother Nate found it impossible to say no to. It had been Jax who'd stayed up with Nate through the night as he'd mourned their mother and, to a lesser extent, his father. Jax who'd brushed away his tears and tenderly kissed his forehead. Jax who'd climbed in beside him, gently rocking him until he'd fallen asleep, his cheeks still wet with grief. There was no good time to lose a parent. All his brothers had suffered immeasurably, but to lose your anchors at the tender age of twelve was a fucking bitch.

With a resigned sigh, he tossed his phone to one side. Five days. He could survive that long in New York without wanting to rip his heart out, along with everyone else's. See, that was the problem with betrayal… once it had gotten its claws buried deep, it was virtually impossible to disentangle without causing serious damage to some very vital organs.

He took his glass of water back into the bedroom. Dawn had broken, the yellow light from the sun lancing through the gaps in the blinds. Dex had turned over, buried herself inside the comforter so the only thing visible was the top of her head. Nate sat beside her, the mattress moving under his weight. Dex gave a soft sigh and burrowed farther into the bed.

An idea pricked at the back of his mind, inching forward as he watched her sleep. Maybe New York wouldn't be so bad if he had a companion. Someone who could distract him with her captivating body and her keen mind, not to mention her sharp wit.

Except if he mentioned it too early, she'd refuse. He didn't know how he had come to that conclusion, but his instincts weren't usually far off the mark. He needed to demonstrate that he wanted to get to know her, which wasn't a lie, and let her see a little of him. Not too much, though. Not enough that he risked letting the wrong thing slip when doped up on her sweet pussy.

She stirred and drowsily lifted her head. She blinked a couple of times and then rubbed her eyes.

"Morning," Nate said, leaning down and pressing a kiss to her forehead, the kind of intimacy he'd never afforded any of his other bedmates. Yeah, yeah. He'd noticed he was being different with this one. But Dex looked so petite, so fragile, so fucking gorgeous lying there with her tousled hair and flushed face that he hadn't been able to resist showing her a little tenderness.

"What time is it?" she said, stretching. The covers slipped, revealing her pert tits and rose-tipped nipples, the areolae pebbled from the cool air blowing through the AC unit overhead.

Nate bent over and sucked one hard nub into his mouth. Dex groaned and clasped the back of his head, urging him to suck harder. He grazed the tip with his teeth, not enough to cause too much pain but enough to make her gasp.

"Jesus, good morning to you, too," she breathed.

He smiled against her skin and then raised his head. "Half after six."

Another groan, this one not steeped in desire. She turned on to her stomach, burying her head in the pillow. "It's Sunday." The sound came out muffled, widening his grin. She was adorable: funny and sweet, and deliciously different. He rarely allowed women to stay the night, but on the odd occasion he had, after a quick—and usually unsatisfactory—morning fuck, he couldn't wait to see them on their way.

With Dex, he wanted the exact opposite. Not the morning fuck part, obviously, because that was non-negotiable. But the part about wanting her to leave? Yeah, not happening. Not for a good few hours.

He tugged at the covers, but she held on, her fingers curled tightly around them. Guess Dex wasn't a morning person. Nate gave a yank, and the covers came away easily, revealing her nakedness. He slapped her ass. She squealed and flipped over, hitting him with a stern glare.

"That stung."

"But you want more, don't you, little Dex?" He burrowed into her neck, his lips leaving a trail of open-mouthed kisses. He nipped along her collarbone, inching farther down, his fingertips gently brushing her waist as he sucked on her tits, left, right, left again. Starved for her, this woman he barely knew, he devoured her, his cock thickening and lengthening when she made those adorable keening sounds and writhed beneath him.

"Oh yeah." She breathed the words in his ear. "I definitely want more."

NATE'S EYES sprang open to a room drenched in daylight—and an empty bed. He leaped up, not bothering with his boxers this time, and dashed into the kitchen. He suppressed an enormous sigh of relief as he spotted Dex, dressed in one of his shirts that almost reached her knees, beating eggs in a bowl. His cock stirred to life—again—at the sight of her ass wiggling beneath the cotton.

"Plenty of salt in mine."

She jumped and spun around, the bowl tucked into the crook of her arm, yellow liquid dripping from the fork she held in midair.

"Salt is bad for you," she said, waggling the piece of silverware at him. "And you scared me."

He wandered over to her, his erection jutting forward as if it was as desperate to reach her as he was. Her gaze fell south, and her tongue dampened her lips. Well, fuck if that didn't make him harder. He removed the bowl from her hands and set it down beside her. He snaked his arms around her waist. When she tipped her head back, he bent down for a kiss.

"Morning, again," he said. "I like the idea of you wearing my clothes and cooking my breakfast."

"Do you now?" she said, arching an eyebrow at him in reproach.

"Mm-hmm," he replied, moving his lips from her mouth to her neck. She owned him. She'd cast a spell on him that meant he burned every time he wasn't touching her, or close enough to touch her. "My cock is raw from being inside you all night, and yet I want you again. What have you done to me, Titch?"

A slight tremor ran through her body, and her hands stroked his back, then she anchored them in his hair.

"Is this a dream?" she murmured.

He drew back, and as he gazed into her huge, gray eyes, framed with dark, naturally thick lashes, an alien feeling stirred in his chest. He felt something for this woman, something more, something… scary.

"More like a nightmare," he said with a grin. His teasing broke the spell, and she gave him a playful punch on the arm, then turned her attention back to beating the eggs.

His phone rang, and he gave it a cursory glance, then grimaced. Calum. No doubt he was calling to see why Nate hadn't responded to Jax's last text.

"Aren't you going to get that?" Dex asked.

"No."

Her eyebrows raised at his curt tone. She looked down at his phone. "Who's Calum?"

"My brother."

"Don't you want to talk to him?"

"No."

"Why?"

He closed his eyes and pinched the bridge of his nose. Irritation swirled in his gut, but he held back from snapping at her. It wasn't Dex's fault that the closer it got to Jax's wedding—and his subsequent return to New York—the shorter his fuse became, and the sicker he felt.

"Nate?"

His eyes sprang open. Concern laced her features, and something moved inside him. Something warm and good, and addictive.

She set the bowl on the countertop. "Is everything okay?"

He slipped his arms around her waist, stealing another kiss. "All good, Titch."

Nate returned to the bedroom and quickly dressed. He went into the bathroom and picked up his toothbrush, a grin threatening the corners of his mouth as he noticed the damp bristles. Dex must have brushed her teeth with it when he'd still been asleep. The idea was oddly thrilling.

He finished getting ready, and by the time he got back to the kitchen, Dex was plating up. Such a domestic scene for a very undomestic man, but he found he didn't mind as much as he imagined he would.

He sat at the counter and shoveled eggs into his mouth. He was starved. Must be all the sexercise coupled with eating Dex's pussy instead of the steak last night.

"These are pretty good, Titch," he said, picking up a piece of crispy bacon and biting it in half. "Same time next Sunday?"

A blush crept across her cheeks, and she wrinkled her nose. "You'll have gotten bored of me by then, Nate. In fact, I'll give it another few hours and I doubt you'll remember my name."

Despite the fact she said the entire sentence while wearing a hint of a grin, a spear of anger shot through him. He tightened his hand around the fork while curling the other one into a fist. His eyes bored into hers, his jaw clenched so tightly together his teeth ached.

"Yeah, you're probably right," he snapped, wanted to maim, to hurt, like she'd hurt him. It didn't matter that he deserved it. It didn't matter that his reputation definitely preceded him, which gave her comment some validity. He was different around her. She made him different, and he wanted her to notice that on her own. Except she hadn't.

Her smile fell, and she turned away, her teeth grazing her bottom lip. Her fork clattered to her plate, despite the fact she hadn't eaten a bite. She shoved the plate to one side and climbed down off the stool.

"Well, don't worry, Nate. I'll be out of your hair in thirty seconds. I wouldn't want to take up any more of your precious time."

She stomped into the bedroom while he sat like a fucking statue and let her think he didn't want her there. That he didn't *need* her there. How had their morning turned from sweaty sex, stolen kisses, and a breakfast she'd cooked for him, to a petty argument that meant she was getting ready to walk out?

You, a familiar and all-too-truthful voice whispered in his ear. *Because whenever anyone gets within a mile of maybe uncovering the man behind the mask, you have to go and fucking ruin it.*

True to her word, Dex appeared within the half-minute, her purse slung diagonally across her body, her hair pulled back into a ponytail. She flashed him a look of complete loathing and then marched to the front door, her spine erect, shoulders back as though to say, "You won't break me, motherfucker."

But as the door opened an inch, as a spear of light cast a triangular glow across the oak flooring of his living room, Nate launched himself off the chair. His palm hit the door, slamming it shut, and his body closed over hers, his hands cupping her waist.

"I'll remember your name today, tomorrow, next week, next fucking month," he whispered in her ear. "I'll remember your name for the rest of my miserable fucking life because nights like last night don't happen to men like me."

Her body, so stiff when he first put his arms around her, yielded ever so slightly. He eased her around in his arms, and when he saw how bright with unshed tears her eyes were, he wanted to take his balls in his hand and twist those fuckers until he passed out from the pain.

"Please stay," he said, cupping her trembling chin. He caressed her face with the tips of his fingers, relishing the softness of her skin, the fullness of her cheeks, so different to the skeletal, haunted-looking women this town was too full of. Her eyes fell shut as he continued to explore her face, and so he did what any other asswipe of a man would do when faced with a woman they'd hurt: he kissed her, hard and deep, sweeping his tongue inside her mouth, probing, seeking the warmth, the comfort, that she gave so willingly.

She broke off their kiss. "I have things to do, Nate," she said softly, crushing his hope with those few words.

"But you haven't finished breakfast." Yeah, that'd make her stay. The offer of a cold breakfast—that she'd cooked. What a catch he was. *Fucking smooth, dickhead.*

She offered him a glimpse of a smile. "I'll grab something at home. Can you give me a lift back to my car, or would you rather I called a cab?"

He pressed his lips together and blew an irritated breath out through his nose. "No, I don't want you to get a goddamn cab. I'll take you... on one condition."

Disappointment flickered across her face, and she gave a slow shake of her head. "What's the condition?"

"You agree to come to dinner with me tonight."

Disappointment was replaced with surprise, her forehead creasing as she looked up at him. "I'd like that."

Relief rushed through him so fast it made his head spin. He grabbed his wallet and keys and ushered her outside. They made a dash for the car, the rain splattering down, soaking them. They drove back to the supermarket in companionable silence. Nate pulled to a stop and reached across her to open her door.

"I'll pick you up at seven-thirty. Drive carefully."

He drove away without looking back. If he did, he'd never leave.

CHAPTER 7

Dex gently lowered herself into the bath and rested her head on a folded-up towel. Her whole body ached from the exertions of the previous night, but she wouldn't change a single thing, not even their fight that morning, because it made it all seem *real*. Every time she thought about the last twenty-four hours, she wanted to hug herself, to scream, to dance around with excitement. To hope beyond all hope it wasn't just a one-night stand.

She'd been thoroughly fucked by Nate Brook. She'd more than tripled her previous sexual experiences in one freaking night, and she'd had so many orgasms she'd lost count.

Her stomach flipped deliciously as she thought back to Nate's hands on her body, his mouth in the most intimate of places, how he'd felt inside her. How he'd tasted. She shuddered and closed her eyes, savoring each and every one of the wonderful memories she'd shared with Nate.

But then something he'd said nudged at her, made her curious. *Because nights like last night don't happen to men like me.* What could he have meant—men like him? TV stars? No, surely not. Nights like that must happen to famous actors all the time. Could he have meant cruel or heartless men? Well, he definitely had a mean streak. The way he'd taken her semi-joke literally and let her almost walk out before he made a move told her that.

And then to say those wonderful words. How he'd remember her name for the rest of his life.

She groaned, dipped a cloth in the hot water, and placed it over her face. No wonder she didn't understand Nate. They'd done things the wrong way around. Dinner and a little sharing of information should have come before the night of hot, sweaty sex. At least he wanted to see her again. She wouldn't have been surprised if he'd dumped her after she'd put out when they hadn't even gone on a single date.

A date. Was that even what tonight was? Or was it Nate's way of apologizing for his behavior before letting her down gently?

Urgh... she was getting on her own nerves.

Dex pulled the plug and got out of the bath, toweling herself dry. She'd wanted so much to stay when he'd asked her to, but as she wasn't working this Sunday, she wanted to spend more time with Mom. Elva would have taken the kids for a visit that morning, but it would have been the usual rush in, quick chat, rush out. Not that Dex could blame her sister. It wasn't easy bringing up two hyperactive kids virtually alone because Andy, Elva's husband, worked so hard trying to provide for his family.

Dex got dressed, fed Milo—giving him an extra cuddle to make up for being out all night, not that he cared—then made some sandwiches, throwing in a bag of chips and a couple of cans of Coke then set off for the nursing home. Mom loved it when Dex brought a picnic, although it could hardly be counted as such. Not that Mom cared. It was as though she'd regressed to her childhood, and the smallest of things seemed like an exciting treat. If it wasn't so cruel, it would be endearing.

She barely remembered the drive over to Oak Ridge Nursing Home, but as she parked her car and ran up the driveway before she got soaked, past the neat, tended lawn and pretty spring flowers, the exhaustion from trying to keep her head above water and the debt collector from the door melted away. It was all worth it to keep Mom here. Oak Ridge was one of the best nursing homes in the state, and Dex would spend the next fifty years paying off the debt if it meant Mom died happy.

She signed in, shared a few words with the receptionist on duty, and then headed for the sun room where Mom spent most of her time. As she got closer, manic chatter bled through the doors, and Dex smiled. A lot of the residents here may be extremely ill, but they didn't let it affect them. She knew the minute she rounded the corner she'd see all manner of activities going on: a couple playing poker, a table set up for chess, complete with timer, the odd game of Monopoly or even Trivial Pursuit.

She spotted her mother gazing out into the rain-soaked gardens, chatting with her friend Norma, a glass of iced tea on a table to her side. Dex wandered across and pulled up a seat, giving her mom a kiss on the cheek.

"Hi, Mom. Norma. Terrible weather, isn't it?"

Her mother looked up and squinted at Dex, her brow furrowing in confusion. And then she gave a bright grin that reminded Dex of what she'd looked like before she'd been diagnosed with early onset Alzheimer's. "Oh, Sally," she said. "It's lovely of you to come."

Dex's heart clenched. Sally had been her maternal grandmother. "Where else would I be?" She played along because to correct her mother usually resulted in confusion, anguish, and then tears. "It's Sunday. And look what I brought?"

She held up the bag with the sandwiches and snacks inside. Her mom's face lit up like a child on Christmas morning when they first cast eyes on a mountain of presents, so carefully wrapped and placed with love beneath the tree. Anxious to tear through the gift wrap, yet wanting to savor the moment, to draw it out as long as possible.

Her mom peeled the Saran wrap off a cheese and ham sandwich and took a bite.

"My favorite," she said, tearing it in two and giving half to Norma, despite the fact there was plenty to go around. "Thank you, Sally."

A trickle of blood seeped from another laceration in Dex's heart. There had been so many in the last three years, each one more painful than the last. Life was unbelievably cruel at times, and some people seemed to suffer much more deeply than others. To take Dex and Elva's father from them before he reached forty was bad enough, but now, at the age of forty-seven, Dex's mother didn't even recognize her own children, her brain ravaged by a terrible illness that shouldn't have been her future.

It wasn't *fair*. It just was.

"Dex, do you have a moment?"

Dex tore her gaze away from watching her mom extort such pleasure from something as simple as meat and cheese between two slices of bread, to see Jennifer, the manager of the home standing behind her.

"Sure." With dread curling in the pit of her stomach, Dex got to her feet and squeezed her mom's shoulder. "Won't be a minute."

Her mom didn't even flinch. Lunch was far more interesting than a daughter she didn't even remember.

Dex followed Jennifer into her office, taking a seat when one was offered.

"She's doing well," Dex said, rubbing the space between her eyebrows as she waited for Jennifer to say what Dex already knew. She was behind with the payments for her mother's care, and Jennifer was running a business after all, not a charity.

Jennifer nodded. "Extremely well. I know it isn't easy to see her like this, Dex, but from your mother's perspective, nothing is wrong. To her, life has become very simple. I hope you can take some comfort in that."

Dex picked a stray piece of white cotton off the sleeve of her sweater, briefly wondering where it had come from. "I do."

"But there is something I need to discuss with you."

Dex let out a resigned sigh. "I know, Jennifer. I'm doing my best, honestly, but it's not easy. I will get you the money. Somehow."

Jennifer's lips pulled to the side in a sympathetic way. "I understand, Dex, but I have bills to pay, too. Staff, food, utilities." She ran her fingers along the edge of her desk and blinked slowly, then hit Dex with the hammer blow. "Fees are going up at the end of the month. Five percent."

"No!"

Despair rolled through her, and she found herself on her feet. She began to pace. The pay rise that Nate had forced Bernard to give her would have helped with the arrears, but even that wouldn't cover an increase in costs. "I can't afford that. I can barely keep up with the current fees."

"I know. Look, I can give you a month. Maybe two. But that's it, Dex. I can recommend somewhere cheaper…" Jennifer's voice trailed off, and she bit her bottom lip and stared out of the window. "I'm so sorry."

"It's not your fault," Dex mumbled, her shoulders sinking as if a ton of concrete had been added to the weight her body was already bowing under. "I appreciate you giving me some leeway."

Dex almost stumbled down the hallway, back to Mom. How was she going to deal with such a mess? She couldn't take on a third job. There simply weren't enough hours in the day. Oh God, it was hopeless.

An hour later, she found herself outside Oak Ridge with disbelief and fear and, yes, hatred in her heart. Not for Jennifer, but for the situation. If she moved her mother now, at this stage in her illness, she'd decline. Forcing Mom to leave behind everything she knew was a death sentence on a woman already desperately short of time.

She climbed into her car and let her head drop to the steering wheel. It didn't matter which way she tried to cut things, there simply wasn't enough money to go around. There was nothing else for it. She'd have to leave Los Angeles and move back to Wisconsin—taking Mom with her. What would that mean for Elva?

And, almost as importantly, what would it mean for her fledgling relationship with Nate?

CHAPTER 8

After numerous wardrobe changes, Dex gave up second-guessing the right attire for her dinner with Nate and went with a simple off-the-shoulder top and a pair of skinny jeans. Her height, or lack thereof, meant that slinky dresses and willowy, flowing skirts would never suit her. One of the many consequences of barely scraping five feet tall. She'd inherited Mom's diminutive stature, whereas Elva had been blessed with Dad's genes, meaning she was a good half a foot taller.

She slipped a pair of silver studs in her ears then added a dash of perfume to her neck and inside her wrists. Sliding her feet into a pair of four-inch black heels, she frowned at her reflection in the mirror. Her hair didn't look right, not with this top. She stuck it up into a high ponytail. Yeah, better.

A knock at her door shocked her pulse into overdrive. Oh God, he was here. She took a deep, steadying breath through her nose and, with a final glance at her reflection, went to answer it.

"Ready?" he said with a leisurely eye-sweep that—thankfully—didn't end in a disappointed grimace.

She returned the favor, hungrily drinking him in. He'd gone with casual, too, wearing black jeans paired with a black shirt left open at the neck, giving her a glimpse of smooth tanned skin which she now knew tasted as good as chocolate ice cream —with a cherry on top. And whipped cream. Oh, and crushed nuts.

"Dex?"

His question, accompanied with a raised eyebrow had her vigorously nodding. "Yes, ready."

She snatched up her purse, barely having time to shove the strap over her shoulder before Nate captured her hand in his. The earlier rainstorm had finally passed by, although it had left behind a heavy thickness in the air.

He held open the car door for her and then walked around to the driver's side. Dex used the few spare seconds to calm her racing heart. Why was she panicking? She'd spent a night in his bed, and he'd seen, not to mention touched, kissed, and licked every part of her body, and yet the idea of sharing a meal with him had her tied up in knots—and not in a good way.

"Where are we going?" Goddamn, her voice sounded breathless.

"To the emergency room if you don't slow your heart rate, Titch," he said with a brazen grin.

"Cocky bastard," she muttered.

His grin widened. "Yeah, so you've said, once or twice." He gripped her chin and turned her to face him, planting a hard kiss on her mouth. "I missed you today, Titch."

Despite the stress of visiting her mom and the looming difficult decisions ahead, her heart soared.

"You can say you missed me, too," he continued. "I know you did."

She narrowed her eyes at him. "There's cocky, and then there's over-confident."

"Yeah, and you find both versions irresistible."

A smile tugged at her lips, but at the same time, she shook her head. "You are incorrigible."

He fired up the engine. "Wow, that's a big word, Titch, especially for someone of your size."

She scowled at him. "Isn't that joke getting old yet?"

He picked up her hand and kissed her knuckles. "Not even close."

Staying annoyed at Nate was like swimming against a riptide —impossible. And he knew it, too, because those dimples stayed in place the entire drive to the restaurant. But when Nate parked in front of a smartly dressed valet outside one of the best restaurants in town, Dex inwardly groaned. This wasn't a jeans and top kind of establishment—at least for the women—but more a cocktail dress purchased from some exclusive place on Rodeo Drive.

She bit the soft skin inside her mouth and turned her eyes on Nate. "Can we go somewhere else?"

He frowned. "Don't you like Italian food?"

"Oh, it's not that." She fiddled with the hem of her top, putting a crease in the material. Terrific. Now she'd look even scruffier.

"Then what?"

She offered him an embarrassed smile. "If I'd known you were planning on bringing me here, I'd have put on a dress or something. I mean, I don't have any that are very smart, but smarter than jeans and a—"

He cut her off, not by interrupting, but by kissing her. And not simply a peck either. No, a full-on heavy-duty kiss that had her stomach vaulting with lust and her toes scrunching inside her shoes.

"You're fucking adorable," he said drawing back, his eyes boring into hers. "And if I have a single complaint about the way you're dressed, it's that you're wearing far too many clothes for my liking." He shrugged. "As for this place, if they have a problem with you, then I'll have a problem with them."

He climbed out of the car. Her eyebrows shot upward. Nate Brook was a full-of-surprises kind of guy, and the more she saw of him, the more she liked him. He opened her door, helped her out, and tossed his keys to the waiting valet. He didn't even wait for a ticket, like normal people. She guessed they knew who he was so there wasn't the same need as for a stranger.

"Mr. Brook." The maître d' smiled broadly and held out his hand. Nate released her so he could shake it. "How wonderful to see you again."

"Hey, Charlie. How's things?"

Charlie tapped on a keyboard and then picked up two menus. "I can't complain. Follow me, please."

He led them into the restaurant. Dex tried to keep her head facing forward, but she still caught the odd stare cast their way. *They're staring at him, not you.* At least she hoped that was the case. Nate cut a much more dashing figure than her, so it made logical sense that he'd draw the eye. He drew her eye. All the damn time.

"Is this table satisfactory, Mr. Brook?"

Nate glanced around and then pointed at a booth a few feet away. "We'll take that one."

Charlie followed his gaze while Dex shrank in on herself, horrified. She rarely went to restaurants, but she never, ever questioned the table she was given, yet Nate had dismissed the one they'd been offered out of hand. Charlie, though, seemed unperturbed. He simply nodded then briskly changed course. Nate let her sit down first, and instead of sitting opposite, he slid along the bench next to her.

"Thanks, Charlie," he said, taking the menus. "Do you want some champagne, Titch?"

She shook her head. "I don't like champagne. Tastes like vinegar."

Nate laughed while Charlie's eyes widened in shock at her blunt response. Well, too bad. She wasn't putting on airs and graces for anyone.

"Wine instead?" Nate asked.

She nodded.

"Some still water and a bottle of Montrachet it is then, Charlie."

While Nate buried his head in the menu, Dex took the opportunity to look around. This is what Dad would have called a *fancypants* place, all marble and granite and expensive lighting. If only he could see her now. And wait until she told Elva. Her sister would probably turn green with envy.

But when she checked out the menu for herself, an uncomfortable feeling stole over her. The price of a single steak would almost pay for a day of her mother's care. It was obscenely over-the-top, especially as steak cost less than five bucks a pound at the store where she worked. Her stomach growled at the smells coming from the kitchen and nearby tables, but she couldn't, in all good conscience, stuff her face with overpriced food in a pretentious restaurant that only existed because the rich and famous wanted to feel special. And then she turned the menu over—and her stomach flipped in a really nasty way. How much? For a bottle of *wine?* Oh no, no, no.

"What'll you have?" Nate said, oblivious to her dismay. "The filet is good, obviously, but the sea bass isn't bad either if you prefer fish." When she didn't say a word, he frowned. "I haven't tried the vegetarian menu, but I'm sure it's perfectly edible. And there's always pasta."

"I want to go, please," Dex said, her voice small and quiet.

"What the hell are you talking about?" Nate said. "We only just got here."

How did she begin to explain her feelings to him without spilling the entire details of her sorry-ass life? However attracted Nate was to her, he'd run a mile if she allowed him a peek of her reality. She couldn't stay here, eating this disgustingly overpriced food and drink, and pretend it was okay. It wasn't okay. Not by a long shot. *Play it cool, Dex.*

"The prices are ridiculous," she said. "Why don't I cook us a meal back at mine?"

Nate scratched his cheek, confusion marring his features. "Stop worrying. It's on me."

"It's not about who's paying," she whispered under her breath. "But that bottle of wine would pay a family's food bill for a month. A *single bottle of wine*. I'm sorry, Nate, but I can't do it."

"Jesus." He grimaced. "Chill the fuck out, Titch. I never pegged you for one of those principled types."

Irritation prickled her skin. "Why do you say *principled* as though it's a curse word? I appreciate the value of money, Nate, because, unlike you, I don't fucking have enough."

She clapped a hand over her mouth, horror at her stupid reveal widening her eyes. Nate, in response, narrowed his.

"What do you mean?"

She inwardly cursed. *You're an idiot, Dex.* "Nothing. It doesn't matter. Please, just let's go." She shoved a hand against his arm, but she might as well have been trying to move a stone statue.

"Is this why you're working a second job?"

Lying wasn't her style, so she remained mute instead, worrying her lip with her teeth as she stared into space.

Nate grazed the back of his hand over her cheek, the caress so warm, so tender, that the urge to spill every worry, every panicked moment that kept her up at night was so strong, she had to clamp her jaw shut. Nate wasn't her boyfriend. He wasn't even a friend. He was just a guy she had the serious hots for, who she'd panted over for months. A guy she'd spent a hot, sweaty night in bed with, followed by this fuck-up of a so-called date.

There certainly wouldn't be a second one.

"Talk to me."

She closed her eyes for a brief moment, but they flew open when Nate put his mouth on hers. It wasn't an urgent, passionate kiss like the one he'd given her in the car. It was a gentle kiss meant to coax and reassure.

She gave him a wry smile. "I bet you didn't expect tonight to turn into an impromptu episode of Dr. Phil." She chuckled, determined to put him off the scent. "Forget it. I'm an idiot. Let's order."

Nate's hand sliced through the air. "We're not ready."

Dex frowned, and then realized he was talking to the approaching server. The man spun on his heel and headed back the way he'd come from, the move so smooth that being dismissed in such a manner must be a regular occurrence.

Nate stared at her without saying a word, his eyes searching her face, although she didn't have a clue what he was hoping to find. And then he sighed. Scooched down the bench. Stood. Held out his hand.

"Come with me, Titch."

"Where to?"

His lips twisted to the side. "Get your ass moving and you'll find out."

FUCK, fuck, fuck. You are a fucking idiot. A self-absorbed dick with your head so far up your own asshole, you can lick your own goddamn tonsils.

He should have realized that someone who worked their butt off all week for a cock like Bernard, and then spent their weekends slaving away at a supermarket checkout wasn't exactly flush with cash. But that wasn't the only reason taking Dex to his go-to haunt had been the wrong move. Dex was different, unique, special. She wasn't a fame-hungry sycophant with grabby hands. If he'd stopped for one second to think about it, he would have guessed her reaction to such unnecessary affluence.

He risked a glance sideways. Dex was staring out the side window, a faint blotching on her neck, although whether it was from embarrassment or annoyance, he couldn't know. Her hands were lying still in her lap, fingers laced together, and she was chewing the inside of her lip.

Five minutes later, Nate pulled off the highway and stopped in front of a local diner. "Better?" he asked, turning to Dex with a grin.

She grinned back at him, her eyes lighting up with delight. His insides did the same. "It's *perfect*," she said, her hand already on the door latch. "Come on. I'm *starving*."

"If my ass sticks to the plastic seat, you're in deep shit," he said, getting out of the car to the sound of Dex's throaty laugh.

They walked inside the diner, her hand firmly clasped in his. He pushed the door open. A bell above the door tinkled. Nate refrained from rolling his eyes. The podium was unmanned, although a sign stated: Please wait to be seated.

On one side was a line of booths covered in red plastic—yep, as clichéd as he'd expected—and on the other side, a line of tables, some seating four, others two. At the counter, sitting on a chrome stool, was an obvious homeless guy, his clothes dirty and scuffed, nursing a steaming cup of coffee.

The waitress came over. "Just the two is it, lovelies?" And then came a squint followed by a squeal that had every single diner looking their way. "Oh my God. Wait there. Don't move. I have to get Susan." She dashed off, her white sneakers squeaking on the checkered floor. "Suze!" she yelled. "Get out here now. You're gonna want to see this, babe."

Nate glowered down at Dex, whose grin couldn't get any wider, and he muttered in her ear, "You owe me a blow job for this, Titch."

She licked her lips. "Doesn't sound like much of a punishment."

He almost groaned. "Fuck me."

"Later," she whispered as the waitress came barreling in with another woman, a platinum blonde in her mid-fifties, he'd guess.

"Oh. My. God," she cried. She grabbed his hands. "Oh, I love you in that show."

"Thanks," Nate said, pasting on a winning smile. "That's nice of you to say."

"I need you to sign something." She cackled and gave him an

over exaggerated wink. "Don't worry, sweetheart. I'll keep it clean."

Dex stifled a laugh, hiding it with a cough. At the rate she was going, he'd be getting blow jobs for a month. He gave her the side-eye. Her forehead crinkled, all innocent.

"He wouldn't mind if it wasn't. Isn't that right, Nate? Anything for his fans."

I'm gonna kill her.

"How about a napkin, or your cap?" he suggested.

She whipped off the cap—thank fuck—and thrust it at him, along with a pen. He addressed it to her and signed his name.

"Can you add a couple of kisses on the end?" she asked.

Dex snorted.

"Sure." He handed it back to her with a broad smile. "Could we take the booth at the very end? My *friend* and I have a few things to discuss."

"'Course you can, sweetheart. You sit yourselves down, and I'll bring a couple menus across."

"Thanks." With his hand firmly pressed in the small of Dex's back, he propelled her to the far end of the diner. Her body shook beneath his palm, and one look at her face told him it was with laughter not desire.

"Keep going, Titch, and you'll be giving me that blow job right here."

She stuck out her tongue. "You're not that brave."

He cocked an eyebrow. "Try me."

She ignored him and slipped into the booth. He followed her, sitting on the same side. "What'll you have?" he said, scanning the menu.

"The Dino burger," she said, licking her lips. "And a chocolate milkshake."

Nate couldn't contain his amusement. "You're much more comfortable here, aren't you?"

"Yep. I'm a sweats and sneakers kind of girl." She gave him an impudent grin. "I bet you're not feeling as comfortable, though."

She couldn't be more mistaken. He was more at ease sitting in a cheap diner with her than he had been with anyone in years. Ever since his life had turned upside down, he'd avoided intimacy, including with his family, in case he slipped up and shared what he knew.

He nudged her playfully with his shoulder. "Actually, you're wrong. I admit, I fucked up taking you to Alessandro's." He shrugged. "I guess I wanted to take you someplace special. But if you're happy here, then so am I."

"Even with *Susan* fawning over you." She laughed. "Your face was priceless. I bet you thought she was going to ask you to sign her boobs." More laughter. "Now *that* I'd have paid to see."

His insides warmed at her genuine happiness. When he'd picked her up, her mouth had been pinched at the sides, and she'd seemed tired and more than a little overwrought—which he hadn't helped with by taking her to the wrong restaurant. But now, even though she was still pale, her color had picked up, and she looked a lot better. Freer even.

He curved one hand around the back of her neck, leaving his other free to explore. "Oh, Titch. Payback time."

"Wha... oh."

"Yeah, oh," he said, flicking his thumb over her nipple a second time. "Why do you think I chose this seat?"

"What can I get for you, lovelies?"

Dex jumped and tried to squirm out of his reach, but Nate held her in place as he lazily turned toward Susan who was proudly sporting her baseball cap with his signature scrawled across the peak.

"Two Dino burgers and two chocolate milkshakes. And if that man at the counter hasn't eaten, tell him to pick whatever he wants and put it on my tab."

"Oh my." Susan clasped a hand to her chest. "Well, aren't you the gentleman. That's real good of you. I'll be back soon with your burgers."

"No rush." He turned back to Dex. "Now, where were we, Titch?"

"I can't believe you did that," she said, her eyes all soft and misty. "Carry on like that, Nate Brook, and you'll find yourself mistaken for a nice guy."

He shrugged, even though he was secretly pleased at her response. Making Dex happy was fast becoming his favorite pastime.

"Even if he orders one of everything off the menu, it'll still be cheaper than two steaks at Alessandro's." He wanted to ask her to expand on the comment she'd made about being short of money, but instinct told him he wouldn't get anywhere. Not with the direct approach anyway. Lucky for him—and unlucky for her—he had a plan for exactly how to make her talk.

Susan came across with their burgers and shakes, and Dex's eyes lit up. "They look fabulous," she said, sending a grin Susan's way.

"Best thing on the menu," she confirmed. "And there's a piece of apple pie waiting after that. My treat for being so generous to Terry." She jerked her head back toward the homeless man who was tucking into a burger of his own, along with a huge side of fries. "He's ex-military, you know. Down on his luck. When you think of what he did for this country, too." She shook her head sadly. "Terrible how we treat some of our veterans."

Dex and Nate finished their burgers and the promised apple pie. She flopped back in her seat and rubbed her belly. "I couldn't eat another thing."

Nate wrapped her ponytail around his hand and tugged her head back. "That's too bad, Titch, coz you owe me a blow job."

Dex blinked rapidly. "You're not serious?"

His lips brushed hers. "Deadly."

He stood and wandered over to the counter to pay. He gave

Susan a large tip, which earned him a dazzling smile and a kiss on the cheek. Weirdly, he didn't mind at all. In fact, he might bring Dex here again.

As they walked to the car, he didn't have to look at Dex to feel her beside him, almost buzzing. Good, because if she'd balked, he'd have taken her straight home. He wasn't in the business of pressuring women to do anything that made them uncomfortable —at least when it came to sex. Talking? Now that was a different prospect all together.

Tonight, Dex was gonna spill what her issues with money were. And Nate was going to fix them.

CHAPTER 9

Nate grinned down at Dex gasping for breath. She yanked on the restraints securing her to the bedframe—a suggestion he'd made and one she'd eagerly agreed to. He plucked another piece of ice from a glass on the nightstand and stuck it between his teeth. Bending his head, he rolled it over her nipple.

"Oh God," she cried, her back arching off the bed when the cold hit her sensitive flesh.

Nate switched to her other nipple and then dropped the ice cube in her navel. "He won't help you."

He sucked the cold nub into his mouth and laved it with his tongue. Her legs writhed, and she tried to get some friction against his thigh—which he denied her.

"Ready to tell me yet?" he murmured, his mouth on her skin, his eyes fixed on hers.

She shook her head. Nate grinned again. Her determination in refusing to share why she needed money, what drove her to work two jobs, pushed her damned high in his estimation. She could have come right out and asked him for money—it wouldn't be the first time a bedmate had asked for a handout—but instead, she'd remained stubbornly mute. It wouldn't do her any good in the long run. She might not spill tonight, but she would eventually.

"Then it's only fair to warn you that I can keep going all night. And the next night. And the one after that. Your choice, Titch."

She groaned and bucked off the bed. The ice cube slithered down her body, leaving a trail of wetness behind. It fell on the sheets. He picked it up and circled it around her nipple once more.

She hissed. "Why do you care anyway?"

He twisted his lips to the side. "That's a good question, Titch. One I don't know the answer to. But soon as I figure it out, you'll be the first to know."

He parted her legs and trailed the ice along her inner thigh. She shivered, goosebumps breaking out all over her smooth golden skin while her little snatches of breath captivated him. He slipped his tongue between her folds.

She gave another long, drawn-out groan, squirming beneath him, pushing her eager pussy into his face. "You're killing me."

If he'd have been able to, he'd have smiled. From scared little girl to fucking sex kitten in twenty-four hours. More than he could have hoped for. Less—far less—than he craved. She'd been a great student, but she had more to give, and he was going to take it.

She came quickly which, considering she was several orgasms into their marathon session, impressed him. With her body still jerking and trembling, Nate straddled her waist and grabbed another piece of ice. He trailed it across her stomach, on the underside of her breasts, down her neck, rivers of water running over her sweat-dampened skin.

"Hmmm, well, if you're not going to make this easy, I think it's time we changed things up. I'm going for a record of orgasms with you, little Dex."

Her eyes widened. "I can't."

He gave her a wicked grin. "Oh, you can. Want me to show you?"

He clamped his teeth around the ice cube and inched down her body. He pushed her thighs wide and circled her clit with the ice, and then pushed the half-melted cube inside her with this tongue. She cried out both in agony and ecstasy, her head rocking from side to side, her thighs straining against his palms. He plunged his tongue inside her, over and over, taking absolutely no mercy. She would tell him in the end, if only to stop the death by orgasm he was subjecting her to.

"Nate, it's too much. I can't. I just can't. Oh fuuuuck."

She came again, her wrung-out body pulsing and throbbing on his tongue.

"You're a bastard."

He straddled her thighs, palming his erection with slow, regular strokes. "Ready for the next round?"

She shook her head violently. "Okay, okay. I'll tell you."

He sat up with a triumphant grin that had Dex rolling her half-hooded eyes. He untied her restraints and rubbed her wrists, even though they hadn't been on very tight.

She sat up, too, pulling the comforter up to her neck. He chuckled under his breath, but if it made her feel at ease, and gave her the confidence to tell him what the hell was going on, he'd let it slide. Her earlier question of why he cared was an intriguing one, and he'd been honest when he'd said he didn't know. Chivalry wasn't his style, but something about this little pocket rocket had him absolutely fascinated.

"Can I have a drink?"

Nate grazed his knuckles down the side of her cheek. Her red locks were an unholy mess of knots, her face flushed, her eyes heavy with sated desire. She'd never looked more fucking beautiful. How had he not noticed her before? He must have had blinders on.

"You can have anything you want," he said gently.

"A glass of water would be good."

"You got it."

He slipped off the bed, pulled on a pair of boxers, and padded into the kitchen. Grabbing a bottle of cold water from the fridge, he then snagged a glass off the drain board.

By the time he got back to the bedroom, she'd smoothed her fiery auburn hair into some semblance of order, and her knees were tucked into her chest with her arms hugging them. Damn, she was so young, so innocent—and he'd corrupted her. Her teeth grazed repeatedly over her bottom lip, her anxiety obvious. Maybe he was a bastard for pushing her. After all, the money thing could be something and nothing. For all he knew, she could have run up a bill on Rodeo Drive on clothes and jewelry she couldn't afford, and now the bank was pressing for payback. But something in her eyes told him it wasn't anything like that. *She* wasn't anything like that.

Keeping secrets had shredded him. He didn't want that for her.

"Here you go, Titch," he said, pouring some of the water into the glass for her. He swigged straight from the bottle then set it on the nightstand. He sat right in front of her, cross-legged, his forearms resting over his knees.

She eyed him over the rim of the glass as she greedily drank the entire contents. She wiped the corners of her mouth with her thumb and forefinger and set the glass beside the half-empty bottle.

"My mom is sick."

As she bluntly made the statement, her chin dropped to her chest, and her eyes cut away from his.

"How sick?" he coaxed.

She blinked slowly and then lifted her head. "Very. She'll die long before her time."

"What's wrong with her?"

"Alzheimer's."

Nate's eyebrows shot up in surprise. Dex was only twenty-two, so even if her mom had her later in life, that would only put her in her early to mid-sixties, surely? Very young for such a disease. As if guessing his thoughts, she added, "She's only forty-seven."

Tears welled up, but Dex being the stubborn, tough, little fireball she was, she refused to let one single tear fall.

"And the money thing. It's for her care?"

She nodded, her chin trembling as she stared over his shoulder. "I'm behind on the payments. With the pay rise you got me, I could have just about managed, but they're putting the fees up." She let out a heavy sigh. "I can't afford that, so I'm going to have to try and get a job back home in Wisconsin and move her. I won't get paid as much there, but I've found a home that's much cheaper. It's not as good. Still…" A shrug. "My sister is going to be devastated."

"Can't she help?"

Dex shook her head. "She helps as much as she can, but she's got two kids. She can't work because the childcare is too expensive, so they've only got her husband's income to rely on."

For the first time, she released the death grip on her knees as her hands came to her face. She rubbed hard and then offered him a wry grin. "So now you know why I was so mad outside that club. And why the price of a bottle of wine offended me."

He tucked a stray curl behind her ear, an idea slowly forming in his mind. A way for him to get what he needed, and for him to help her out, without it looking like she was some sort of charity case. Dex was a proud girl. Determined, hardworking, tenacious. Independent. Yep, very independent. If he didn't handle this the right way, the mouthful she gave him at the club would pale into insignificance to the tongue lashing she'd unleash on him now.

"I have a proposition for you."

She leaned forward, her eyebrows furrowing and then releasing. "Oh yeah?"

"Don't look so worried, Titch. It's a quid-pro-quo kind of

arrangement. I have a problem you can help me with, and in return, I might be able to help you."

She narrowed her gaze. "What kind of a problem?"

"Suspicious little thing, aren't you?" He cleared his throat, buying time while he thought of the best way to phrase it. "My brother is getting married. Three weeks on Saturday. I want you to come with me."

Her eyes sprang wide open. "Me? Come to your brother's wedding? With you?"

Nate grinned. "Thanks for the recap, Titch."

"But... but why? Why me? We're practically strangers. Weddings are for friends and family."

Irritation crept over his skin that she could cast aside this weekend as though it was nothing. Odd really, because her comment was accurate. They were strangers. He'd only noticed she existed a week ago, but a week was a long time in showbiz. During that time, he'd grown to care about her. It occurred to him how well she'd get on with his family, how easily she'd fit in. But he must remember he'd be showing her a mirage of his true self. Sharing his reality wasn't a possibility.

He kept his inner thoughts to himself, though, instead sharing a crooked smile and a hint of the truth.

"Let's just say we'll be strangers together. Don't get me wrong, I love my family. But we're no longer close. I find going back to New York... difficult. Having you there to distract me," he gave her a lascivious look that sparked a flash of desire in her eyes, "would make my visit back home more palatable. Believe me, I'm getting the better end of the deal."

She grazed her bottom lip with her teeth and nodded sagely, considering his request. "So, how can you help me?"

"I'll clear your debts—"

"No. I can't—"

"Wait." He lifted his hand in the air to stop her interrupting, as he'd known she would. "I'll clear your debts with the nursing home and cover the percentage increase in fees, as well as whatever that crappy grocery store pays you. It's the other half of the deal, and you're taking it."

To him, it was peanuts, but to her, it meant everything.

She shook her head violently. "No. I can't let you do that. I *won't* let you. It's too much and—"

He put a finger over her lips. "You know, I'm envious. You share such a closeness with your mom, a deep love that, despite her illness, cannot be denied. I was only twelve when I lost my mom. I've never gotten over it. That bond between a mother and their child... it's so special. Let me help, so you get to have that with your mom for as long as possible."

He kissed her to stop her responding. He would not take no for an answer, and by getting her aroused, she'd be pliable and more likely to listen. The more he thought about having her by his side in New York, the greater the idea appealed to him. Sneaking off into quiet corners to steal kisses or, where privacy allowed, easing her to her knees so she could suck him off and release the tension that would ride him hard for the entire weekend. If only she knew: he was definitely the winner in this deal.

He pressed her into the bed, his hands already searching, seeking, his mouth feverishly taking what he needed from her—to forget—because since he'd first put his hands on her, the constant voices in his head had quieted. A soft appreciative noise sounded at the back of her throat, drawing a growl of acknowledgement from him.

His dick throbbed from the number of times they'd fucked over the weekend, but as blood rushed to his groin, it throbbed for a different reason. God, he wanted inside her. Like a fucking drug, she'd gotten him hooked with a few delicious samples.

He quickly donned a condom. "You're coming to New York," he demanded. "And you're coming all over my cock. You don't have a choice, Titch. With either one. You're going to take the deal, no argument."

He thrust inside her, silencing any further refusals. She cried out, probably because her pussy was as sore as his dick, but as he moved, her nails raked down his back and her eyes took on that wild 'you can do anything to me just don't stop' look. The one that had him squeezing his eyes closed so he didn't come in thirty seconds like a fucking horny teenager.

The lack of visuals didn't make a difference. With zero control over his body, he climaxed, his head pressing into the pillow, his lips against her damp neck as pure pleasure rushed through him. Her walls clamped around him, drawing out his own gratification.

"Nate." She spoke on an exhale, her drowsy voice the sweetest thing he'd ever heard. It wasn't a question, just a statement of appreciation, one he felt more deeply than he'd imagined possible, given that he was such a shallow bastard. He pecked her lips then rolled to the side. He clasped his hand around hers and squeezed her fingers, staring at the ceiling.

"Say yes, Titch. To New York, to the money. To all of it. Just fucking say yes."

He held his breath. If she refused again, he didn't know what his next move would be. He'd used every tool he had. She had the power now. She took a breath, and he closed his eyes in silent prayer.

"Yes—on one condition."

Nate twisted his head to find Dex lying on her side. She blinked up at him, her jaw set in a determined fashion.

"Hit me with it."

"The money, it's a loan. However long it takes, I'll pay you back. I won't take no for an answer. That's my condition, and if you don't agree, it's a deal-breaker. So, do we have a deal?"

His lips twitched. Christ, she was unique, someone to cling on to with everything he had.

He held out his hand. "I believe we do, Titch."

She let out a sigh of relief and shook it. "Good, because I'm too tired to go another round, either verbally or physically." She cast aside the covers and swung her legs over the edge of the bed.

Nate leaned up on his elbow. "Where are you going?"

She glanced over her shoulder. "Tomorrow's Monday. I have work."

"So do I. What's your point, Titch?"

"I need to get home. All my things are there."

"Then I'll take you in the morning."

"I have to be in work by eight." She glanced at her watch and groaned. "Fuck, it's two in the morning."

Nate offered her a slow grin and a wink. "No point going home now then, is there?" He held out his arms. "I don't want you to go. Stay, please. I'll make sure you get to work on time. Promise."

After a pause, she got back into bed, defeated, and snuggled up to him. "What's going on here, Nate?"

He kissed her temple. "I don't know, Titch."

And I'm shit scared to look too closely.

CHAPTER 10

Dex stared at the stack of work piled high on her desk with a sense of despair. Since Nate had dropped her off at the office on Monday morning after one of the most exciting and exhilarating weekends of her entire life, she'd come back down to earth with an almighty bump. Whether Bernard was still furious Nate had gotten one over on him, or her boss sensed a flush of happiness in her that he was determined to stamp out, he hadn't given her a moment's breathing space all week.

Not that it mattered. Dex hadn't heard from Nate. At all. And that was giving her more sleepless nights than coping with a big baby like Bernard.

With a sigh, she picked up the first file. Opened it. Closed it again. Gave another sigh. It was as though Nate had stolen her motivation, as well as her attention. His easy dismissal of what they'd shared made her feel cheap, like it hadn't meant a thing. Except to her, it had meant far too much.

Did his silence mean he'd changed his mind about New York? If he had then she had a problem, because Nate had already cleared her debts. Jennifer had called on Monday afternoon to thank Dex for promptly paying her arrears.

As she tried to work through the reason for Nate's lack of contact, her phone rang. Bernard. With a sigh she picked it up. Before she could say a word, he barked, "Get me a coffee. Now."

He slammed the phone down. Dex gritted her teeth but complied without question. Someone must have ticked him off. Best keep her head down, not draw attention to herself, and scour the internet for alternative jobs that paid as well.

Or, just as likely, win the lottery.

She made Bernard's coffee, ensuring she added exactly the right amount of cream and sugar otherwise she'd be subjected to a hissy fit and a tongue lashing. With a tap on his door, she waited for the curt, "Enter," like he was a goddamn king, and stepped inside.

"Here you are, Bernard," she said, setting the cup on the left-hand side of his desk. Never the right, even though he was right-handed. Go figure. He didn't even look up from his computer as he stabbed angrily at the keys. "Can I get you anything else?"

He glared up at her then. "Yeah, you can get the fuck out of my sight. I don't want to be disturbed for the rest of the day. Think you can manage that, girlie?"

Don't punch him. Don't punch him.

"Of course," she murmured.

She turned to leave... and hard stopped. Nate was leaning his shoulder against the open door, a pair of Aviator sunglasses hiding those glacier-blue eyes, his arms crossed over his chest. His dark hair was rumpled and messy, like he'd just rolled out of bed. God, he looked delicious enough to eat. But then she hardened her heart against him. After a week of absolutely no contact, it was no less than he deserved.

"My mother used to tell me manners cost nothing," Nate drawled. "You should try it sometime."

Dex dragged her gaze away from Nate to glance back at Bernard, tensed for an explosion when she caught his expression. Bernard's forehead was scored with a deep scowl.

"I can't see you today, Nate. I'm busy, and we don't have an appointment."

Nate stepped into the room. Right next to her. The sleeve of his shirt brushed her bare arm. A rash of goosebumps appeared, from pleasure rather than a chill. His fingers touched hers so lightly, she might have imagined it.

"I'm not here to see you. I've come to take your assistant to lunch."

"You have?" She quickly slammed down on the spike of hope. It was probably so he could let her down gently. Tell her he'd made a mistake about New York and put an end to their relationship.

Relationship? Pah. A weekend of hot fucking more like.

He pushed his sunglasses on top of his head. "Yep."

"She's too busy," Bernard interjected, even though his eyes narrowed with curiosity. "Hasn't done half the stuff I asked for this week which, considering she's costing me fifteen percent more, I should get fifteen percent more output."

"She's entitled to a lunch break." Nate's smooth voice brooked no argument. "I'll have her back by two-fifteen."

Bernard grunted. "She'd better be."

Nate's warm hand pressed against the small of her back, and he eased her from Bernard's office.

"What are you doing here?" she whispered as Nate closed the door with a quiet click. At least he didn't slam it, although that wasn't Nate's style. He was more the silent assassin type.

"Um, taking you to lunch?" He grinned. "Didn't I just say that?"

Dex planted her hands on her hips. "I haven't seen you all week, and then you turn up here. I'm on the edge with Bernard, Nate. You know how important this job is to me."

His hand curved around the back of her neck, and he bent his head, stealing a quick kiss. "Missed you, too, Titch. Now can we go?"

She refused to show any humorous reaction, even though she wanted to jump in the air. *He's missed me.*

"You are an annoying little shit."

He raised one eyebrow. "After last weekend, you know there's nothing *little* about me." He grabbed her purse, handed it to her, and slung a casual arm around her shoulder. "How about Thai? There's a half-decent place right around the corner. They're fast, too, which considering we only have," he checked his watch, "fifty-six minutes, we'd better get a move on."

Dex found herself being propelled toward the elevator, her short legs struggling to keep up with Nate's loping strides. As they spilled outside into the bright sunshine, he dropped his sunglasses back in place. Hiding his eyes gave him a more enigmatic appearance. On the short walk to the restaurant, her hand inside his, she must have counted at least ten women giving him the eye. Jealousy surged through her, like a swollen river following a torrential downpour. Oh, she was so screwed. If innocent looks from passersby garnered such a strong reaction, how would she feel when Nate moved on—because he would. Nate Brook was a player, a guy who liked to eat from a buffet. He was all about new and exciting and variety. The minute she became old and dull, he'd be gone

Nate secured them a table in a quiet part of the restaurant. He'd been recognized, although no one approached them. The area surrounding her office was full of casting agencies and scouts, and so seeing actors in the vicinity wasn't an unusual occurrence.

They ordered lunch—the two-course special that their server assured them was part of the fifteen-minute guarantee—and a bottle of water, because, well… work. Dex would have preferred to slug back a large glass of wine, but given Bernard's mood, and her tenuous position, water was the safer option.

"Bernard's still being a dick, I see," Nate said with a carefree grin.

Dex shrugged. "I can handle Bernard."

"I don't doubt that for a minute."

Silence fell between them. Dex fiddled with the tablecloth as Nate's keen gaze raked her face.

"What's the matter, Titch?"

She shouldn't have said anything. She should have kept her mouth shut, like a good little girl, smiled, and told him she was fine. Fine was a good word, right? Especially to a man. The male of the species was comfortable with *fine*.

But she didn't. Instead, she made a complete and utter fool of herself with a diatribe she couldn't have remembered afterward, even if someone put a gun to her head.

"Have you changed your mind about New York? If you have, then we need to sort out how the fuck I'm going to pay you back. Jennifer called me. She's the manager of the home, in case you didn't know. She told me my arrears have been cleared. So if New York is off, then A, you should have had the courtesy to tell me and you didn't, which makes you a bastard, and B, I need to pay you back. And before you say a word, I know I said pay you back twice. I know, okay, but, well, fuck... And I know last weekend probably didn't mean a thing to you, but I'm not in the habit of jumping into bed with strangers, pouring out all my troubles because of their superior sexing skills, and then have them come up with some sort of a... a... an indecent proposal that they then don't allow one party to pay their half."

She gulped in some air, damned sure all those words had come out on one single breath. Where was the water? Her mouth was dry as a cracker. She looked around for their server while shredding a napkin that she couldn't remember picking up.

"Dex."

She couldn't face him. Didn't want to hear the truth spill from those delicious lips that had touched every single inch of her. Wouldn't allow him to shatter her hopes for something more between them.

"Dex. Either fucking look at me or I'm gonna do something that'll embarrass you a whole lot more."

She snapped her eyes to his. Nate didn't have the embarrassment gene, so she had no doubt he'd follow through on his threat. The details of what it could entail was anyone's guess, but she wasn't about to test him.

"I haven't changed my mind about New York."

"You haven't?" Her voice came out more like a squeak.

"No."

"Oh."

"I've been pulling sixteen-hour days. We're up against a deadline to get the latest episode of my show in the can. I haven't had time to do anything except work, sleep, and eat."

Her face burned. "Oh." She dropped the ribbons of paper that used to be a napkin onto the table and stared at her now-empty hands.

"That's partly why I called round today, actually." A pause. A sigh. A curse. "Will you fucking look at me."

She slowly lifted her chin.

"What on earth is wrong with you?"

Nothing. Apart from the fact I'm falling too deep, too fast, and I'm going to bear the scars for a lifetime.

"I'm sorry. For ranting. It's been a stressful week."

Nate leaned forward and caressed her cheek with the back of his hand. "It's all good, Titch."

Their soup arrived, preventing her from reacting to the tender moment. The server also set down a jug of water Dex had needed five minutes ago. The minute her glass was full, she downed it in one.

"Thirsty?" Nate asked with an eyebrow arch and an amused smirk.

She ignored him and instead dug into her soup. The flavor hit her taste buds, and she made an appreciative noise. Best. Soup. Ever.

"Stop taunting me. It's mean."

"I like taunting you, though."

She stuck out her tongue. His eyes flared.

"Point that in my direction again and I'm sucking on it."

A sound came out of her that was a cross between a gasp and a snort. "You wouldn't dare."

He bent his head to the left and licked his top lip. "Oh, Titch."

Desire curled in the pit of her stomach. There was something so decadent about Nate, and she couldn't get enough. He would corrupt her. That wasn't in doubt. Up for question was to what extent.

She cleared her throat. "So, you were saying, about why you came by."

He laughed. "Was I?"

Dex pouted. "Stop it."

He nodded at her bowl. "Eat your soup."

She growled, which had him laughing harder. She almost inhaled the rest of her appetizer. Dropping her spoon, she gestured with a flourish. "Ta-da."

Nate finished at a much more leisurely pace. By the time he pushed his bowl to one side, she was almost fizzing with anticipation and a healthy dose of annoyance.

"Enough, already. What's going on, Nate?"

He gave her an innocent stare. "What, I can't take you out for lunch?"

"You're playing games."

He rested back in his chair and dropped his napkin beside his bowl. "I wanted to see you. I needed to eat. It seemed like a good idea to do both things simultaneously. Plus..." He shifted in his chair. Jesus, Nate Brook actually looked uncomfortable. Her skin prickled. "We're doing a night shoot tonight. It'll probably finish about two a.m. I wondered if you wanted to swing by the set, and maybe after, we could grab a bite to eat and you could come back to my place."

Her mouth fell open. Actually dropped almost to the table, like a scene from a cartoon. "You want me to come… to come…"

He beckoned to her and whispered, "Yes, I want you to come and come and come, but not until I've finished work."

Intense heat almost burned the skin off her face. Nate was so comfortable with dirty talk. She had some serious catching up to do.

"I'll text you the details of where you need to go. Security will direct you when you get there, and then I'll come fetch you. Deal?"

Railroaded yet thrilled, she nodded. "I'll be there."

CHAPTER 11

Dex stopped the car at the security gate. She gave her name to the guard, who checked down a list, nodded, then gave her directions where to park. The red-and-white striped barrier lifted, allowing her access onto the set. It felt odd being there, especially as she'd done her best to avoid all things Hollywood since coming to Los Angeles in search of a better life for Mom.

She turned left at the end of the road. A yellow sign with large black lettering that read 'Visitors' told her she was in the right place.

Where was Nate? He said he'd be there to greet her, but apart from a few people hanging about with clipboards and various filming paraphernalia, she couldn't see him.

Cutting the engine, she sat for a moment and took a deep breath. Being invited here by Nate felt like a shift in their relationship, as if the tectonic plates were grinding together, and she wasn't sure whether the earth moving beneath her feet was something to cling to or run from.

A tap on her window startled her. Nate's winter-blue eyes and white-toothed grin peered through the glass, drawing a happy smile from her. He opened the door.

"Come on, Titch. I'll show you around."

She took her keys out of the ignition and then climbed out of the car. Locking it behind her, she slipped her hand inside Nate's.

"I've never been on a set before."

Nate began walking toward a huge building that resembled an aircraft hangar. "It's not nearly as glamorous as you might think. This job is ninety-five percent hanging around and five percent acting."

He pushed open a door and gestured for her to go ahead. "Let's get some caffeine in you, and then I'll take you through to where we're shooting tonight's scene." He strode to the far side of the building, waved at a couple technicians who were unwinding an enormous reel of cable, and then opened another door that led into a kitchen.

A few people were sitting at a table drinking coffee and chatting. One of them Dex recognized as Nate's co-star. She racked her brains trying to remember her name but came up empty. She rarely watched TV, and had only tuned into Nate's show because, well, Nate was in it. If asked to recall the storylines, or who the other actors were would result in an epic fail.

"This is Dex," Nate said. "You fuckers—be nice. She's coming on set tonight for the shoot."

"Hey, Dex," his co-star said. "I'm Sharla. Sadly for me, I have to work with this prick five, sometimes six days per week."

Nate threw a sugar sachet at Sharla, hitting her square on the side of her head. She laughed and threw it back, her aim not nearly as true.

"Ignore her," Nate said, flinging one arm around Dex's shoulder while pouring coffee into two paper cups with his free hand. "She loves me really."

Sharla snorted, but her eyes twinkled. Dex took to her immediately.

They finished their coffee, and Nate got to his feet. "Come on,

Titch." He pointed his finger at Sharla. "Don't be late. I want to be out of here by two at the latest."

She gestured dismissively. "Yeah, yeah."

Nate led her around the back of the building, and she was almost blinded by the number of lights. Although it was dark, it might as well have been daytime. And so many people wandering about with cameras, microphones, cables. It was like a community all of its own.

Nate grabbed her a chair and set it up against a false wall. It wasn't long before he was called away, so after a final check she was okay, he wandered over to the director.

Dex took out her phone and sent her sister a text, along with a picture of the set. Not that it would be exciting for Elva. She'd visited sets in the past. Still, it was nice to share this moment with her. She needed to tell her that their money worries were fixed, too—at least for now—although Dex was determined to pay Nate back. Accompanying him on a trip to New York—that he was insisting on paying for—did not make them equal. Whatever he thought.

She slipped her phone into her pocket and tried to spot Nate. She couldn't see him, though. Nate hadn't been joking when he'd said there was a lot of hanging around. And then an excited buzz went around as people started moving into position. A tall, thin guy ambled toward a car, holding a huge boom. It looked heavier than him, although he wielded it like a pro.

And then Nate appeared, his arm wrapped around Sharla's waist. She was looking up at him, her face lit with desire. Nate drew to a halt. His lips moved, but she couldn't hear his lines from this far away. The director gesticulated, and Nate bent his head, taking Sharla's mouth in a passionate kiss.

Jealousy slammed into her, and her stomach hardened. It didn't matter that what they were doing was only make believe. She couldn't help it. He was like a book she'd loaned from the library. Hers to thumb through, to hold, to pore over, but eventually, her time would be up, and she'd have to return him.

She wanted to turn away but found herself staring, almost like watching an accident about to happen. It was impossible to tear her gaze away. Then she heard a faint voice yell "Cut". Nate broke away from Sharla, and the two co-stars shared a few words.

And it was then she heard someone mention Nate. Coming from behind the false wall. A guy speaking. She held her breath, her ears on high alert.

"Did you see that girl with Nate? Talk about deviating from his usual fuck."

A snort, followed by, "Understatement of the century," from a second guy.

"Poor cow. I bet she hasn't got a clue."

"Yeah, although I bet it brought Sharla to heel. She might be more willing to spread her legs for him now."

Laughs. Lots of laughs. At her expense.

Dex dug her fingernails into her palms. Pure rage had black and white dots appearing in her vision. She barely heard the rest of their conversation because one line kept playing on repeat.

I bet it brought Sharla to heel.

No wonder that kiss had looked so real. It *was* fucking real, at least from Nate's perspective. It seemed as though her part in this little charade was to make his co-star jealous. She must be resisting him, and so Nate decided to up the ante.

A painful tightness constricted her throat, her breath coming in shallow little gulps. She scrambled to her feet. For one brief moment, she considered storming over to where the director was setting up the next shoot and kneeing Nate right in the balls. And maybe stomp on them for good measure. She'd bet he wouldn't be able to fuck Sharla—or anyone—for quite a while after that.

Instead, she quietly slipped away. Five minutes later, she reached her car. Relieved she hadn't gotten lost on the way, she climbed inside, took a few moments to rest her head against the steering wheel while she waited for her tears to recede, and then quietly pulled out of the car lot.

CHAPTER 12

"Cut."

Nate broke away from Sharla and gave her a reproachful frown. "Garlic again? You're such a bitch."

She laughed. "I can't stay away from the things I like to eat, Nate. Even if I do adore you."

Nate grinned. "Remember, two can play at that game."

She spread her arms wide. "Bring it."

"When you least expect it, sweetheart."

She laughed again, linking her arm through his as they walked over to their next marker. "So, Dex is the special one then?"

Nate frowned. "I have no idea what you're talking about."

"Sure you do. I've been working with you for two years, Nate. You've never brought a woman to set. Not once."

He shrugged. "She's different. Fun. I like her."

"Then try not to fuck it up."

"I'll do my best," he said, his voice dripping sarcasm as he sought out where he'd left Dex. Except she wasn't there. He scanned around, but he couldn't see her.

"Where the hell is she?" he said, more to himself than Sharla.

He poked his head behind the fake wall she'd been sitting in front of. No sign.

"Relax," Sharla said. "Maybe she's gone to the restroom."

"How long do we have before shooting the next scene?"

"Five seconds," Jonathan, their director said, appearing by Nate's shoulder.

"Fuck," Nate muttered. He forced himself to concentrate on delivering his lines. The second Jonathan shouted "Cut!", he shot over to where he'd left Dex. He questioned a couple of the crew who were hanging about, but they hadn't seen her.

He scouted the set, eventually deducing she wasn't there. What the hell was going on? She'd been fine when he'd left her. Maybe she'd been bored and gone home, but he doubted it. Rudeness wasn't Dex's thing. She'd have waited for a break and then spoken to him.

What if something had happened, with her mom, maybe, or her sister? He called her cell. It went straight to voicemail. Damn it. He was stuck there until they finished that night's schedule. His mood darkened, and he found himself snapping at a couple of crew members.

Finally, at five to two in the morning, Jonathan called a wrap. Nate didn't say goodnight to a single soul. He called her again on the way to his car. Still no answer.

Forty minutes later, he parked up outside Dex's apartment. On his way upstairs, he tried calling again. Lucked out.

With his heartbeat thundering in his ears as concern set in, he banged on her door. Silence. He knocked again. Nothing.

"Dex, are you in there? It's Nate. Open up. I'm worried." When he couldn't hear anything from inside, he tried one final time. "Dex? Is everything okay?"

Finally, he heard a sound, a shuffling. Maybe she'd felt unwell and hadn't found the right break in filming to let him know.

But the door didn't open. Instead, she decided to hold a

conversation through the damned thing. Well, conversation was a bit of an overstatement, because all he got was, "Fuck off, Nate."

His eyebrows shot up. *What the hell?*

"Open the door."

"No."

He clenched his jaw. He wouldn't mind her being pissy at him if he knew what he was supposed to have done. "Open the goddamn door."

"Go home."

He picked up on the slight waver to her voice. Time to press his advantage.

"Not without you, Titch," he said softly.

All fell silent, and he expected to hear the rattle of a chain, the click of a lock. He got neither.

"Aww, Sharla turned you down again, has she? So you thought you'd come take out your frustration and your hard-on with me? Because *of course* I'd be willing. *Of course* I'd be grateful. Superstar Nate Brook noticing little old me. Except I'm only a tool for you to use to make Sharla jealous. Right?"

Shock slammed into him, and he actually took a step back, as if he'd been physically shoved in the chest. What. The. Actual. Fuck?

"Wrong," he bit back. "So fucking wrong, Titch. Where the hell did you get such a crazy idea?"

This time he heard a lock being turned, but instead of Dex's door opening, the one next door did. Nate found himself faced with a furious neighbor in her late sixties. She was wearing a floor-length pale-green nightgown—with a white bow no less—and a head full of hair curlers. He suppressed a grin. He guessed it wouldn't be welcome.

"What is going on out here? Do you know what time it is, young man?"

"Sorry, ma'am."

"Sorry won't help me fall back to sleep without a cup of hot milk now, will it? It's obvious to anyone with half a brain that Dex doesn't want to talk to you. Go home, son. Come back tomorrow, at a more reasonable hour."

She disappeared inside with a huff, slamming her door behind her.

Well, shit.

"Dex," he hissed through the door. "Open up, will you, before Jessica Fletcher comes out and chastises me again."

He hoped slipping in some humor might soften her. He needed to find out what the hell she'd meant about Sharla. She'd obviously been fed some misinformation, and he couldn't allow that to fester. He'd stay out here all night if he had to.

Finally, he heard the chain rattle and the lock turned. She drew back the door. Oh, she was mightily pissed, arms crossed over her chest, hip cocked out to one side.

Humor didn't work then.

"Can I come in?"

"Sorry. My vagina isn't open for sympathy fucks this evening."

He held back a grin that threatened. God, she was infuriating, but also magnificent. Angry Dex definitely turned him on, although right then probably wasn't the best time to share that thought.

"Let's talk."

He took a step forward, testing the water, his eyes locked on hers.

She exhaled through her nose, spat, "This should be good," and then plunked herself on the tiny sofa.

He clicked the door shut and sat beside her, his ankle resting over his knee in a show of nonchalance, even though he was anything but. He tried to pinpoint when this thing between them had moved from a bit of fun to something much... more. Where he cared. A lot.

"Okay, let's start with you telling me what is going through that gorgeous head of yours."

Her lips flattened into a thin line. "Don't think you're getting out of this with throwaway compliments."

Nate offered her a crooked smile. "As soon as I know what I'm supposed to be trying to get out of, I'll adjust my approach accordingly."

A hard glare, followed by a sigh, and then her chin dropped to her chest. "Is something going on between you and Sharla?"

"No."

"Liar."

He clenched his jaw. "I don't lie." *Not directly, anyway. Keep secrets, yep, absolutely. But that was for my brothers, to protect them and Mom's memory...* "But in the spirit of full disclosure, Titch, we did sleep together. Once. Over two years ago. What I'd like to know is, who told you?"

She lifted her chin. "I heard a couple guys talking when you were doing that scene. The one where you kissed. They basically implied I was only there as a way to get Sharla to sleep with you."

She almost turned green. He liked the fact she was jealous because it meant she gave a shit, but regardless, if he found those two fucks, he'd rip them a new asshole. He grazed his knuckles down her bare arm. "Titch, TV and movie sets are hotbeds for gossip. You can't believe anything you hear."

She bent her head forward, her hair covering her face. He tucked it behind her ear to get a better look at her.

"Wouldn't it have been easier to just ask me, instead of all this... drama?"

She twisted her lips to one side. "Probably."

"Then why didn't you?"

She exhaled slowly. "I don't know, Nate. All this," she swung her hand between them, "it's so unbelievable. I'm out of my depth here." She nibbled on her bottom lip. "I can't go to New York with you. I'll find a way to pay you back, I promise."

His pulse jolted. No way. She *had* to come. He needed her. She'd stopped being a distraction to take his mind off being back home, instead becoming someone he wanted to introduce to his family, to show her where he'd grown up, the places he'd hung out when playing hooky. The alley where he'd had his first fumble beneath a girl's skirt. Okay, maybe not that, but the rest of it. Yep, he wanted it all.

"You have to come."

She raised her eyebrows. "Pardon me?"

Fuck. Wrong approach, dickhead.

He rubbed his fingertips over his lips. "That came out wrong. What I meant to say was I really want you to come. I get it, Dex. This is new for both of us, but what better way to get to know someone than a short vacation."

She bit the inside of her cheek and closed her eyes, a soft sigh spilling from her lips. "I don't know, Nate."

He took her hand and prayed the right words came out of his mouth.

"I'm so twisted up over you. I can't even figure out when it happened. Maybe when you called me out that night at the club, or maybe the quiet dignity you showed in front of Bernard, when you'd have had every right to twist his balls until the fucker passed out. Or when I first got inside you and you looked up at me with those beautiful eyes that begged me not to stop moving." He knitted his fingers into her hair and tilted her head back. "Tell me you feel the same, Titch."

Their eyes met, her dove-gray one's doing funny things to his insides. "I don't want to get hurt, Nate."

He sensed a weakness and pressed his advantage with a soft brush of his lips against hers. He couldn't promise not to hurt her, and damned if he was going to lie.

"I don't know where this is going any more than you do. But if we don't try, how will we know what might have been? Don't leave me hanging. Come to New York. Be mine, Dexter Nolan."

She closed her eyes, and when she opened them, they were full of tears. Surprise sent his eyebrows shooting up. Dex wasn't the teary type.

And then she climbed on to his lap and flung her arms around his neck.

"I'll be yours."

CHAPTER 13

Nate knocked on Dex's door, and the minute she answered, he waved the airline tickets in the air. "We're all booked. We leave on Thursday."

Dex grinned and snatched the tickets from his hand. She scanned them, her eyes glistening with excitement. "Oh, this is so cool. My first trip to New York. It's gonna be *awesome.*" She twisted her lips in pause. "We'll have time for sight-seeing, right?

Nate rubbed his chin in thought. "Hmm, wonder if it's too late to get a refund on your ticket."

She gave him a playful punch. "You wouldn't."

He cocked an eyebrow. "Don't bet on it, Titch."

"Well, if all you came over for was to tease me, I've got better things to do."

She spun on her heel. He followed her inside and snagged her around the waist, pulling her against him.

"Not so fast, little Dex." He kissed her neck and snaked his hand over her breast.

She arched into him, groaning when he scraped a fingernail over her nipple. "You don't play fair."

"Correct. Now get your sneakers on."

She twisted in his arms. "Where are we going?"

He tapped his nose and repeated, "Get your sneakers on. It's Saturday, and we're spending it together. You'll be seeing your mom tomorrow, and I'm not going to have a minute before Thursday, so stop defying me, otherwise I'll have to take you in hand."

She pouted and flounced off. He smiled at her retreating back. She was fucking adorable. He was definitely keeping her, at least for now. Was his record three or four dates? He wasn't known for sticking around—he got bored far too easily—but Dexter Nolan had piqued his interest. These past three weeks had been a revelation.

She finished tying her shoelaces. "Do I need anything else?"

"Yep, a hat. And sunscreen."

She donned a baseball cap that had *I might be small, but I'm ballsy* stitched on the front, and slotted a tube of sunscreen in the front pocket of her shorts.

"Okay, ready."

He flicked the peak. "Apt."

She grinned. "I know, right?"

The traffic was hideous, and it took him an hour to reach Santa Monica pier. On the whole journey, Dex chattered excitedly about everything she wanted to see in New York. Despite his dread about the upcoming visit, he had to admit her enthusiasm was catching. He instinctively knew the trip back east wouldn't be nearly as bad with her by his side.

He parked as close to the pier as he could. Pulling on his own baseball cap, he grabbed a pair of shades and then took Dex's hand. Five minutes later, he stopped outside the bike rental shop.

"Excellent," she said with a wide grin. "I want to do this in New York, around Central Park, although I haven't ridden a bike since I was a kid."

"Then this'll be good practice for you," Nate replied.

"Where are we going?" she asked once he'd paid the rental and they'd both been sized up for bikes.

"The Strand. We'll cycle down to Redondo Beach, stop for some lunch, and then cycle back."

Her brow crinkled. "That's pretty far."

Nate shrugged. "Forty miles or so, give or take. It's flat, though, so you'll be fine."

She didn't look convinced, but as they set off down the path, with the beach communities on their left and the Pacific Ocean on their right with the sun twinkling off its surface, she seemed to forget her worries about the distance.

Nate pointed out a few sights along the way, and they stopped for a few minutes at Huntington Beach to watch the surfers and drink some fluids.

"Can you surf?" Dex asked.

Nate nodded. "I learned when I first came out here. It's kind of a religion. I'm nowhere near as good as the locals who started surfing as soon as they could walk, but I can hold my own. I'll teach you if you like?"

She shook her head. "No way. I don't like open water. I like to be able to touch the bottom."

He tossed his empty bottle of water in the recycling trash can. "Why don't you like open water?"

Her gaze became shuttered as she looked out to sea. A gust of wind blew her hair across her face, momentarily hiding her from view. She tucked it behind her ear. "When I was nine, I almost drowned."

Nate stepped closer to her and rested his hand on the small of her back. "What happened?"

She let out a deep sigh. "I followed my sister and her friends to a lake not far from our house. Mom had strictly forbidden me to go swimming, saying I was too young. I ignored her." She glanced up with a wry grin. "I wasn't the best-behaved child."

"Shocker," he said.

She laughed, the darkness which had momentarily clouded her features receding.

"Anyhow, I spotted Elva and her friends splashing about and having fun, so I jumped in and started swimming toward them. My legs got caught up in some reeds. Elva saved my life. It's one of the reasons we're so close. I love her to bits." She shook her head. "I don't like to think about it very much. So yeah, no open water for me."

Despite the sad story, envy curled deep within him. He used to have that kind of relationship with his brothers, and if he let them in, he could have it again. But he couldn't take the risk. By staying away, he limited the chances of dropping his guard and spilling what he knew. That was the worst thing he could do. To destroy his brothers so heartlessly... no. Better for them to think he was a brooding, miserable asshole than risk telling them the truth.

"Hey." Dex touched his arm, jerking him from his thoughts. "You disappeared on me."

He curved his hands around the back of her neck and bent his head to kiss her, only briefly, but it had the desired effect of halting further questioning on her part.

"Shall we go?" he asked.

She smiled. "Sounds good."

A couple of hours after they'd left Santa Monica, they arrived at Redondo Beach. The path continued a little farther, down to Torrance Beach, but Redondo, in his opinion, had a little more going on.

They secured the bikes and wandered around. Knowing Dex as he now did, he suggested hot dogs and ice cream for lunch which, if her beaming smile was anything to go by, scored a plus point for him.

After an hour or so, they returned to their bikes and headed back to the path. It was much hotter on the journey back to Santa Monica, and after they'd been cycling for ten miles or so, Dex slowed down. By the time they reached Marina Del Rey and turned off the path to skirt the marina, she called a time out.

She kicked out the bike stand and stretched her legs.

"My knees are stiff, and my cooter is *killing* me from that saddle."

Nate raised an eyebrow. "Cooter?"

"Yeah, you know." She pointed to her pussy. "Cooter."

Nate threw back his head and laughed. "You are one crazy woman."

"You can laugh, but if I'm in pain down there, you won't be able to visit, will you?"

"I'll lick it all better," Nate said. He took a step—to tease her.

She threw her hands out in front. "Don't even think about it."

He laughed again. "Okay, I'll wait until we get home. A hot bath, and lots of tongue action, and you'll be good as new."

"You are so bad."

He caught her around the waist and bent down for a kiss. "Yeah, so you keep saying. Still here, though, aren't you, Titch?"

"Cocky bastard," she muttered, adding, "Anyway, if my cooter is sore, your cock and balls must be, too, surely?"

"All in full working order," he said, grinning. "When I first came to LA, I took up cycling as a way of getting my cardio in. Better than running on a treadmill in a gym, and if you get up into the mountains, you burn an insane number of calories. Anyway, the first couple times I went, I pushed myself pretty hard, cycling for four, five hours at a time. On the third time I went out, after an hour or so, I noticed I couldn't feel my balls. I'm telling you, I shit myself."

She leaned forward, interested in the story. "What happened?"

"I quit the ride, walked the damn bike home. And then I got on the internet. Turns out it's pretty common, and I fixed it by changing the seat on my bike. It also helps if you change position regularly, and occasionally stand up to cycle, which is what I did today, because these rental bikes don't have the best seats."

"Well, if we do this again, I want a cooter-safe seat."

Nate saluted. "Noted. I'll make sure I call ahead and ask for one specifically. I'm sure they have stock out back."

She shoved him in the chest. "Stop teasing me."

He grabbed her wrist, yanking her up close against him. They were both sweaty from the bike ride, but he didn't care, and from the way she pressed herself close, neither did she.

"But it's so much fun, little Dex," he said, capturing her mouth. He licked along her bottom lip then slid his tongue inside. Kissing Dex could become his new hobby. At least the hobby he undertook when he couldn't fuck her. *That* was his new favorite thing to do.

"Think you can make it back?" he asked, loving how disheveled she looked, her face flushed, and her hair mussed from the wind and his fingers.

She nodded. "I might take your lead and stand up a bit."

After arriving back in Santa Monica, they dropped off the bikes and strolled back to the car. As he drove away, heading back to Dex's place—because she had a bath and he didn't—he curled his fingers around hers and lifted her hand to her mouth.

"Next stop... Operation Cooter."

CHAPTER 14

Dex couldn't stop her legs from bouncing as the plane began its descent into JFK. Even though Nate had become more and more monosyllabic the longer the flight went on, she couldn't wait to see *everything*. Her one worry was that she'd miss her usual Sunday trip to see Mom, but Elva had allayed Dex's concerns by promising to make an extra visit that weekend.

She and Nate were staying in New York Thursday through Tuesday—the wedding was being held on Saturday—and Dex had already planned out an entire itinerary, much to Nate's chagrin.

"I wonder if Bernard is over his snit yet?" she mused, referring to her boss's fury when she'd finally plucked up the courage to ask for a long weekend. He'd said no at first—until Nate had made a call.

"Who gives a shit?" Nate said, staring at the seat belt sign as if it held the answer to who'd win best actor at that year's Emmy's.

"What's the matter?" Dex asked, wondering if he was scared of flying and that was the reason he'd barely spoken a word in over three hours.

He didn't look at her. "Nothing."

"Really?" she snapped. "Cat got your tongue then?"

The closer she and Nate had become over the last few weeks—since the whole *Be Mine* speech as she'd now chosen to think about it—the more she'd become herself. Those early days of watching every word—even if she occasionally slipped—were over. Not that Nate seemed to mind. In fact, the more combative she was, the more he liked it.

His eyes cut to hers, and what she saw in his face had her worried. Gone was the over-confident man with a permanent cocky smirk that she sometimes wanted to smack right off of him. In his place was a sullen, morose guy who gave the impression he was heading to a funeral rather than a wedding.

She caressed his arm and softened her tone. "What's wrong, Nate?"

For a split second his mask fell, and behind the brooding façade she saw a man who was deeply troubled. Then the curtain dropped back into place, and he became unreadable once more.

"I've told you before. I don't really like coming back here."

"Yes, you have told me that. What you've omitted to mention is why."

"Bad memories, that's all."

"You mean your parents dying?"

He shrugged one shoulder. "That, among other things."

She should have stopped there, but she'd always found knowing when to quit a challenge. "What other things?"

"Fuck's sake, Dex. Just leave it."

He returned to staring at the seat belt sign, a ticking nerve in his jaw giving away his annoyance.

"I'm a good listener."

"Then hear me. Drop it."

She sighed heavily and turned away to look out of the window. The clouds parted, giving her a view of the ground below. They'd be landing soon, and despite Nate's black mood, she was still so excited. She refused to let him steal her joy.

As they walked through the arrivals hall toward baggage reclaim, Nate entwined his fingers around hers.

"Sorry."

She expelled a deep breath through her nose. "You should be sorry. You wanted me to come, Nate, and yet from the moment we got on the plane, you've been moody and distant."

He offered her a crooked smile. "Apart from my brothers, you're the only other person to call me out on my shit, you know that?"

Thrilled with his admission, she beamed. "Get used to it, mister. My sister doesn't call me Mouth Almighty for nothing." Except with bastard Bernard. She only minded her manners around him because she needed the money.

Nate threw back his head and laughed. His arm came around her shoulder, and he pulled her into his side. "I'm glad you're here, Titch."

She playfully bumped his shoulder. "I'm good with moods, Nate. Look at who I work for. But don't shut me out. I'm here to listen anytime you're ready to talk."

He gave her a wide-eyed look and then slowly shook his head. "You know what, Titch? One of these days, I might take you up on that."

NATE STARED out of the cab window as the Manhattan skyline grew closer. Dex remained silent, but he sensed her buzzing with excitement each time a new sight came into view. The contrast with his own pit of dread that increased with every mile the cab ate up wasn't lost on him, but fuck, couldn't he put his own feelings aside for a few days? Didn't she deserve a fun-filled vacation, especially with all the shit going on with her mom?

Except the familiar black cloud had descended, dragging him to dark places he didn't want to visit. Somehow, he found it easier to forget back home in LA. But faced with his brothers, and the city he used to adore, the memories always flooded in. If only he could gouge out the part of his brain that had found the letter. The part that made him so fucking miserable.

The Williamsburg Bridge loomed ahead—he'd asked the driver to go that way so Dex could see a few sights as they traveled through Manhattan to the upper east side—further darkening Nate's thoughts and tightening the band around his chest. Not long now until he had to play the part of his life—the same part he played every single time he came home.

"Oh look, it's the Empire State Building," Dex enthused, clutching his arm.

Nate forced a smile. Her excitement was so contagious. Each day that passed made him thank his lucky stars he'd gotten her fired that day. If he hadn't, she wouldn't have come after him at the club, and she wouldn't be sitting beside him now.

He sought out her hand, threading his fingers between hers. "I'll take you if you like."

She turned to him, face shining. "Oh, would you? It'd be like Sleepless in Seattle. I love that movie."

He laughed. "Sure, Titch. Whatever you want. I'll even see if I can get us a table at the Rainbow Room."

A furrow appeared between her eyebrows. "What's the Rainbow Room got to do with Sleepless in Seattle?"

He stared at her in mock horror. "Call yourself a fan? It's only the restaurant where Meg Ryan's character sees the heart on the top of the Empire State Building and she knows she has to break up with her fiancé to be with the man she truly loves."

Dex gave him an incredulous look and then broke into a fit of giggles. "Nate Brook, I wouldn't have taken you for a chick-flick fan."

He cleared his throat. "Well, I wouldn't say that exactly."

"Oh yeah?" Still smiling. "What would you say?"

He hitched a shoulder. "I had a crush on Meg Ryan, okay? When I was a kid."

Dex clasped a hand to her chest. "That's so sweet."

Fucking sweet?

He unclipped her seat belt and dragged her across his lap. He cut off her squeal with his mouth, ignoring the irritated grumblings from their driver.

Drawing back, he nipped at her bottom lip. "Nothing *sweet* about me, little Dex. As you'll find out later."

"Promises, promises," she said with an over-exaggerated wink.

He kissed her again, because every time he did, she stopped him thinking—with his brain, anyway.

The taxi jolted to a stop as the damned driver slammed on the brakes. Nate's hand shot out against the seat in front to steady himself and to stop Dex sliding off his lap.

"Jesus," he said as the driver tapped his forefinger against the red counter showing the fare. "Not the way to get a fat tip, buddy."

He dug out his wallet and handed over the fare as Dex got out of the cab. Nate opened his door and walked around the back to grab their luggage from the trunk.

"So, this is your hotel?"

"Yep." Nate slung his bag over his shoulder and picked up Dex's suitcase—the woman did *not* travel light. He slipped his free hand inside hers. "Deep breath, Titch, coz you're about to enter the lion's den."

She giggled. "I think that happened a few weeks ago."

He raised an eyebrow. "Indeed. And I'll definitely be taking a bite out of my prey later."

Jax jogged down the steps to meet them, preventing her from responding. "You made it," his brother said, pulling him into a rough hug followed by a hard clap on the back. "And you must be Dex." He briefly hugged her. "Come on in. Champagne's on ice."

"I'd rather have a beer," Nate said while Dex gave him a dig in the ribs.

"Champagne sounds lovely," she said politely.

"Stop being a sycophant," he muttered under his breath. "You don't even like champagne."

"Stop being an ass," she hissed, tugging her hand from his.

"Beer it is then." Jax went to walk back inside the hotel. "Everyone's downstairs. They can't wait to meet you, Dex."

Dex trotted after Jax, leaving Nate lagging behind. "Thank you so much for letting me come to your wedding."

"Any friend of Nate's is welcome here," he said.

"And so it begins," Nate muttered uncharitably.

Dex glanced over her shoulder, a wide-eyed glare getting her message across perfectly.

Nate rolled his eyes, gritted his teeth, and prepared himself for the longest few days of his life.

CHAPTER 15

Dex glanced around as Jax led her into a hallway, past a lounge that was buzzing with guests. He waved at a woman serving drinks to a couple of patrons sitting at the bar then carried on. He pushed open a door on his left marked Private.

"Be careful going down the steps."

She followed him downstairs. At the bottom, it opened up into an enormous open-plan living room with a kitchen at the far end and a large table that seated twelve. Five pairs of eyes swiveled her way, three women and two guys. It took a moment for her to realize the two guys were twins. Identical twins. She did a double-take, her mouth dropping open a couple of inches. And then she blinked and forced her jaw shut before anyone noticed.

One of the women got up and came toward them wearing a beaming smile. "You must be Dex." She clasped Dex by the shoulders and kissed her cheek. "I'm Indie. Jax's fiancée. We're thrilled you could be here for our wedding."

The other four people all rose to their feet and were now making their way over.

"I'm Calum," the first guy said, also kissing her cheek. "This is

125

Laurella." He tugged a dark-haired, olive-skinned beauty to his side as if he couldn't bear not to touch her.

"It's so lovely to meet you," Laurella said, a European accent shining through.

Dex couldn't place it. She made a mental note to ask Nate later as it seemed rude to ask Laurella.

Calum's mirror image followed on behind. "I'm Cole, and this is my girlfriend, Millie. And over there," he pointed to a bassinet Dex hadn't spotted until then, "Is our little girl, Aimee."

The pride in Cole's voice, and the way he gazed adoringly at Millie, had envy curling in Dex's belly. She had no doubt Nate was attracted to her—the amount of sex they'd had was testament to that. But Cole looked at his girlfriend as though walking over hot coals wouldn't be enough of a sacrifice to prove his devotion and love.

"It's so great to meet you all," Dex said. She peered inside the bassinet at Aimee whose face was serene in sleep, her hands at either side of her head. "She's gorgeous," she said to Millie. "You must be so proud."

"Fuck's sake," Nate grumbled, finally appearing at the bottom of the stairs, hauling their suitcases behind him. "What the hell you got in here, Titch?"

Dex watched with fascination as the faces of Nate's brothers lit up, and he was enveloped into the bosom of his family. Even the girlfriends joined in with the group hug. It reminded her of a rugby game she'd seen on TV once where all the players piled on top of one another. She frowned in confusion. Why would he not want this? There was so much love for him that she almost felt like a voyeur, peering in on a private moment that wasn't hers to share. And yet he'd freely admitted he didn't like coming home.

Eventually he muscled his way free. He scuffed a hand over the top of his head and straightened his shirt. His eyes cut to hers.

"Sit down, Titch."

"Both of you sit down," Jax said. "I'll get the drinks. Champagne, Dex?"

Dex opened her mouth to respond, but Nate beat her to it. "She was being polite earlier. She doesn't like champagne. She'll have a beer."

She glared in his direction. *I'm going to kill him.*

Nate didn't even bat an eyelid at his rudeness, or her death stare. Instead, he shrugged.

"*She* is perfectly capable of speaking for herself," Dex said. Nate's lips twitched at her snippy attitude. The man was incorrigible. "I would love a Corona if you have one."

"Ha!" Nate said.

Dex showed him her middle finger.

Calum barked out a laugh. "You're going to fit right in, Dex."

Jax rolled his eyes at Indie. "Here we go."

Jax and Indie walked over to the kitchen area, and Nate flopped down beside her. His little finger brushed against hers. "Doing okay, Titch?"

"You didn't tell me you had twin brothers," she whispered as embarrassment at her open-mouthed stares of a few minutes ago finally hit her. "*Identical* twin brothers."

Nate twisted his lips to the side. "It never occurred to me."

Dex suppressed an urge to elbow him in the ribs, but only because Laurella and Millie started asking her about her job, and how many famous people she got to see on a daily basis. Neither of them seemed to think of Nate as one of those *famous people*, which Dex guessed was fairly natural when referring to someone they knew well.

"So, bro," Calum said. "It's been a while. What's new?"

Nate shrugged, disinterested. "Not much."

"Work okay?" Cole asked.

"I guess."

Dex squirmed at his monosyllabic responses to perfectly legitimate questions. She pressed her thigh against his in warning. It had absolutely no effect.

"We're really glad you made it," Jax said.

Nate cocked an eyebrow. "I wasn't aware I had a choice."

"You didn't," Jax replied, grinning. He seemed indifferent to Nate's curt attitude, which meant this wasn't unusual behavior.

Her curiosity increased at the same rate as her embarrassment. Nate's relationship with his brothers was an odd dynamic, yet the restraint was all on his side.

Nate yawned loudly when fewer than thirty minutes of his brothers trying to tease information from him—which he refused to share—had passed. "It's been a long day, and Dex is shattered." He unfolded his long legs and got to his feet. "Come on, Titch. Let's go to bed."

Dex narrowed her eyes. She wasn't remotely tired, and neither was Nate, but the silent pleading in his expression had her rising to her feet.

"Thank you for such a lovely welcome," she said.

"We're glad you're both here," Jax said. "Your usual room is all ready for you, Nate, but if you'd prefer your own space, Dex, you can take the one next door. It used to be Calum's room before he and Laurella moved in together, but don't worry, I changed the sheets."

His twitching lips told her he was joking, but Nate's glowering expression said he didn't find the quip remotely funny.

"She won't be needing that," Nate said, capturing her hand. He grabbed their bags and towed her—and them—toward his bedroom, his brothers' chuckles ringing in her ears.

"Why were you so rude out there?" she asked as soon as they were alone. "And for the record, I'm not tired."

Nate parked her suitcase by the wall and tossed his own bag on the floor next to the bed. "You will be, by the time I'm finished with you."

Her stomach vaulted when he crooked a finger, beckoning her, but despite her body's eagerness to strip naked and get down to business, she couldn't let it lie.

"You were really short with them, and they were so happy to see you. I think you should apologize."

Nate curved one eyebrow. "Do you now?" His tone held a hint of ice—which she ignored.

"Nate! What is wrong with you?"

He pinched the bridge of his nose. "Nothing. They're used to me. It's fine."

"It is *not* fine. I was embarrassed."

"Don't be. Not on my account."

She planted her hands on her hips and glared. A few seconds scraped by, and then Nate expelled a frustrated sigh.

"Oh, for Christ's sake. Fine. I'll apologize in the morning. Now can we go to bed and fuck?"

She stayed on her side of the room. "We should unpack."

"The only thing we'll need tonight is condoms." He reached into his jacket and pulled out several, which he dropped on the nightstand. "Well, would you look at that."

Despite her annoyance, she smiled. It was impossible to stay mad at Nate for long. It wasn't her place to call him out on his relationship with his brothers. If they had a problem, it was theirs to solve.

"What if they hear us?"

He unfastened his belt. "If it bothers you so much, then keep quiet."

She nibbled on her bottom lip. "You know I like it noisy."

Nate eased the belt through the loops on his jeans and casually flung it on the bed. "Then maybe I'll have to gag you."

Yes, please.

Oh, where did that come from? Her face must have spoken a thousand words, because Nate slowly grinned. "You like that idea, do you?"

She fiddled with the hem of her shirt. "Maybe."

He sauntered across to her side of the bed and slipped his arms around her waist. His erection nudged at her, and her thighs trembled as a surge of excitement heated her blood. Nate always had this effect on her, like her insides were on fire.

"Such a revelation," he murmured, briefly touching her lips with his. "Dex Nolan. My perfect woman."

His perfect woman? A lightness spread through her chest, and she wanted to fist pump the air and shout "Yes!" But that would *not* be cool. Instead, she pretended to faint.

"Nate Brook, giving out compliments."

"Grab 'em while you can," he said, unfastening the buttons on his shirt. His eyes never left hers as he shucked it from his shoulders and let it fall to the floor.

Her gaze inched lower, over his firm chest, the hard ridges of his abdomen, the thin line of hair disappearing behind the waistband of his jeans.

Nate groaned. "Don't look at me like that, otherwise this will be over quicker than either of us want."

She flicked her tongue out to wet her lips, eliciting another groan from him. He gripped the hem of her T-shirt and pulled it over her head. Her bra went next, then her jeans were peeled down her legs. She kicked off her sneakers so he could remove her jeans completely.

"Get on the bed," he ordered.

She didn't hesitate. She *loved* it when Nate bossed her around —at least in the bedroom. If he tried laying attitude on her outside, he'd find his balls in a vise, but in here, where it was just the two of them, she was more than happy to cede control.

"Open your legs."

She complied, but he shook his head. "Wider. Yep, just like that."

He slipped off his shoes, and his jeans followed. She swallowed at the sight of his thick erection through his boxers. He crawled on to the bed and lay on his side, his hand propping up his head.

His eyes were firmly fixed on the apex to her thighs. He tongued his top teeth. "Pull your panties to one side."

Unlike the previous time Nate had asked her to do this, this time, Dex didn't hesitate. During the last few weeks, trust had developed between them, and now she knew that by pleasing him, she would ultimately please herself.

"Touch yourself."

Oh, this was a step up. She'd masturbated several times thinking of Nate, but never when he'd been present. Her hand crept toward her core, and she glided her middle finger over her folds. Nate remained completely still, his eyes following every move of her hand. Dex touched her clit, the bundle of nerves already so sensitive that her legs writhed of their own accord. Nate sat up and gripped both ankles, holding her thighs apart.

"Make yourself come."

Beset with embarrassment, she felt the blood rush to her cheeks. Masturbating herself to climax in the privacy of her own room back home was one thing. To do that with Nate's ice-blue, unwavering gaze on her was quite another.

"I-I don't know if I can. Not with you watching. Not with your family on the other side of that door."

His lips curved to the side in a crooked smile. "Forget my family. Close your eyes if it makes it easier."

"Why do you want me to do it, rather than you doing it?"

"Because it's fucking sexy. It turns me on. Big time."

When she chewed uncertainly on her lip, Nate moved between her legs and kissed her.

A few seconds later, he drew back. "How about I join in?"

Her eyes widened as his meaning became clear. The thought of Nate stroking himself while she did the same... oh yeah. Now she understood why he might find it a turn-on to watch her.

She tilted her head in affirmation, and he stood and removed his boxers. His erection bobbed as he climbed back onto the bed. She expected him to lie beside her. Instead, he kneeled up, between her thighs. She wouldn't be able to close them now, even if she wanted to. Which she didn't.

He wrapped his hand around his shaft and moved it in slow, leisurely strokes, but his eyes were on her rather than him. She followed his lead, touching, pinching, rubbing in faster and faster circles. Lost in the moment, she inserted two fingers inside, eliciting a long moan from Nate.

"Jesus, Titch." He caught her wrist and sucked on her fingers.

Dex gasped at the surprise move, and then she giggled. "You're a bad man, Nate Brook."

He gave her a lecherous grin, all the while moving his hand faster and faster. "You fucking love it."

I love you.

The thought came out of left field, and, like a shovel to the side of her skull, it knocked her sideways. She didn't love Nate. She was in an emotional state, that was all. He was introducing her to a side of herself she hadn't known existed, and she was feeling extra sensitive. She liked him. She was glad they'd met. She was grateful he was helping her with Mom. But love?

"I'm close," he groaned out, sweat gathering on his top lip.

Dex dragged herself back to the here and now and filed away the little nugget her subconscious chose to reveal for another, more appropriate time. With her eyes fixed on Nate, magnificent in his aroused state, she moved her fingers faster against her clit, brushing her other hand over her erect nipples. Heat grew in her belly as she built to the inevitable climax.

"I want to come on your tits. Tell me now if you'd rather I didn't."

At his admission, her orgasm broke. "Come wherever you like," she moaned, her head rolling back against the pillows. She meant every word.

"Fuck."

She opened her eyes in time to see Nate's seed spill over her chest. Hot spurts of warm, slippery cum dripped between her breasts. She thought she'd be grossed out. She wasn't. In fact, it turned her on so much, she'd definitely be revisiting this particular fantasy. His abs twitched and clenched as he emptied himself. God, he was beautiful.

He grinned down at her, still semi-hard. She raised herself and licked the moisture off his tip. His cock jerked in approval.

"You're a fucking revelation, Titch," he said, bending down for a quick kiss. "Don't move. I'll get a cloth and clean you up."

He disappeared into the bathroom. Dex couldn't resist a quick taste. She dipped her pinkie into the liquid pooled on her boobs and sucked it off. She grinned to herself. It'd be her little secret.

Nate returned a few seconds later with a facecloth. God bless him, he'd dipped it in warm water. Thoughtful Nate was also a revelation. He cleaned her up, returned the cloth to the bathroom, and joined her on the bed.

"Pass me those condoms, Titch. It's going to be a long, hard night."

CHAPTER 16

Dex snuggled into Nate's side as the early morning sun rose over Manhattan, bathing his bedroom in light. He stirred and rolled over, tucking his arms around her.

"Morning," he murmured against her ear, sending a shiver of desire down her spine, despite the fact they'd stayed up half the night exploring each other intimately.

"What are we going to do today?" Dex asked.

"Fuck," Nate replied lazily. Dex nudged him in the ribs, drawing a loud groan. "Ow."

"Be serious," she said.

He rubbed the offending area. "I was."

Dex raised her eyes heavenward. "We're guests here. We can't spend all day in bed. Plus, I want to see New York."

"We're not guests. I'm a twenty-five percent owner, so if we want to spend all day in bed, we can. However," he added when she opened her mouth to interrupt, "there are some things I want to show you today that don't involve the area below my waist."

She couldn't help laughing. "You are so bad."

He tickled her until she squealed and tried to scramble away, but Nate soon had her pinned to the bed, both her wrists clamped in one of his large hands, leaving his other hand free to roam.

"I'm very, very bad, Titch. You don't know the half of it."

He nuzzled between her breasts, and she involuntarily arched into him. And then, as quickly as she'd found herself imprisoned by his lean, firm body, he released her.

"Let's shower."

He wandered into the bathroom, and seconds later, the sound of flowing water reached her. She eased herself out of bed and stretched, her body stiff and sore. In a few short weeks, she'd turned into a goddamn nymphomaniac. She couldn't get enough.

I love you.

Last night she'd managed to thrust the thought aside, but here it was again, crashing into her. She'd never been in love, so how could she possibly know whether the feelings she had for Nate were love or some misplaced infatuation with a man who made her body hum with a pleasure so addictive, she wasn't sure she could survive without it?

She'd ended up in bed with him too fast, but she knew herself well enough to recognize her feelings as deeper than purely physical. She loved spending time with him. She craved his smile, would do just about anything to make him laugh. When he was happy, she was ecstatic. He was her anchor in the middle of the stormy sea of life, and she'd do anything to cling on, to never let go.

She wandered over to the window and took a few deep breaths to calm herself. Nate wasn't ready for this. Hell, *she* wasn't ready. To fall in love with anyone was scary enough, but an actor, a man expert in playing a part... the road ahead would be paved with pain if she wasn't careful.

Was Nate even capable of such deep feelings? If he couldn't embrace the love of his brothers when they so obviously adored him, what chance would she have of putting a dent in his armor?

But she couldn't pull away now. She was in too deep. She'd have to try to protect herself and focus on having fun along the way. Whatever happened, happened.

"Titch, get in here."

Pushing aside the deep thoughts, she obeyed his instruction. The bathroom was filled with steam, and Nate stood, shoulder braced against the glass door as he waited for her. He opened it and gestured for her to go ahead, then followed.

She stepped underneath the spray and wet her hair, but when she reached for the shampoo, Nate took it from her. He squeezed a dollop in the palm of his hand and rubbed it in her hair. God, it felt good as he massaged the soapy suds into her scalp. She let out a shallow moan of appreciation, drawing a hiss from him.

"How do you manage to make every little whimper sound so goddamn sexy, Titch?"

He dug his fingertips in harder, and she moaned again. "How did you learn to wash hair so good?"

He chuckled. "Tip your head back."

She did as he'd asked. He washed out the soap until the water ran clear. Reaching for the shampoo again, he passed it to her. "Your turn."

She squeezed the bottle. "You'll have to bend forward. I'm never going to reach."

She expected him to lower his head, but instead, he lifted her and hooked her legs over his hips, bringing them eye to eye, his hands cradling her ass. "Now you can reach."

She laughed and began to wash his hair. "You're crazy, you know that?"

"You wouldn't have me any other way."

Not true. I'll have you any way I can get you.

They finished their shower. Nate passed her a huge towel that she wrapped herself in, taking another one to swaddle around her head. He dried off and strolled, fully naked—and fully erect—into the bedroom. She'd expected him to want sex in the shower, but one thing she was learning about Nate was that he often did the complete opposite of what she thought he'd do.

"There's a hairdryer underneath the sink in the bathroom if you need it," Nate called through.

She joined him in the bedroom. "No wonder you can travel so light. Half your stuff is here."

He heaved her suitcase onto the bed, making a big production of its weight. "And you brought half your belongings with you."

She nudged him out of the way and opened it. "A girl never knows what she'll need."

Nate peered over her shoulder as she started to unpack. Like a hawk, he pounced on her best set of underwear, a navy-blue lacy number that left very little to the imagination. It had been a birthday gift from Elva a couple of years ago, but Dex had never found a reason to wear it. She'd hummed and hawed about whether to pack it, but in the end, had thrown it in.

He dangled it in the air. "Oh, Titch, here's an outfit you'll *definitely* be needing. In fact, you could have just packed this and nothing else."

She snatched it from his grasp and stuffed it into the nightstand drawer, her face burning. "Get dressed."

He laughed and ambled over to the dresser. She gawked at his firm, muscled ass, and when he turned around unexpectedly and caught her peeking, her skin colored up once more. She grabbed her own hairdryer—she was fussy like that—and her curling iron, and scuttled back to the bathroom with Nate's chuckles ringing in her ears.

It took thirty minutes to dry her hair, and a further fifteen to add a few waves. When she returned to the bedroom, Nate was nowhere to be seen. She quickly dressed in jeans and a top and shoved her feet into her sneakers. If they were going to be doing a lot of walking around, she'd need comfortable footwear.

She tentatively opened the door and peeked into the living room, only to find it empty. She'd expected it to be full of people, like last night. The smell of coffee reached her, and she tiptoed over to the kitchen to find a pot already brewed. After opening several cabinets—and feeling more than a little audacious—she found a stack of mugs. She poured a coffee, added a dash of cream, and wandered into the living area. She set her coffee on the table and plunked down on the sofa. A few magazines were haphazardly strewn over the low-level table. She picked one up and flicked through, but it didn't hold her attention.

Where the hell was Nate?

"Oh, you're up. Sleep well?"

Dex turned her head to see she'd been joined by Indie. "Um, yeah." She held up her mug of java. "Hope you don't mind."

"Of course not. Make yourself at home. Do you want some breakfast?" Indie grabbed a pan and put it on the stove. "I'm making an omelet if you'd like one."

"I'm okay, thanks." She scrambled to her feet. "Have you seen Nate?"

Indie nodded. "He's upstairs talking to Jax. Asked me to come down and check on you."

"Oh."

"He'll be down shortly." She cracked an egg into a bowl. "Are you sure I can't make you something?"

"I'm good." Dex wandered over to the breakfast bar and slipped onto a stool. "I'm surprised you're not rushing around like crazy, especially with the wedding being tomorrow and all."

Indie smiled. "Luckily, I'm a pretty organized person. It's all done."

"Thanks for letting me share your special day."

Indie patted her hand. "I'm glad you're here. Any friend of Nate's is always welcome."

Dex leaned her elbows on the counter and rested her chin in her hands. "How long have you known Nate?"

Indie briefly looked up. "Four years, give or take."

"What's he like?"

At that, Indie put the bowl down and fully focused her attention on Dex. "You tell me," she said, quirking an eyebrow. "You're the one sleeping with him."

Dex blushed, but then she noticed Indie's teasing expression and laughed. "Doesn't mean I know a single thing about him."

Indie nodded. "True." She sighed, considering Dex's question. "Out of all of Jax's brothers, Nate is the one I know the least, and the one I'm not at all close to."

Dex tilted her head. "Why's that?"

"Partly because he lives on the other side of the country, but I think it's more to do with Nate himself. He's… difficult to get to know. You saw him last night. Not even his brothers can get much from him, and Jax virtually raised him."

Dex nodded. "I told him off for how rude he was when we arrived."

Indie raised an eyebrow. "You did? Brave girl."

"He took it well," she said, irony lacing her voice.

Indie laughed. "I can imagine."

Dex paused, wondering whether she should push harder. Whether Indie had an insight into why he hated coming to New York so much. Oh, what the hell. In for a penny and all that.

"Why does Nate hate being here so much?"

Indie came to sit beside her. "I don't know. Over the last four years, I can count on one hand how many times he's visited, and whenever Jax has suggested we go to visit him, Nate always has an excuse."

Dex shook her head. "I don't understand it. If you were all horrible, then yeah, I'd get it."

"Have you asked him?"

"Oh yeah," she said. "He either responds with brooding silence or a snippy comeback."

"I wish I had some insight." She sipped some coffee. "I'll tell you one thing, though. He's the happiest I've ever seen him."

Dex frowned. "What makes you say that?"

"His smile." When Dex's frown deepened, Indie elaborated. "I find Nate a little intimidating if I'm honest. I remember when I first met Jax, something made me want to give Nate a wide berth. But upstairs just now, I saw him smile three times. *Three*. In the space of ten minutes. I don't think I've seen him smile that much in four years. Whatever you're doing, I say keep doing it."

A shot of warmth rushed through Dex. Could she be making a difference in Nate's life? He certainly laughed with her. A lot. Yet from Indie's experience, laughter was a rarity. She flashed a quick grin. "I'll try."

"Okay, food." Indie went back to cracking eggs. "Last chance. Sure I can't tempt you?"

"I'm taking her out for breakfast."

Dex twisted around to see Nate sauntering casually across the living room. Like a clichéd heroine in a chick-lit movie, her breath caught in her throat, and her heart sped up. His hair was still partially damp from their earlier shower, and the black button-down shirt he'd paired with jeans showed off his muscled physique to perfection.

He dropped a kiss on the top of her head. "Shall we go?"

"Sure."

"Enjoy, kiddy-kins. Be good," Indie said with a grin.

"Very fucking funny," Nate said, although his lips tugged upward with a hint of a smile as he caught Dex's hand in his.

The sunshine from the previous day had been replaced with a thick blanket of cloud, which was just as well because she'd left her sunglasses in Nate's bedroom. It was still humid, though, and her T-shirt stuck to her skin after trying to keep up with Nate's loping strides.

"Can you slow down a bit," she said, yanking on his hand. "I'm small, remember."

Nate lazily cast his gaze over her. "Yeah, but perfectly formed."

She rolled her eyes at him but was secretly thrilled. She kept wanting to pinch herself to make sure all this was real. She was on vacation. In New York. With Nate Brook. And they were walking down the street hand in hand. The odd passerby cast a curious glance their way, probably trying to place Nate, but he stared straight ahead without making eye contact. She realized after a few minutes that this was a tactic he'd used in LA, too. It must be an approach he'd discovered worked because they weren't accosted by a single person.

He stopped in front of a café with a green awning that read *Evergreen*. "This place serves the best pancakes in New York," he said, pushing open the door.

A bell jingled overhead, alerting the waitress behind the counter who was serving coffee to men in suits.

"Sit anywhere you like," she said. "I'll be over in a sec."

Nate slid into a booth. Dex followed. She'd figured, after the several meals they'd shared, that Nate preferred for her to sit beside him rather than opposite. He caressed her inner thigh and hit her with a smile that melted her insides.

"You're learning, Titch."

Dex had never thought of herself as subservient enough to be a people pleaser. She was too mouthy, too opinionated, to need outside validation. But pleasing Nate was becoming an addiction. She chased his smiles, craved his approval. She loved making him happy, because it made her happy.

After they'd ordered pancakes, eggs, and coffee, Dex turned to Nate. "What are we doing today?"

Nate tapped the side of his nose. "Wait and see."

Dex grinned. Let him have his fun. "As long as the Empire State is on the list, I'm good."

"It might be," he said, leaning back to allow the waitress to set down two steaming mugs of coffee.

"Are you sure Jax doesn't need you to help with the wedding? We can easily sightsee on Sunday and Monday."

Nate flashed a look of horror her way. "That sounds like my idea of hell. I'm here. I'll turn up tomorrow and smile and make small talk with dicks I couldn't give a shit about. But as for anything else," he shook his head vigorously, "nope. Not a fucking chance."

Dex rolled her eyes. "Jeez. Chill, will ya."

Nate narrowed his eyes, but beneath the fierce stare he shot her way was a mischievous glint she couldn't resist. She flung her arms around his neck and kissed him, a quick peck rather than a passionate clinch, but as she began to pull away, Nate held her arms in place and deepened the kiss.

"The taste of you is becoming addictive, Titch. Luckily our pancakes will be here soon, otherwise I may have gotten on my knees and eaten you instead."

A couple of customers at nearby tables looked over. Dex's face burned, not because of what Nate said, but the volume at which he'd said it.

"Shhh," she said, giving him a nudge.

"What?" When she cocked her head, Nate made eye contact with a man sitting adjacent who had decided the conversation happening to his left was a lot more interesting than his plate of eggs Benedict. His sleazy gaze swept over her, and he licked his lips.

Nate straightened in his seat and picked up his fork. "Buddy, if you don't take your eyes off my girlfriend, I'll fucking gouge them out."

Dex stared at the floor, willing it to open and swallow her whole.

The guy cleared his throat. "No offense meant." His chair scraped backward, and he got to his feet, mumbling an apology.

Once she was sure he'd gone, she lifted her head, expecting to see the entire café watching the show. Thankfully, Nate's glowering expression must have put off any other interested parties - not one person was paying them any attention.

And then Nate's words hit her like a ten-ton truck. *Girlfriend.* He'd only gone and called her his girlfriend. Her mouth opened and closed, but she was saved from conjuring up any words when their breakfast arrived. Nate seemed oblivious to her bewilderment as he picked up the maple syrup and poured it over his pancakes.

"Take a bite and tell me they're not the best damn pancakes you've ever tasted."

Dex stared at her plate, then at him. "I'm your girlfriend?"

Nate frowned, and then his forehead wrinkled, sending his eyebrows shooting up. "Fuck. Yeah. Shit." And then he broke into a smile. "Guess you're stuck with me, Titch. How do you feel about that?"

She swept her tongue over her dry lips and swallowed. "I guess I can cope. Once I've trained you up a bit."

Nate threw back his head and laughed. "Trained me up?"

She grinned. "Yeah. I mean, you could be boyfriend material. It'll take a shitload of work, but I'm up for the challenge if you are."

Nate shook his head, but the smile was still very much on his lips. "Sold."

Her heart began thrumming against her ribcage. She'd just become Nate Brook's girlfriend. Oh, dear God, she was going to hyperventilate.

"Now eat your pancakes before they go cold."

NATE PAID the check and opened the door for Dex. His heartbeat still wouldn't slow down. He had a girlfriend. Him. Nate Brook: playboy, manwhore, skirt-chaser extraordinaire. He was off the market, and fuck, if that thought didn't make him the happiest he'd ever been. When the hell had this happened? This thing with Dex had started out as a bit of fun with someone who perked up his dick without effort more than any other woman had ever managed. The last thing he'd expected was to end up in a relationship—and be happy about it.

Dex linked her arm through his. "Okay, boyfriend, lead the way."

Nate grinned. "First stop, Empire State."

Dex's eyes gleamed with excitement. "I *knew* it."

A short subway ride later, they emerged onto the street. A few spots of rain were in the air, but nothing could dampen his spirits. The little dynamo bouncing on her toes beside him had chased the clouds away, at least right then. Experience told Nate he wouldn't shake the dark thoughts forever, but if being with Dex could push them to the far recesses of his mind and heart—only to emerge when he was alone—well, he could live with that.

They joined the end of the line, but thankfully, they didn't have to wait too long for tickets. During the entire ride in the elevator to the top, Dex didn't stop babbling. Whereas once, constant chatter from a female companion would have irritated the fuck out of him—and he'd have made some inane comment about sticking his dick in their mouth to shut them up—with Dex he found he didn't mind one bit. Her enthusiasm was contagious, so much so he found himself looking forward to getting to the top, despite the view being something he'd seen several times.

The viewing platform on the eighty-sixth floor was crowded, but not overly so. Give it another hour and it would be impossible to move for tourists.

"Wow, I can see *everything* from up here."

"Yeah, it's pretty cool." He slung his arm around her shoulders and pulled her close. "There's Madison Square Garden. I used to go there fairly regularly with Jax to watch the Knicks. Not so much these days."

She gave him a look. "I didn't know you liked basketball. I used to go watch the Bucks with my dad before he passed away."

Nate leaned in close, his mouth next to her ear. "Oh, Titch. A basketball fan? You're definitely getting several orgasms later."

Her dainty pink tongue appeared and dampened her lips. Fuck. His cock jerked as the memory of what she'd done to him with that tongue the previous night came rushing back. He shook the image from his mind. He had several things he wanted to share with her today, and while his cock was most certainly one of them, it'd have to wait until later.

They walked around the entire observation deck. Dex took so many photos, she'd need to buy extra storage to house them all. Nate checked she'd seen enough, then the two of them headed back down onto the street.

"Where to now?" she asked.

He glanced down at her footwear. Sneakers. Good.

"Let's walk over Brooklyn Bridge. There's a cool pizza place on the other side that I love. We can grab lunch. And the view back to Manhattan from the waterside is really cool."

She laughed. "I'm still full from the pancakes."

"You won't be after we've walked over to Brooklyn."

By the time they'd crossed the bridge, checked out the waterfront, eaten lunch at his favorite pizzeria, and arrived back in Manhattan, it was already four in the afternoon. Sightseeing in New York always took longer than expected. Jax had arranged dinner at a local restaurant for them all at eight, but that still left plenty of time for one final stop. The one he most wanted to show her.

Their third subway ride of the day culminated about a quarter mile from the hotel in a tree-lined street with rows of attractive-looking brownstones lined up like soldiers. Nate's chest hurt the closer they got to the final destination. He clutched Dex's hand, her soft skin and warm touch soothing him from the pain blooming inside.

Five minutes later, he turned a corner and stopped.

She glanced up at him, a confused frown drawing her eyebrows together. She didn't say a word. Instead, she squeezed his fingers.

"This was the place I grew up," he finally said, the words sticking in his throat, his voice hoarse and rough. "The house we lived in before my parents were killed." Pain scored his heart, and he suppressed on a wince.

"It's a lovely home," she said gently.

"Yeah." He sighed. "Jax sold it within weeks of their passing and moved us a few blocks away, but I used to come back here regularly. This place grounded me when everything else turned to shit. It was the wrong decision to leave here so quickly. I hated the other house. It was never my home. Jax knows he made a bad decision, but at the time, he thought he was doing the right thing."

He sat on the stone steps, tugging Dex down beside him, hoping the owners weren't home and might, at any second, come out to ask him what they hell he was doing on their property.

"I was twelve when they died. Can't remember if I already told you that. It's so weird how when you're that age, you go through life not even aware of how fragile it all is. And then bam! Your whole world is turned upside down in an instant."

She stroked up and down his arm, her soft fingertips alleviating the ache inside. "I'm so sorry, Nate. Not that it makes a difference, but I know exactly what it feels like."

He rested his head against hers. "It does, though. Make a difference."

They sat in silence for a few minutes, each lost in their own memories. Then he got to his feet and helped Dex up. "I don't know why I brought you here." He shrugged. "I guess I wanted you to see where I came from."

"I'm honored you brought me." She pressed a kiss to his cheek, her lips so warm, so inviting.

He turned his head, capturing her mouth. With a groan, he

buried his hands in her dark-red hair, digging his fingers into her scalp as he angled her exactly the way he needed. When they broke apart, both were panting. He glanced at his watch.

"Come on, Titch. Dinner isn't until eight. I reckon that gives me a good ninety minutes to start on those orgasms I promised you."

CHAPTER 17

Dex checked herself in the mirror one more time. She always felt strange wearing a dress, but a shirt, jeans, and sneakers wasn't acceptable attire for a wedding. The cornflower-blue knee-length fitted dress went well with her red hair and complexion, so all in all, she hadn't scrubbed up too badly.

She applied a little more lipstick and patted her lips on a folded tissue. After slipping her feet into four-inch stilettos—she needed height from somewhere—she picked up the silver clutch bag and took out her cell phone. One text from Elva to let her know Mom was okay and Milo was missing her. She smiled and tapped out a quick reply.

As she dropped her cell back into the purse, Nate appeared behind her. He slipped his arms around her waist and rested his chin on her shoulder. Dear God, the man rocked a tux better than anyone she'd ever seen, and if they had time, she'd be peeling it off and helping herself to a piece of what she craved.

"Don't," he murmured, nibbling on her earlobe.

"Don't what?"

"Look at me like that, otherwise we're not going to make this wedding, and Jax is going to spend a lifetime making me pay."

She turned around in his arms and brushed imaginary dust from his suit jacket. "You're damned handsome, Nate Brook."

"And you're sexy as fuck." He bent to kiss her.

She turned her head. "I've just put lipstick on."

"So? You've got more, haven't you?" His mouth took hers in a kiss that left her breathless. When he drew back, he was wearing more of her lipstick than she was. She giggled and grabbed a tissue from her purse, wiping it away.

"That's better."

She reapplied her makeup, then took Nate's proffered arm.

"Ready?" he asked.

"Are you?"

He shrugged. "You're making this trip a whole lot more bearable, Titch."

She twisted her lips to one side. "I don't get it, Nate."

"Get what?"

"Why you hate coming here so much. Your brothers clearly adore you, and you're surrounded by so much warmth and love. That shit's addictive, yet you push it away."

His jaw tightened, and his eyes darkened, a dangerous glint in their depths. He yanked his arm away. "Don't pull at that thread, Titch. Not if you know what's good for you."

Her eyebrows shot up, and she planted her hands on her hips. "What's *good* for me? Is that a threat?"

A nerve beat in his cheek, and she was sure she could hear him grinding his teeth. "I'm not talking about this, so either drop it and we can go enjoy the day, or carry on and seriously piss me off. Your choice."

He slowly turned away and headed for the door, leaving Dex standing there, anger building deep within her. "Stop right there, Nate Brook, or so help me, I'm going to kick your ass."

He froze in place, one foot in front of the other, mid-step. She moved in front of him, her neck craned back. Goddammit, what she wouldn't give for a few more inches so she could have this conversation eye-to-eye.

"I will let this drop, not because you *ordered* me to, but because I can see you're a hot mess of anger and rage. I don't know what the hell is going on here, but I'll tell you one thing: the day will come when whatever issues you have with your brothers is going to erupt. And if you don't take control of that shit, it's going to blow up in your face."

And this time, *she* left *him* behind. She wrenched open the door and stormed into the living room. Cole and Millie were sitting on the sofa. Millie was cradling Aimee who looked absolutely adorable in a soft pink dress, matching shoes, and a pink bow in her dark hair. Their eyes widened when met with a furious redhead stomping around. Cole glanced over her shoulder where she guessed Nate was standing, and then looked back at her.

"Everything okay?" he asked, concerned.

"Fine," she spat. "Except your brother is a dickhead."

Cole's forehead wrinkled, and Millie smothered a grin. "Well, we know *that*," Cole said, laughing. "And now you've caught on, you're definitely part of the family."

Cole's jokey demeanor stripped the tension right out of the room. Dex's shoulders relaxed back in place, and as she joined in with the laughter, she sensed Nate behind her, his eyes boring into the back of her head. Deciding to ignore him, she turned to Millie, who she'd sat beside at dinner the previous evening. The two girls had developed an immediate rapport, and Dex hoped they'd become friends, albeit long-distance ones. Still, that was what social media was for.

"I love your dress, Millie," Dex said. "It really suits your coloring. And Aimee looks so cute."

"Thank you," Millie said with a smile, adding, "You don't think it makes my skin appear too pale?"

Dex shook her head. "Not at all. You'll steal the limelight from Indie at this rate. Talking of which, where is the blushing bride?"

"She stayed at Alana and Paul's last night."

"Oh, that's right. She did say."

"Jax okay?" Nate finally spoke, but when Dex turned her attention on him, he refused to meet her gaze.

Well, screw him. He could spend the rest of the day in a snit for all she cared. Except she *did* care. She just wished he'd talk to her. They'd had such a breakthrough yesterday, and she was finally beginning to feel secure and not be constantly waiting for him to end things between them. Maybe she needed to wait until he had a couple of drinks inside him. Might make him more pliable. Or ask him again after sex. Nate was always more agreeable when his balls were empty.

"No, he's panicking," Cole said.

"I'll go see if he needs a hand."

Nate disappeared into Jax's bedroom, leaving the three of them alone.

"Jesus, did you refuse to put out or something last night?" Cole asked, earning a sharp dig in the ribs from Millie's elbow.

Dex giggled, not in the slightest bit offended at Cole's remark. "No, but I will be tonight if he carries on behaving like a child."

Cole laughed. "Y'know, Dex, you're exactly what he needs."

They chatted for a few minutes, and Dex even managed to sneak in a quick cuddle with Aimee before Jax and Nate joined them. Jax's face had a green tinge to it, and Dex couldn't help feeling sorry for him. Although the wedding would be a small, intimate affair, it mustn't be easy to stand up in front of everyone. If it were her, she'd be worrying about forgetting her lines, or tripping up on her dress, or being sick over the pastor.

"Oh, Jax, you don't look at all well. Shall I get you something to settle your stomach?" Millie asked.

"Mightn't be a bad idea," Nate said. "Coz if he pukes over me, I'll kill him." The latter was said with the hint of a smile as his eyes searched for Dex.

Whatever he and Jax had spoken about, it had lifted Nate's

mood. Her annoyance withered under his warm gaze, and she went over to him as Jax followed Millie into the kitchen.

"Truce?" she said.

He caught her hand and lifted it to his mouth. "Sorry."

"Me, too. I shouldn't have pushed."

"I'll go see if the car is outside," Cole said, taking off upstairs. He was back a couple of minutes later. "Yep, we're all set. I've checked with Calum, too. He and Laurella are on their way to the church."

"Oh God," Jax muttered. He rubbed his stomach.

"Fuck's sake," Nate said. "You've been living together for four years."

"Yeah, but *marriage*." The green tinge was back.

"Okay, let's go." Cole took hold of Jax's arm and propelled him upstairs.

Dex and Nate followed along with Millie.

By the time they reached the church, Jax had calmed down. Paul, his best man, met them outside. He clapped Jax on the back. "Ready?"

"As I'll ever be," Jax muttered, heading inside.

"Want me to have a bucket on standby?" Calum called after him, receiving a cutting glare from Laurella for his trouble.

"Thank Christ I'm not best man," Nate said, taking hold of Dex's hand.

"Why aren't you? Or Cole, or Calum?"

"Imagine having to choose and then explain to the ones who missed out? Nah, we all agreed weeks ago that it should be Paul. Easier all round."

She wrinkled her nose. "Yeah, I guess. At least I won't have that problem. Elva will definitely be my maid of honor."

Nate's gaze cut to hers. "I don't remember asking, Titch."

Oh shit!

Heat flooded her face, which was damned annoying. She wasn't a blusher, yet since hooking up with Nate, the blood rush to her cheeks was turning into a regular occurrence. "I-I didn't mean that. I meant—"

Nate gave her a nudge. "Chill. It's all good."

"Oh." She made a dramatic sweep across her forehead with the back of her hand. "Phew."

"Phew indeed. I doubt I'll ever get married."

A wave of disappointment crashed over her. Her stomach clenched, but she kept her face straight. It wasn't that she wanted to marry Nate or anything, but for him to one day call her his girlfriend, and the very next basically tell her they didn't have a future was a bitter pill to swallow.

"Just as well, coz I'd pity the poor girl."

Nate pinched her side. Despite a despondent feeling weighing her down, she giggled. They took their seats, and moments later the wedding march rang out. As Indie started her walk down the aisle, Nate let out a huge yawn. Despite his bad manners and her dark mood, Dex suppressed a smile. Nate was his own man, and that went a long way in her book. Still, she flashed a glare his way —which he studiously ignored. His eyes did follow Indie, though, as she passed by them, and there was the smallest curve to his lips.

It wasn't a long ceremony, and in no time at all, Indie and Jax were walking back up the aisle, their faces shining as they looked at each other with mutual adoration, Jax's earlier nausea nowhere to be seen. As the congregation followed the happy couple outside, Nate slung an arm over Dex's shoulders and whispered, "Come on, Titch. Let's get drunk."

AFTER THE WEDDING breakfast and the speeches were out of the way, Nate led Dex onto the dance floor. He folded her into his arms and rested his chin on the top of her head. She nuzzled into his chest, breathing him in. He smelled delicious, of vanilla body wash and woodsy cologne. She burrowed her hands beneath his jacket, the soft cotton of his shirt warmed by his skin.

"You survived," she said.

"Only just." She felt his grin.

"It was a lovely wedding."

He leaned back and coaxed her chin up. "What I said before, Titch, about marriage. I meant every word. I'm not the marrying type, but that doesn't mean I don't value what we have. I wouldn't have made it through the last forty-eight hours without you. I might not be the guy to put a ring on it, but you are deeper inside my head than any woman I've ever known." He hitched up a shoulder. "I just thought it was important to tell you where my head's at."

I love you.

Fuck, there it was again. It *had* to be infatuation. She couldn't possibly be in love with a guy she'd only known for a few weeks. She liked him, a whole lot, but insta-love only happened in chick-lit books and sloppy movies.

"Dex?"

She blinked a couple times. "Sorry, I kinda disappeared there for a moment."

He gave her a crooked grin. "Where'd you go?"

She touched a hand to his face. "It doesn't matter. Life is short, Nate. You and I know that better than most. I try not to focus too much on the future but live for the here and now." She laughed. "And to anyone over thirty, that probably sounds crazy coming from a twenty-two-year-old, but you get where I'm coming from."

"I do. I guess I wanted to be honest, especially after the whole girlfriend and boyfriend conversation yesterday."

"And you have been. Now show me your moves."

———

"OH MY GOD," Indie lamented, collapsing onto the sofa. She

kicked off her high heels and rested her feet on Jax's lap. "Husband, rub my feet."

Nate snorted. "You're fucked, bro. Pussy whipped until you shuffle off this mortal coil."

Warmth filled Dex's insides. The more time that passed, the more Nate slowly dropped his cold, distant attitude toward his brothers. Determined to keep the atmosphere light, she let her shoes fall to the floor and stuck her feet in Nate's lap. She made sure to graze his cock with her heel. "Boyfriend, rub my feet."

Jax threw back his head and laughed. "No, bro. I think *you're* the one who's fucked."

Nate gave her a look that said she was in so much trouble. But that didn't stop him kneading at her soles with his thumbs. Her head rocked back, and she groaned. "God, that feels good. You'd make a good masseuse. And with your looks, you might even pull in a little extra on the side."

Indie joined in with Jax's laughter. "Dex, you are priceless."

"She's fucking dead," Nate grumbled.

"Who's dead?" Cole asked, appearing with Millie and Aimee.

"Where'd you get to?" Jax asked him.

"I got the munchies," Millie said, pointing to a bag full of chips and dips that Cole had a hold of. "I'm always hungry after champagne. I'm going to put the baby to bed and then I'm tucking in. You guys want some?"

"Not for me," Indie said, getting to her feet. "Come on, Jax. Early start in the morning."

"When are you guys going on honeymoon again?" Nate asked.

"Not until after the summer season is over." Indie rolled her eyes. "The joys of running a hotel. Good thing we're only newlyweds and not newly relationshipers." She giggled. "I think I just made up a word."

Jax rose from the sofa and swept Indie into his arms. She squealed. "What are you doing, you crazy man."

"We might not be going on honeymoon for a few months, but

that doesn't mean I can't carry you over the threshold." He strode over to their bedroom, Indie's giggles only cutting off when the door closed behind them.

"Think we'll turn in, too," Nate said, standing.

"Night, you guys," Cole said. "See you in the morning. And try to keep the noise down," he added, earning a one-fingered salute from Nate.

Once they were inside his bedroom, he kicked the door shut and fell onto the bed. He loosened his laces and kicked his shoes across the room where they thudded against the wall underneath the window. "What a fucking day. I thought sixteen-hour shooting days were torturous. Turns out weddings top trump that shit all day long."

Dex collapsed next to him. "I love your family."

Nate grunted and then rolled onto his side and got to his feet. He wandered over to the dresser and took a box out of the top drawer. An oblong black box tied with a pink bow. He tossed it on the bed.

"I got us a present."

Dex sat up and crossed her legs. "You got *us* a present?" she said with a frown. "Why?"

Nate smirked. "It's definitely for us. Open it, and all will become clear."

Dex tugged on the ribbon. She peeled it away from the box and put it on the nightstand. Lifting the lid, she peered inside. It took her a millisecond to figure out what Nate had gotten them both, and then her eyes widened.

"You can't be serious?"

"Deadly. I can't wait to use this on you. I bet you'll come like a fucking freight train."

Nate removed the vibrator from its satin casing. He pressed on the non-business end, and it buzzed loudly.

Dex grabbed it out of his hands and quickly turned it off. "Stop it! Your family will hear."

Nate shrugged and snatched it back. "So? If you're that embarrassed, I'll tell them it's your toothbrush—and you're a thorough brusher." He laughed.

Dex did not.

"You are not using that on me here." *Back in L.A.? Hell yeah. But with his family in the next room? Nope. No. Definitely not.*

Nate set it on the bed. He grabbed hold of her ankles and parted her legs. He burrowed beneath her dress and pressed a kiss through her underwear to her sex. Her body jerked with pleasure. "Have you used one before?"

"No."

He eased aside her panties and gave her another kiss, then slipped his tongue through her folds. She groaned loudly and then clamped a hand over her mouth. She could hardly call him out for switching on Victor the Vibrator if she was going to make such a racket.

"Aren't you curious?"

She raised up on her elbows. Her stomach clenched deliciously at the sight of Nate between her legs. "Yes, I'm curious. But let's wait until we get home."

"I'm curious, too. I'm wondering how much I can torture you with this." He picked Victor up once more. He didn't turn it on, but he did roll the end over her clit.

Her legs writhed beneath her.

"A lot, I'm guessing," she gasped.

"Let's see."

He pressed the button, and the buzzing noise started up again, this time with the tip of the fake penis against her clit. Oh, the sensation... so intense... so fucking amazing. She arched her back, moans of pleasure spilling from her lips, all thoughts of denying him this... denying *her* this experience... gone.

"Let's get you out of this dress," Nate said.

He left the vibrator buzzing beside her and stripped off her clothes. He undressed himself, then tossed their clothes on the floor. He picked up the vibrator once more and trailed it over her stomach. It tickled, and she giggled. Except when he moved north and pressed the tip to her left nipple, she didn't giggle.

No, she shouted, "Fuck me!"

Nate burst out laughing. "I guess we can stop worrying about being overheard now. Worst is over."

Her face burned. She had no idea how she was going to face everyone in the morning. Nate, though, clearly didn't care because he stuck to his word. He tortured her. By the time he'd finished with Victor, she could barely recite her own name. She'd come so many times, she was completely wrung out, and wet? God, so wet, that when Nate pushed inside her, he almost slipped straight out. She clenched her core, anchoring him deep within. He groaned.

"Shit, Titch, if you're gonna clamp down on my dick so hard, I need to use that on you more often."

"Shut up and fuck me, Nate," she said, tilting her hips.

"I love it when you talk dirty," he said, grinning against her mouth.

And then he kissed her, deep, hard, using lots of tongue. She'd loved the battery-operated help, but nothing matched the feel of Nate moving inside her. She clutched him tightly to her. Her body built toward climax once more. Holy fuck. How was that even possible? She peaked, then crashed, wave after wave of pleasure washing over her.

She opened her eyes as Nate came. His eyes were clamped shut, and a faint sheen of perspiration dampened his forehead. His lips parted. He gave a throaty groan and then buried his face in her neck.

A few seconds later, he pulled out of her and rolled onto his back, breathing heavily. "You kill me, Titch, but fuck if I can't get enough."

Pleasure at his admission rushed through her. She leaned up on her elbow. "Ditto."

He reached for the vibrator and waved it in front of her face. "You got over your embarrassment pretty damn quick."

She poked him in the ribs. "Cocky bastard."

"You love it."

I love you.

Not again. Her brain needed to take a goddamn vacation. Time for a change of subject. She snuggled into his side, her cheek resting on his shoulder.

"I enjoyed today. Your family are wonderful."

"Yeah."

She twisted her head so she could look at him. "I know you were annoyed with me this morning for bringing it up again, but I've always been a tenacious bitch. Please tell me why you hate coming here so much."

A muscle ticked in Nate's cheek, and his eyes stayed firmly fixed on the ceiling.

"Drop it, Dex."

She pressed a hand to his chest. "Please, Nate. I—"

"I said drop it, and I meant it."

"I only want to help."

"You can help by shutting the fuck up." He pushed her hand away and swung his legs over the side of the bed.

She rested her palm on his back, feeling the tension radiating off him, his muscles bunching. "Don't shut me out."

He turned to her, and what she saw in his eyes scared her. *He* scared her. "I'm warning you, Dex. Either stop pushing this subject, or it's over."

She widened her eyes then scrambled to her feet, pulling the sheet around her nakedness. How had they gone from such mind-blowing sex to talk of them splitting up? "You don't mean that."

He stood, too. "What's it to you anyway? Why do you care so fucking much?"

"Because I care about you," she said quietly. "And an idiot can see you're carrying the world on your shoulders, but I don't understand why. If your family were horrible, or they talked down to you, or were mean and nasty, I'd get it. But they're not. They're a family to be proud of, and *you* should be proud to be part of it."

Nate's eyes flashed with such venom, she recoiled. He dragged on a pair of jeans and a T-shirt and shoved his feet into his sneakers. "You haven't got a fucking clue what you're talking about. You know what? Go fuck yourself, Dex."

He stormed out, slamming the door so hard behind him she jumped. Tears sprang to her eyes, but she refused to cry. After what they'd shared, she couldn't understand how he could be so cruel. So cold. Her early impressions of Nate Brook were dead-on. That was the real man. Nasty. Narcissistic. Thoughtless and selfish. Arrogant prick.

Mentally exhausted, she pulled on some clothes, fetched her suitcase, and began packing her things. If Nate thought she was going to hang around here waiting for him to calm down and apologize, well, he could fuck right off. She wouldn't be *that girl.* She opened the dresser drawer as a soft tapping sounded on the door. Definitely not Nate returning to beg for forgiveness. He'd have barged in and expected her to fall to her knees in gratitude.

"Come in," she called out.

Millie popped her head inside. "Are you decent?"

Dex shrugged. "Not sure I can claim that, but I'm dressed if that's what you mean."

Millie closed the door behind her and came farther into the room. "So, I just had the skin burned off my face by Nate as he stomped out of here at full pelt." She gave Dex a warm smile. "Want to talk about it?"

Dex plunked herself on the bed and rubbed her eyes. "I'm not sure I have an explanation for what happened."

Millie sat beside her. "Take your time."

Dex flopped onto her back and hooked her arms behind her

head. "Nate didn't want to come here. To New York, I mean. Not just the wedding."

Millie laid down, too, and mirrored Dex's pose. "Nate never wants to come here."

Dex twisted her head, hope spiking within her. "Do you know why?"

Millie shook her head. "He visits so rarely, and when he does, he's usually monosyllabic and brooding. These past couple days is the only time I've seen him say more than a handful of words, not to mention smile. I wasn't sure he had teeth."

Dex chuckled. The more time she spent with Millie, the more she liked her. "Indie said the same the other day." Her cheeks puffed up as she blew out a breath. "We argued because I questioned his reasons for staying away. I mean, you're all so fabulous, I don't understand why he's so reluctant to spend time with you. Clearly, I hit a nerve. Or several."

Millie sat up and crossed her legs. "Nate's hiding something so poisonous, it's eating him up from the inside."

Dex frowned. That was exactly what she thought, but the fact Millie had picked up on it, too, when, by her own admission, she rarely saw Nate, piqued Dex's interest. "What makes you say that?"

Millie bit down on her lip. "Has Nate ever mentioned my past?"

Dex snorted. "Nate doesn't talk about any of you. He didn't even mention Calum and Cole were twins, hence my stupefied look when I arrived on Thursday."

"Oh dear."

The two girls laughed. Then Millie grew serious. "I went to school with Calum and Cole. I actually dated Calum for a few weeks, before he grew tired of me and moved on."

"Wow," Dex said, adding, "Poor Laurella."

"He's grown up a lot since then, although I think Laurella dragged him kicking and screaming into adulthood. Anyway, I was sore when he dumped me, but I soon got over it because the captain of the football team started paying me lots of attention. I wasn't even a cheerleader, so you can imagine how that went down with the other girls. Tanner was the dream. Good-looking, fit, the envy of the school, and he was interested in little old me." She stared off into the distance, lost in her own thoughts. "Stupidly, I married him. I was eighteen. For a while, things were good. He secured a tryout with the Chicago Bears, so we moved to Michigan. Then he damaged his knee and bam! Promising football career over. His way of coping with his terrible disappointment was to abuse me."

Dex sucked in a breath. "He hit you?"

She shook her head. "Believe me, it would have been easier to deal with if he had. No, Tanner had a special way of breaking down my confidence, my self-esteem until I didn't even know who I was anymore. He got inside my head, and he systematically destroyed me."

"I'm so sorry," Dex said, wondering why Millie was choosing to share all this with her.

"Oh, I'm not telling you for sympathy. My story ends well because Cole saved me. But I kept my secret for a long time. I thought people would blame me if they knew. *'That stupid girl who let her husband walk all over her. I'd have kicked him into touch years ago. Why didn't she? Maybe she liked him ruling over her.'* Yada yada. Anyhow, what I'm trying to say is I recognize the signs of someone carrying a terrible truth inside them. One they daren't let loose, because they're terrified of what will happen if they do."

"Nate," Dex said, more to herself than Millie, but the other woman nodded anyway.

"Don't give up on him. He's such a sad person, yet with you I see more than glimpses of… peace, I guess. Cole was my savior. I think you're Nate's."

She yawned and got to her feet. "Sorry, honey, but I need my bed. When he comes back—and he will—try not to be too hard on him. But at the same time, don't let him hide from the truth. If he's ever going to tell anyone what's bugging him, I think it will be you."

Dex stared at the ceiling long after Millie had left, even though she was exhausted. But eventually, her eyes fell shut, and she slept.

CHAPTER 18

"**F**uck!"

Dex's eyes snapped open in time to see Nate hit the wall as he staggered through the bedroom door. She sat upright, watching him lurch toward her, reeking of booze. His hair stuck out at all angles, as though he'd been running his hands through it, he had a bruise on his right cheek, and his shirt was missing a couple of buttons.

"What the hell happened to you?" she whispered, conscious of Cole, Millie, and their baby sleeping right next door.

His unfocused gaze fell on her. With a stupid grin plastered over his face, he took another unsteady step—and collapsed onto the bed. "There you are," he mumbled, clawing his way closer. He rested his head in her lap. "You smell gooood."

She shoved him off her. "You're drunk."

He giggled. Nate did *not* giggle. Ever. A chuckle perhaps, or a snort of laughter.

"Drunk on you, Titch." He tried to raise himself up, but couldn't manage it, and collapsed back into his previous position then rolled onto his back. He closed his eyes.

"How much have you had to drink?" she asked, wondering

whether he'd need his stomach pumped. When he didn't respond, she punched his arm. "Nate!"

"Ow." He turned onto his side, curling his knees into his chest. "Make love not war, Titch."

She struggled to figure out what he'd said, because he was slurring all over the place. Her heart clenched. Poor Nate. He must be hurting really bad to get this wasted. Sure, he liked a drink, but from what she'd seen of him these past weeks, he was always in control.

"Shall I call a doctor?"

He violently shook his head. "No doctor."

"Your brothers, then? Shall I get Jax, or Cole?"

A deep frown scored between his eyebrows. "What brothers?"

Jesus. He was utterly loaded. "Your brothers, dickhead. Shall I wake Jax or Cole, or call Calum?"

"Not my brothers," he muttered. "Not proper brothers."

"Nate." Another arm shake followed by a second punch. "What are you talking about?"

He swatted the air with his hand. "Need sleep."

And before she could say another word, he turned over. In seconds, he was snoring.

But Nate's untimely arrival had put paid to any sleep she was likely to get. She got out of bed and tiptoed across the room, not that it made a difference to Nate. A pneumatic drill starting up right next to him would be unlikely to even stir him. He'd have a hell of a headache the next day, though.

The living area was quiet as she strolled into the kitchen. A cup of hot milk with some sugar might help her drop back off, but usually, once her sleep was disrupted, she always struggled to get back to dreamland.

She put the pan on the stove and half-filled it with milk. Within a couple of minutes, tiny bubbles formed. She removed it from the heat in case it got a skin and poured it into a cup. She added two spoonfuls of sugar and took a seat at the breakfast bar.

What on earth had Nate meant, not proper brothers? When she was younger, she'd occasionally disowned Elva as a sister, usually when she wouldn't do as Dex wanted, but Nate wasn't a child, and he hadn't fallen out with his siblings. He'd fallen out with her. She rubbed her forehead. None of this made sense. Not his immature tantrum which resulted in him storming out, nor his refusal to have a proper discussion on the subject. And now he'd gotten so drunk he could barely speak.

She finished her milk and, with a heavy sigh, went back to bed. She must have fallen asleep eventually because the sun woke her. Groaning, she glanced at her watch. Seven-thirty. Nate had rolled in around two, which meant he wouldn't be awake for a while. He was still dressed in his clothes and shoes from the previous evening and Dex watched his chest rise and fall, vowing that he could get as angry as he liked, but she wasn't letting him get away with averting a grown-up discussion any longer.

She took a quick shower, dressed, and left Nate still snoring to go out for a walk. She plugged Central Park into the maps app on her cell and set off. Nate had planned for them to visit the park today, but given the sizeable hangover he would have, chances were he'd spend the day slouching around on the couch, no doubt feeling sorry for himself. Well, screw him. She'd sightsee on her own. No way was she coming all the way to New York City without ticking off every single must-do item on her list.

The park came into view, and she spotted a bike rental shop down a side street. A selection of bikes was already lined up outside, which meant they were open. She wandered inside and, after filling out a form and paying a deposit and rental fee for an hour, she set off toward the park.

She stopped when she reached the Alice in Wonderland bronze sculpture. She'd read about this when researching where to go, and it was at the top of her list. She loved that book so much. Taking out her phone, she shot a couple of pictures, but as she got back on her bike, her cell rang. She glanced down at the screen.

Nate.

Keeping her voice slow and steady, she answered. "You're awake then?"

"Where are you?"

In usual Nate style, his tone was brusque and commanding, and whereas she usually didn't mind, this morning, it grated.

"What's it to you?"

A pause, followed by a deep sigh. "How long are you going to make me grovel?"

"Well, seeing as you haven't even started yet, that's difficult to answer."

She could have sworn she heard a low chuckle, but then he sighed. "I'm sorry for snapping, okay? And for running out on you."

"And for getting wasted. And for saying some horrible things, like telling me to go fuck myself."

"Jesus, you really are milking this for all it's worth. I didn't fucking mean it, you crazy woman."

"Do you remember what you said to me last night, after you came home stinking of booze and staggering all over the place?"

"Whatever it was, I'm guessing it wasn't good."

She propped up her bike on its stand and perched on one of the toadstools in front of the Mad Hatter.

"Dex?" Concern and worry laced his voice when she didn't respond.

Good. Let him stew and think he'd been horrible when, in fact, his comments had simply caused confusion.

"You still there?"

"You were so drunk, you could barely stand. After you collapsed on the bed, I was worried about you being sick and choking. I asked if you wanted me to fetch a doctor. You were very adamant in telling me no. So I asked if you wanted me to get your brothers. Your response, and I quote, was 'Not my brothers. Not proper brothers'. What did you mean by that?"

Dead silence greeted her. She couldn't even hear him breathing. She looked at her screen in case they'd been cut off. Nope. Still connected.

"Nate?" Now it was her turn to sound worried.

He laughed, but it sounded husky and raw, and very forced. "No idea what I meant. I was hammered."

"You're lying."

She didn't know how she could sense he wasn't being truthful with her, but her intuition was firing like crazy.

"Where are you?" he eventually said.

"Central Park. I'm coming back now."

"No, don't. I'll come to you. Meet me outside the main entrance to The Plaza. Can you find that?"

"Yeah."

"On my way."

He hung up, leaving Dex with a very uneasy feeling. He'd sounded exhausted, beaten, scared even. Why wouldn't he want her to come back to the hotel where they could talk in private? It didn't make any sense. *He* wasn't making any sense.

She returned the bike to the rental shop, recovered her deposit, and walked to The Plaza. By the time she got there, Nate was already waiting. He must have sprinted to get there so quickly, but he didn't look out of breath, only wary.

He sauntered over to greet her, meeting her halfway.

"Hey." He offered her a wry smile. "You didn't punch me."

"You're lucky I didn't smother you while you slept."

"Then the fact I fell asleep with that as a potential outcome must mean I trust you."

She twisted her lips to the side, considering his comment. "Do you, though? Do you trust me enough to tell me what's really going on? And don't even think about denying it. We might not have known each other long, but I'm not stupid, Nate."

He let out a sigh, and his eyes briefly closed. "Come with me."

She allowed him to take her hand. He walked into The Plaza, right across the lobby, stopping in front of the reception desk.

"We need a room."

Why do we need a room? She went to ask, but Nate gave a brief shake of his head and squeezed her hand in a silent no.

The man behind the desk glanced up, recognition evident in the slight bow to his head. "Certainly, Mr. Brook." He put out his hand which Nate shook. "I'm Andrei, the assistant manager. Anything you need, rest assured I'm at your service."

Dex suppressed a giggle at his formality while Nate responded with, "Thank you."

Andrei tapped on a keyboard. "Our junior king suite is available. It comes with full butler service, of course."

"A regular room will be fine."

Andrei swiped his card then handed it back to Nate. "Our normal check in time isn't until three p.m., but for you, Mr. Brook, I'm sure we can make an exception."

"Great."

"How many keys will you be requiring?"

"One."

"Certainly." He coded the key and passed it over. "The elevators are right over there, sir."

"Thanks."

A few minutes later, Nate opened the door to their hotel room, except it wasn't like any hotel room she'd ever stayed in.

"This is bigger than my apartment," she said. "Why have you brought me to a hotel?"

Nate sagged wearily onto a sofa positioned at the end of the bed, his legs sprawling in front of him. "I don't want our conversation to be overheard, and don't give me a hard time about extravagance. I refused the suite, didn't I?"

Dex chuckled, taking the seat beside him. "I thought I might have had something to do with that."

Nate hitched a shoulder. "I learned my lesson." He knitted their fingers together. "I really am sorry, Titch. I shouldn't have spoken to you like I did last night."

Something about his demeanor scared her. Fear turned her stomach. Millie was right. Nate needed to share his inner turmoil about his family with someone before it slowly ate him alive. Might as well be her. She could cope with whatever it was... couldn't she?

She squeezed his forearm. "I'm very discreet, Nate. You *can* trust me. Whatever you tell me stays between us." She crossed her heart. "I will take it to my grave, on my mother's life."

He covered his face with his hands and rubbed hard. "I'm tempted. It'd be good to say the words aloud instead of listening to them screaming inside my head for the last seven years, but I'm scared to." He expelled a sharp, bitter laugh. "I bet that's a turn-off, right? I'm the man. I'm supposed to be the strong one."

She shook her head. "Showing you're vulnerable is actually a huge turn-on, Nate. At least for me. I don't want a boyfriend who pretends to be something he's not. I want the real you."

He touched his forefinger to his bottom lip and stared at the wall opposite, lost in thought.

"If you tell a soul, I swear to God—"

"I won't. Trust me, please. I won't let you down."

He turned to her then and reached out for a lock of her hair, letting it run through his fingers. "What is it about you, Titch? We've only known each other a month, yet I feel like we've been together for years."

Her heart skipped a beat because that was exactly how she felt. "I guess with some people, time is irrelevant," she said gently. "And then there are others who spend their whole lives together and never really know the other person."

"Yeah, I guess." He took a deep breath through his nose and then exhaled slowly. "Let me finish before you speak, okay?"

When she nodded, he began to talk.

"Jax, Calum, and Cole aren't my full brothers. Mom had an affair, and I was the by-product. When I see my brothers now, I'm reminded that I'm an outsider, an interloper, and the woman I adored more than life itself was a liar and a cheat. That's why I hate coming to New York. Because it fucking hurts."

Whatever she'd expected him to share, that was not it. The pain in his eyes cut through her, and she automatically reached for his hand, squeezing for all she was worth as he continued.

"Seven years ago, I came home from RADA for Thanksgiving. I was looking through bits and pieces of Mom's stuff that Jax had kept around. He'd put most of it in storage, but there was a box of trinkets and cards we'd made her when we were little, that kind of thing, which he'd kept on hand for some reason. There was a letter inside an envelope containing a birthday card. I've no idea how it got there." He grimaced. "Not that it matters."

His gaze returned to the wall. As he hadn't given her a sign he'd finished, she kept her silence, but her grip on his hand remained steadfast. She hoped he'd take some comfort from it. What a terrible thing to find out, and then to keep to himself all these years. Her heart ached for him. To have everything you believed to be true torn apart. More than a minute passed, and still he didn't carry on with the story.

"What did the letter say?" she asked as gently as she could.

His head dropped, chin curved into his chest. She wanted to hold him, to take his pain and make it her own.

"It was from *him* in response to her ending their affair. She'd sent him a letter which he'd sent back to her with one of his own agreeing to leave her alone. Apparently, my dad—and by that, I mean the man who raised me—had found out everything. He'd given Mom an ultimatum. End the affair and they'd never speak of it again, or he'd throw her, and me, out on the street and make sure she never saw Jax or the twins again. My sperm donor didn't mention me at all, as though I didn't even exist. From the date on the letter, I'd just turned six months old."

171

"Jesus," Dex muttered.

He rubbed his eyes and then his forehead, as though he was trying to scrub away the hideous memories.

"It all became so clear to me then: the way Dad kept me at a distance, yet was so close with the others; how he'd be much harder on me over everything. My grades at school, how tidy I kept my bedroom, telling me I couldn't have friends over, yet my brothers were allowed as many as they liked. Mom overcompensated for his behavior. She'd tell me how special I was, how gorgeous, kind, bright, clever. But I always knew something was different. That *I* was different." His eyes cut to hers, and the depth of hurt in them broke her heart. "So, yeah, now you know."

It was her cue to talk, but instead, she climbed on to his lap and hugged him as tight as she could manage. She wanted to take the agonizing memories festering inside him into her own body, cleanse them, and give them back to him, almost like money laundering for the mind. Except she couldn't. All she could do was silently tell him that she was there for him, that it didn't matter to her what terrible things lurked in his past. She wanted him regardless, every fucked-up, wonderful, amazing part. His past shaped the man he was today—sometimes angry and hurtful, but always magnificent.

"What do you need, Nate?"

He drew back, his eyes searching her face. She didn't know what he was looking for, but he must have found it because he gave a small nod, curved his hands beneath her ass, and stood. Without saying a word, he carried her to the bed and set her down. His mouth searched for hers, and as their tongues came together, his touch became urgent. He undressed her quickly, and then himself, but as he nestled between her parted thighs, he slowed down as though her compliance to giving him what he needed had soothed an ache she couldn't see but could definitely feel.

His hands cupped her face, and the way he looked at her, with such reverence and desire, sent her pulse into overdrive.

"I can't wait, Dex."

"I don't want you to wait."

With a groan, he pushed himself inside, but instead of taking her hard and fast, as she'd expected, he moved with slow, deliberate thrusts. His eyes never left hers, and as his hips moved, stroking the part of her that made her toes curl, she had an epiphany. Nate wasn't fucking her. He was making love to her.

I love you.

She wanted to say the words out loud, but fear held her back. Just because he was making love to her didn't mean he actually loved her. Nate was a man who felt deeply, that much was obvious, given what he'd told her about his background, but she instinctively knew he was also a man who didn't love easily. To tell him how she was feeling was a risk she simply couldn't take. If she lost him now, it would punch a hole in her heart that she couldn't hope to fix.

Her stomach clenched, and then warmth rushed out from her center. She hugged Nate to her as he found his own release. He muttered something unintelligible in her ear, his breath hot against her skin. He held her close for a while, then rolled to the side. His fingers crept toward hers. He knitted them together, his gaze fixed on the ceiling.

"I know being with me isn't easy. I'm fucked up, moody at times. I can sulk with the best of them. I have serious issues that I'm working through. All I ask is for you to accept me for the man I am. Not the actor, or the public figure, or the youngest of four brothers who doesn't know who his dad is."

Dex swallowed past a huge lump in her throat. If one tear dared to fall, she'd gouge out her own eyes. This wasn't about her - it was about Nate and his deeply rooted feelings of rejection from his birth father and betrayal by his mother, a woman he adored.

"Why have you never told your brothers?" she asked softly.

A shadow crossed his face. "I don't want to talk about it."

"But, Nate, don't you see? It'll free you from the terrible burden you're carrying."

"No, it won't."

"How do you know if you don't try?"

"What's it to you anyway?" A cold, stark statement said without an ounce of inflection.

"What's it to me? Are you kidding me?"

Nate got off the bed and began to get dressed. A flush of anger reddened her skin. He really could be a complete asshole at times. She got out of bed, too, but instead of getting dressed, she stood in front of him, stark naked. Her hands went to her hips, and she jutted her chin forward.

"You're right. Being with you isn't easy. But let me make this real simple. In case it's escaped your notice, I actually give a shit about you. And a fucking idiot can see this secret is eating you alive. Jesus, like I've said a hundred times before, I'd understand your reticence if your family were a bunch of dicks, but they're wonderful. They'll understand."

He went to walk around her like she hadn't even spoken. She shifted to stop him. Poked her finger in his chest. "Don't even think about walking out on me."

He towered over her, his eyes almost black, fury in their depths. "I fucking knew it was a mistake to tell you. Get off my back."

"No."

He made another move. She countered it. Like two mismatched boxers facing off at the pre-match press conference, he stared her down. And she refused to bow to his dominance.

"Get out of my way."

She shook her head and planted her legs wide in case he tried to shove her off balance.

"Talk to me."

"I did!" he yelled, pushing a hand roughly through his hair. "You think it was easy for me to tell you something I've kept to myself for seven fucking years? I didn't tell you so you could lecture me on how fessing up to my brothers would make me feel better. It wouldn't. It would make me feel worse."

"How, Nate? Because all I can see is that it would free you. Don't you get that?"

"No, I fucking don't."

She expelled a frustrated breath. "Your brothers love you. And you clearly feel the same way about them. Don't you want to be able to look at them without thinking about what your mom did tainting your relationship? Don't you want to be a real part of the family, instead of standing on the periphery wishing you were and hating that you're not? Don't you want to be able to live without secrets, and show them the real you? To get back the closeness you had growing up?"

He visibly winced. "Fuck, Titch."

Oh shit. Sometimes she wished she could rip her own tongue out. But instead of him railing on her, his anger withered. He sagged on to the bed and let his head fall into his hands. His pain was so raw, as though his skin had peeled off, leaving the exposed nerves to the elements. She rushed to sit beside him and rested her head against his shoulder, half expecting him to shuffle out of her reach. Instead, he curved an arm around her and held her tight. His body trembled, and it was only when she lifted her head that she realized he was crying.

She scrambled onto his lap and let his tears soak her skin. From the way his sobs racked silently through him, she'd guess he'd never cried for what he'd lost. A whole history, a belief system, a sense of belonging. A loss of trust in the one woman every child should be able to have faith in without question. His innate fear he'd be rejected by his brothers when they found out. No wonder he'd kept quiet for so long while his pain grew and festered. And the fact he'd chosen her to share something so painful with her was humbling. It seemed as though they'd known each other years, not mere weeks. But then again, souls who were meant to be together didn't need years to know they'd found the other half of themselves.

He drew back slowly, his red-rimmed eyes seeking her out. His intensity was such that she wouldn't be surprised if he could see right into her soul.

She cradled his cheek, wiping away the remains of his tears with her thumb. "You asked me to accept you for who you are? Well, I do, Nate. The good and the bad. You want to know why? Because I love you. I'm in love with you."

The relief at finally vocalizing the words that had been swimming around her head was immense, like a weight she'd been carrying around for days had lifted.

He brushed her lips with his own. "I don't deserve you, Titch."

She lowered her head, and her shoulders dropped. She'd been brave and shared her feelings with him, and he hadn't reciprocated. Not that she'd expected him to profess his undying love, but a tiny part of her, hidden in a deep recess of her heart, had dared to hope. At least he hadn't run a mile.

She shrugged. "You're right. You don't."

A glimmer of a smile touched his lips. He skimmed the back of his hand across her cheek, his touch soft and tender.

"I feel the same, Titch. You know that, right? I don't know when or how you wormed your way into my heart, but now you're there, I'm guessing there's no getting rid of you."

She gave him a warning glare, but secretly, her heart soared. He did feel the same. *Thank God.* "You can say the words, Nate. They won't burn you."

"You burn me. You're the one, Titch. The only one for me. My everything."

Oh, now *that* would do very nicely. Nate might never be the type of boyfriend who'd tell her he loved her, but if those were the words he'd chosen instead, she'd take them every single time.

"Then do something for me."

He pressed his lips together and gave her a pained look. "I know what you're going to say."

"Good. Then I don't need to waste my breath."

He shook his head. "What have I gotten myself into with you?"

She grinned. "Be honest. I've brought a lot of excitement into your sad and lonely life."

He barked out a laugh. "You've brought stress, I know that much."

She straightened her face. "It will work out, Nate. I know it."

He twisted his lips to the side. "I wish I felt the same."

"Only one way to find out," Dex said.

When he nodded, her pulse leaped. "So you'll talk to them?"

"Will you be there?" he asked.

"I'll be wherever you need me."

He let out a long, exhausted sigh. "At least if I lose it all, I'll still have you."

CHAPTER 19

Nate clasped Dex's hand as he walked through the entrance of the hotel, trying—and failing—to halt the hurricane swirling in the depths of his stomach. He couldn't believe that after seven years of holding his secret close, a few weeks with Dex had broken down his carefully erected barriers and unraveled his silence, resulting in him spilling his guts. He'd had no plans to tell her, but following his drunken slip of the tongue and her determined persistence, he'd had a sudden urge to offload the burden.

This could all go horribly wrong, or it could go perfectly right. He couldn't call it. He wasn't worried for their reaction about his parentage so much as terrified of destroying the memory they all had of their mother. Each one of them held her on a sort of pedestal. Maybe if she'd lived, they'd have seen her flaws, recognized she was as human as the rest of them. But she hadn't. And they didn't.

But he did. He knew exactly how flawed she had been.

Dex increased the pressure on his hand. "I'm with you all the way."

He nodded but couldn't speak. His mouth was empty of saliva, and he found it difficult to swallow past a huge lump in his throat. His heart hammered against his ribcage, the tender muscle bruised and battered by the very cage meant to protect it.

Jesus, the parallel with his own existence wasn't fucking funny.

Jax and Indie were back at work, as though their wedding hadn't happened. Jax was talking to a couple of guests, sharing a joke, his smile broad, open, friendly. Indie was serving a pot of coffee to a man sitting at the bar. Guess it was too early for alcohol, although Nate wouldn't say no to a very large whiskey right at that moment. Fuck the hangover.

Jax spotted them at the entranceway. "Hey, you found her," he said. "See, I told you she wouldn't have gone far."

"I went cycling in Central Park," Dex offered helpfully.

"Can't come to New York and not take a ride through the park," Jax said, turning to Nate with a frown. "Although you could at least have gone with her. Douche."

Nate couldn't summon a smile, and Jax must have noticed because his frown lines deepened at Nate's brooding demeanor. "Is everything okay?"

"I need to talk to you," Nate said, plunging in before his nerve fucked off down the street and never came back. "In fact, I need to talk to all of you. Calum and Cole, too."

A flicker of worry crossed Jax's face, but he didn't delve any deeper. He simply pointed his chin. "You two go downstairs. I'll give them a call. I think Cole has taken Millie and Aimee out for breakfast. No idea where Calum will be, but I'm sure I can round him up."

"No girlfriends. Just the guys," Nate said.

Jax gave him a quizzical look, which Nate ignored. After Jax had left, Dex curved her hands around his neck and forced Nate to look at her.

"Breathe. It's going to be fine. They love you."

"Don't you get it? I'm about to destroy their memory of Mom."

She shook her head. "Your mom had an affair, Nate. That

179

doesn't make her unlovable or any less the wonderful mother she was to all of you. It makes her fallible, like the rest of us."

He pinched the bridge of his nose and closed his eyes. "I hope my brothers see it that way."

She waited for him to open his eyes. "They will," she said gently. "Trust me, Nate. You're doing the right thing."

He briefly kissed her. This girl. He couldn't imagine a life without her. She brought light to his dark, dragged laughter from him when no one else could, made him want things he hadn't expected to.

"Put her down."

Nate's abdomen clenched painfully as Jax walked in. He was alone.

"You got hold of the others?"

Jax nodded. "They're on their way." He crossed to the kitchen. "You guys want a coffee?"

"Yeah." Nate went to sit on the sofa, taking Dex with him. "So how's married life?"

"He only got married yesterday," Dex said.

Jax grinned. "That is true. Although apart from the wedding ring feeling strange, nothing's changed. Not that I expected it to, considering we've been living together for four years."

"What was the point in getting married then?"

"Nate!" Dex elbowed him in the ribs.

Jax rolled his eyes. "It's okay, Dex. We're used to him."

"It's a genuine question."

"It's a stupid question," Dex grumbled, her reprimand pulling at the corners of his mouth.

He'd never taken shit from a woman before, but he loved bantering with Dex. She wasn't a girl who backed down, and he loved that.

Jax brought over the coffees, and he and Dex chatted about nonsensical things—but Nate brooded as time passed. He wanted this shit over now.

"Where the fuck are Calum and Cole?"

"Right behind you, asshole."

Nate glanced over his shoulder. The knot in his stomach tightened. No backing out now. Calum flopped into the chair to Nate's right, and Cole perched on the arm.

"Well, you summoned us, and we're here," Calum said. "What's so fucking urgent that I got dragged over here on a Sunday morning when I should still be in bed with my girlfriend?"

Jax glared at him, but Calum simply returned his stare with one of his own.

Nate's tongue dampened his dry lips. He felt sick. How did he begin? What should he say first?

Dex's hand slid across his thigh, the warmth from her palm bleeding through his jeans, grounding him right when he needed it. He could've kissed her, and not only because it'd distract him, but because when he was kissing her, he forgot everything except how good she felt.

"You have to let me finish." Said for Calum's benefit—Nate knew Jax and Cole wouldn't interrupt. "Or I can't do this."

Calum's eyes narrowed. "You're starting to worry the shit out of me, little brother."

Jax leaned forward, his forearms resting on his knees. "You can tell us anything, Nate. We're your brothers and we love you."

Nate squeezed his eyes shut. The back of his throat ached, and he had difficulty swallowing. His pulse began to race, speeding up with every passing second. *Come on. Spit it out already.*

Slowly, he opened his eyes and looked at each one of his brothers in turn. "That's just it. You're not my brothers. Not full ones anyway. Mom had an affair. I'm the result."

Apart from a buzzing sound coming from the fridge, no one spoke. Sweat coated his palms, and his mouth was so dry his lips stuck to his teeth. God, this was awful. Hideous. He held his breath, waiting for the ax to fall.

Jax's posture stiffened, his spine rigid, and Cole's mouth

dropped open. Calum, on the other hand, shot him a disbelieving look.

"The fuck you talking about?"

Nate's insides boiled at Calum's blunt response, and he curled his hands into fists. "Want me to say it in fucking French?"

Calum's eyes widened, and a nerve ticked in his jaw. "You might as well, because you're talking out of your ass."

"Shut up, Calum," Jax said, beating Nate to it. Except his response would have been "Fuck you."

"Why do you think Mom had an affair?" Jax asked, the question accompanied by a painful wince which Nate mirrored.

"I found a letter. Years ago when I was home for Thanksgiving. It was from *him*. Apparently Mom had broken off their affair, and he was writing back to acknowledge her wishes. Her letter was included with his. That's how I know I wasn't Dad's real son." He flinched again, and his chin trembled. He clamped his jaw tight and tried to breathe through his nose.

Realization crossed Jax's face. "Seven years," he mumbled. "That's when you found it, didn't you?" Nate nodded, and Jax continued. "And that's why you stopped coming home, unless forced."

"Yep."

Jax swept a hand over his head and muttered, "Jesus."

Nate glanced over at Cole who still hadn't said a word, but then that was so like him. He'd hold his tongue until he figured out the right thing to say. Except not even his composed, unflappable brother would be able to find the words to fix this fuck-up.

"Where is this so-called letter?" Calum said.

Heat flushed through Nate's body. He poked his finger in Calum's direction. "Fuck you. You think I'm making this shit up?"

Calum must have realized he'd screwed up because he blushed red as a beet. Calum never blushed. Cole glared at him, his eyes glinting with fury. "Shut the hell up, dickface."

"Of course I don't think you're making it up," Calum backtracked, ignoring Cole's interjection. "But if, as you say, you discovered this information years ago, then you've had years to come to terms with it. Remember, we're hearing this for the first time."

"Come to *terms,*" Nate said through gritted teeth as his anger reached boiling point. "You think I've *come to fucking terms* with the fact I'm not a Brook? That we're not fully related? That the mother we all adored had an affair? Jesus, you are a fucking piece of work, you know that?"

All three brothers started talking at once, but Nate was done listening to this crap. He launched to his feet, dislodging Dex's vise-like grip on his arm. He stormed across the room. Cole shot in front of him.

"Don't go. Not like this. We need to talk."

Nate shoved him out of the way, which wasn't an easy feat because Cole was two hundred pounds of solid muscle. "I'm done talking." And with that, he took off upstairs. If one of them dared to follow, he'd knock their fucking teeth out.

He burst out onto the street, his lungs blazing with agony. He shouldn't have let Dex talk him into it. He'd known it would be a complete disaster. Being right hurt like a bitch.

His eyes burned with hot tears, but fuck if he'd stand in the street blubbing like some goddamn loser. He'd lost his brothers seven years ago. Nothing had changed except now they might stop nagging him to come back to New York every five fucking minutes. He'd change his flight and head back to LA in the morning. Dex could either come or stay. Her choice.

Bye-bye, New York. I always fucking hated you anyway.

CHAPTER 20

D ex stared at the space Nate had occupied not ten seconds
since with sorrow and disbelief. Where had it had all gone
so wrong? She didn't think for one moment that Calum had
meant his words to cut as deep as they had, but Nate's over-the-
top reaction spoke volumes. She'd seen his face when Cole had
tried to stop him—a mixture of rage, disappointment, hurt... and
expectation. He'd *expected* this to go badly, so it had. Almost as if
he'd willed it, because believing his brothers would ostracize him
as soon as they found out the truth validated his own beliefs in
himself.

Nate Brook: outsider, loner, good for nothing.

Pain tore through her chest. She scrambled to her feet but was
pulled up short when Calum stopped her.

"I'll go. It's my screw-up. Mine to fix."

He jogged up the stairs but was back a few minutes later. Dex
looked up hopefully, but her face fell when Calum returned alone.

"Damn, that fucker moves fast. I couldn't see him anywhere."

"Leave him," Jax said. "He's hurting and needs to calm down.
When he comes back, we'll sit together as a *family* and have a

proper discussion." He turned to Dex. "Do you know the full story?"

"I know as much as you do." Despite not blaming Calum, she couldn't help flashing an irritated look his way. "I'm the one who persuaded him to tell you. That shit has been eating him up for years, and I hoped by releasing it, he could begin to heal the pain inside." She gave a despairing snort and swept a hand down her face. "What a mess. Did you have to react like that?" The last comment was aimed at Calum, who grimaced and tugged on his collar as though it was choking him. She'd like to choke him right that second.

"Shoot first, think later," he said apologetically. "Yep, I pretty much hate myself right now."

"Does he know who his father was?" Jax asked.

Dex shook her head. "I'm not sure. He didn't say, and I didn't ask."

Cole rose from his chair and paced in front of the couch. "I can't believe Mom had an affair." He raked his hands through his hair, his face twisted with pain as he no doubt struggled to come to terms with such devastating news. "And worse than that, I can't believe Nate thought, for all those years, that it would change one damn thing about the way we feel about him. I couldn't give a flying fuck who his sperm donor was. He's my brother, and I love the fucking bones of him."

Dex caught Cole's eye. "When he gets back, can you please tell him that? Right away. Let those be the first words out of your mouth, because that's exactly what he needs to hear."

Cole nodded while Calum recovered his composure and said, "We'll all tell him that. It happens to be the truth."

"Thank you," she said, her voice husky and raw as she fought to contain the emotion swirling inside. "I love him, too, you see."

Three pairs of emerald eyes turned on her, so very different to Nate's ice-blue, but despite the differences between him and his

185

brothers, there were also similarities. The strong, firm jaws, the straight, perfectly formed noses. The fact they were all insanely good-looking, which either meant both their fathers had been handsome sons of bitches, or they all got their looks from their mother.

"Thank you." Jax was the first to speak up. "For persuading him to tell us. It was the right call. I can't believe he discovered such a devastating secret and kept it to himself all these years."

"He didn't want to ruin the memory of your mom, so he decided he'd be the one to suffer."

Jax rubbed his face, hard, and blew out a heavy breath tinged with exhaustion. "There's nothing we can do until he returns. I'll call everyone as soon as he comes home. Dex, you're welcome to hang out, or leave your number and I'll call you, too, if you'd rather get some fresh air."

She shook her head. "I'm not leaving until he's back."

Jax nodded. "Fair enough."

The day passed with no sign of Nate returning. The brothers all gathered back at the hotel in the evening, trying to decide what to do. Cole had asked his buddies in the police to keep a lookout, but as Nate was a grown man with the freedom to come and go as he pleased, there wasn't a lot they could do.

"Do you think he'd just fly back to LA?" Jax asked after they'd exhausted all other possibilities.

A shot of ice water rushed through Dex's veins. Surely he wouldn't be so cruel. To leave her here with virtual strangers as a punishment for the way she'd pushed him into revealing a secret he'd successfully hidden until she'd come along.

"No," Cole said. "He's hurting, but he's not a total fucker." He squeezed Dex's hand. "He wouldn't leave you here, sweetheart."

"How can you be sure?" she said, her voice betraying the hurt inside.

"I'm sure. I know my brother."

Jax began to pace. "If he hasn't gone back to California, where the hell could he be? He doesn't have any friends here, so it's not like he'd be hanging out with them."

As they all tried to second-guess Nate's whereabouts without any real clue as to where he might be, an idea pricked at Dex. Could that be where he'd gone?

She got to her feet and grabbed her purse. "I think I know where he is."

"Where?" Calum asked, but Dex didn't listen. She shot for the door.

"I'm coming with you." Jax snatched up his phone and wallet. "You guys stay here in case he comes back, and call me the second he does."

They didn't wait to see if the twins agreed before they took off upstairs. Jax had a quick word with Indie who, God bless her, was tending bar the day after her wedding. Some start to a marriage, although she didn't seem to mind one iota. She gave Jax a quick kiss, her face filled with concern. She even managed a friendly wave to Dex and mouthed, "Don't worry", then turned her attention back to the paying customers.

The minute they got outside, Dex set off down the street as fast as her too-fucking-short legs would carry her. Jax easily kept up with her at a slow lope whereas she was almost running.

"Where is it you think he's gone?" Jax asked.

"Your parents' house," she panted back. "He took me there the other day."

Jax's eyes widened. "He did?"

"Yeah."

"Fuck. I wouldn't have ever thought of it. He's never once mentioned a hankering to go back there. I know I moved them too fast at the time, but that was sixteen years ago."

They turned into the tree-lined street with Dex half-expecting Nate to be sitting on the front steps, much as they both had when he'd shown her his family home, but apart from a few kids playing an ill-advised game of baseball in the street, no one else was about.

"Shit," Dex said, glancing up and down the rows of houses as if Nate would magically appear if she willed it hard enough.

"He's not here," Jax said, stating the obvious. "He wouldn't have knocked, would he? Asked to go inside, take a look around maybe?"

"Only one way to find out." Dex jogged up the front steps. She rapped on the front door, exquisitely painted in a deep navy blue with polished chrome fittings, so clean she'd bet she could see her face in them.

A few minutes later, an elderly lady answered the door, balancing on a walking stick.

"Can I help you?" she said, her face open and friendly, which spoke volumes of what a nice neighborhood Nate had grown up in.

"I'm sorry to bother you, ma'am," Dex said. "But we're looking for our friend. He used to live here a long time ago and, well, we're wondering if he came back for a visit."

"Oh, you mean Nate," she said with a bright grin which sent a flood of relief rushing through Dex, but it quickly disappeared with her next words. "He was here, but he left about fifteen minutes ago. Lovely young man. He asked if I minded him taking a look around, which, of course, I didn't at all. And then he stayed for tea and chatted with an old lady for a while. What a lovely boy." She winked at Dex. "If only I were a few years younger."

Despite the weight of disappointment, Dex couldn't help chuckling along with the old lady. "Would you mind if I left my number, in case he comes back?"

"Not at all, my dear."

Dex scrawled hers and Jax's numbers on a scrap of paper the old lady found, and then she and Jax trudged back onto the street.

"Where now?" Jax said helplessly.

Dex raised her hands in the air. "I'm all out."

Jax's phone rang. He answered it, and after two seconds barked, "Don't let him leave. We're on our way back." He turned to Dex. "He's at the hotel. And he's packing."

"Shit."

They ran back to the hotel. Jax kept having to stop and wait for her to catch up. By the time they got there, Dex was seriously out of breath, whereas Jax had barely broken a sweat. As they went inside, Dex shook his arm.

"Let me talk to him first, okay?"

She anticipated Jax might argue. Instead, he nodded. With her heart pounding from both the sprint back to the hotel and trepidation for her upcoming conversation with Nate, both of them headed for the basement. Cole was pacing. Calum was nowhere to be seen.

"Where is he?" Dex asked Cole.

"In his room. Calum's attempting to talk to him."

Dex went inside without knocking. Calum glanced over his shoulder and shot her a helpless look. Nate, on the other hand, didn't even acknowledge her presence as he shoved the last of his things into his suitcase.

"Can you leave us, please, Calum?" she said.

"Sure." He paused by her side and touched her briefly on the arm, whispering, "Go easy. He's raw."

She waited for Calum to leave and then sauntered across the room and peered out the window. A flurry of activity came to a halt behind her.

"Aren't you going to try and stop me?" Nate bit out. "Tell me it'll all be okay, that they love me and accept me, even though it's all bullshit."

Dex turned around slowly. "What's the point? You've already made up your mind."

"Yes, I have," he said, hands planted on his hips, legs splayed wide in an act of dominance.

She yawned. "Then why are we even having this conversation?"

She strolled past him and entered the bathroom, grinning to herself at his befuddled expression. During hers and Jax's mad dash back to the hotel, she'd been thinking of the right way to play the situation. Instinctively she knew if she begged Nate to stay, pleaded with him to listen to his brothers, all he'd do was dig his heels in and do the complete opposite. Whereas if she refused to play that game, let him think he'd gotten his own way, her attitude would confuse him, and he'd want to understand why.

An attempt at reverse psychology. Worth a shot at least.

She washed her hands and splashed her face. When she opened the door to the bedroom, Nate's suitcase still laid open on the bed with him standing frozen beside it. Ignoring him, she went over to the dresser and took out a fresh T-shirt. She quickly changed as the burn from his angry stare almost took the skin off the back of her neck.

"Pack, Dex," he ordered. "Flight leaves first thing tomorrow. We can stay at the airport tonight."

She slowly turned around, leaning against the dresser for support. Her stance was casual, contradicting the inner turmoil churning in her stomach. If this went wrong, she wasn't sure what she'd do.

"*My* flight doesn't leave until Tuesday, and so, until then, I'll be staying in New York and ticking off the rest of my itinerary. You, on the other hand, can continue to run away from your problems if it makes you happy. Just don't drag me into it."

His eyes widened in surprise, and his mouth actually fell open. If the situation wasn't so serious, she'd have laughed. As it was, she stared him down, refusing to budge a single inch. His expression hardened, and he stared at her so coldly she almost lost her nerve.

"Get. Fucking. Packed."

She gritted her teeth. Who the hell did this guy think he was? Nerve back in its rightful place, her face flushed with anger as the gloves came off. "Screw. You."

His nostrils flared, and his stance widened. "Don't push me, Dex."

She strode over and poked him in the chest. "Don't *you* push *me.*"

She went to go past him—with every intention of leaving the arrogant prick to stew until he calmed the hell down—despite her earlier pledge to talk to him calmly, to play the long game. As her shoulder leveled with his, he caught her wrist. She yanked it out of his grasp and marched to the door. She didn't get to open it because his body covered hers. He gripped her hands and held them above her head, holding her in place with his hips, while his tongue traced the nape of her neck.

"You're so goddamn sexy when you're angry."

"Let me go, Nate."

"Never."

He spun her around, and his mouth crashed down on hers. As angry as she was with him, her nipples puckered, and the low-lying muscles in her stomach contracted. But she wasn't about to let him off the hook completely. She bit down hard on his lower lip. He released her with a curse. His lip was bleeding, and he dabbed it with his finger, then pulled his hand away, frowning at the blood on his fingertips.

"You feisty little witch."

"You'd better believe it, asshole."

She waited for his next move, but as was often the case with Nate, he surprised the hell out of her by throwing back his head in laughter.

"What am I going to do with you?"

She grinned. "Listen for once in your goddamn life."

She half expected him to argue, but instead, he took a big

breath and sat on the edge of the bed. His eyes turned to his suitcase, and then to her.

"You won't come back with me?"

She sat beside him. "Sure I will. On Tuesday."

His lips twitched, and he touched his head to hers. Silence stretched between them, and it wasn't uncomfortable so much as necessary for them both to take a breath. Dex broke first.

"Why did you run off to your parents' house?"

He turned to look at her, his fingers entwining with a stray lock of her hair. He fed it through his fingers and then brought it to his nose. The tenderness in the way he did it made her heart clench. "How do you know me so well after such a short period of time?"

She hitched one shoulder.

He sighed softly. "I guess after telling my brothers, I yearned for a different time, when things were simpler. When I was still one of four."

Dex made a frustrated noise. "You *are* still one of four. Don't you see that?"

He stared at the wall opposite, thoughtfully rubbing his chin. "Maybe."

"Did Cole talk to you before?"

"I didn't give him chance. Just stormed in here and began packing. Calum tried to talk to me, to apologize for his knee-jerk reaction, but I didn't want to listen."

"Are you ready to listen now? Because I think you should hear what they have to say before you run away like a spoiled child who hasn't gotten their own way." He cocked an eyebrow at her, but she barreled on regardless. "I understand where Calum was coming from, if not the manner in which he shared. It must be a helluva shock to all of them. But come on, Nate. You're not the only one affected by this. For God's sake, don't let something that happened twenty-eight years ago ruin your relationship with your brothers, or fuck up the memories of your mom. You're better than that."

His gaze dropped to his feet. "Am I?"

She crawled onto his lap and nudged a finger under his chin until he looked at her. "I wouldn't be here if you weren't."

He captured one of her hands and pressed a kiss to the inside of her wrist. "Okay, Titch. We'll do this your way. Let's go face the music."

Nate's brothers weren't alone when they emerged from his bedroom, but as soon as Indie, Millie, and Laurella spotted them, they all got to their feet.

"We'll leave you to it," Indie said.

"No, stay," Nate said. "This affects all of us." He looked at each one of his brothers in turn. "I'm sorry for running out. Guess I still have some growing up to do, as Dex rather gleefully pointed out."

"Someone had to," Dex said, earning a round of laughter from the room and a hard stare from Nate.

"Come sit down," Jax said, pointing with his chin to the sofa.

Calum got to his feet to make room for Nate and Dex.

"Bro," Calum said, clapping Nate on the back. "Again, I'm sorry." Which Dex took to mean it wasn't Calum's first apology— and Nate hadn't listened to the first one. "I didn't mean you'd found it easy when I said you'd had chance to come to terms with it. I can't imagine how awful it has been for you to carry that around for so long. I feel like we've failed you."

Nate offered his brother a crooked grin. "You haven't failed me. I guess I've been shitting myself about this moment for so long. I overreacted, so it's me who should be apologizing."

He took a seat, tugging Dex down beside him. He laced their fingers together, and he kept brushing over her skin with his thumb, as though he needed the contact.

Cole sat on the coffee table and leaned his forearms on his knees. "Nate, I'm only going to say one thing, on behalf of every one of us here, and then I'll shut up and let you talk," he said. "You are *our* brother, our family. Nothing will ever change that. None of us give a flying fuck about genetics. We all love you so very much. All we need now is for you to let us."

Aimee chose that moment to let out a loud wail. Millie gave an apologetic smile and got to her feet. "Sorry, Nate." She picked the baby out of the bassinet and rocked her.

"Can I hold her?" Nate asked.

Dex guessed this was not a normal request when the whole room went silent. She glanced around at a sea of shocked faces.

"Of course," Millie said, the first to react. She nestled the little girl in Nate's arms. He stared down at her, his face a mixture of surprise and wonderment.

A warm feeling spread through Dex's chest. He looked so at peace. After a couple of minutes humming to the baby, she fell asleep.

"You've got the gift," Millie said, grinning as Nate carefully handed the child back to its mother. "I might call on you for babysitting duties."

"I'd like that," he said quietly.

Jax's eyes sparkled with what Dex guessed was happiness. He confirmed it when he said, "I've finally gotten my brother back."

Nate rolled his eyes, his trademark cocky attitude making a comeback. "All right. No need to go all maudlin on me."

Calum laughed. "There's the dick we all know. I suppose this means we'll be seeing your ugly mug around here more often now."

"You might," Nate said. "If only to piss you off."

Calum laughed again. "Bring it."

Dex sneaked a glance at Nate. Happiness shone from every pore as he bantered back and forth with Calum. *Thank God.* She'd been right to push him to do this.

"Feel up to talking now?" Jax asked.

Nate nodded. "Sure."

"Okay, maybe you can start at the beginning," Jax said. "Do you still have the letter?"

"No. I put it back where I found it. It was in that old shoebox you kept at the house that was full of bits and pieces of Mom's."

"Damn," Jax said, crestfallen. "I put that in storage with the rest of Mom and Dad's things when we moved here. Never mind. We'll go to the lockup tomorrow." He cast a look at Nate. "If you don't mind, that is?"

"Fine by me," Nate said with a shrug.

"Do you know who your dad is?" Laurella asked.

Dex briefly wondered if she'd drawn the short straw on that particular question, but then with her soft European accent and gentle manner, it somehow sounded better coming from her.

"Not a clue," Nate said, his expression hardening. "And I don't fucking want to know."

"Don't you?" Dex asked. "Are you sure?"

"Positive," he bit out.

"Even if you did, I'm not sure we'd know where to start," Jax said. "Twenty-eight years is a long time."

"Good thing I don't give a shit then."

Calum chuckled. "You're our brother all right. Full of attitude."

Nate flashed a quick grin, then the room fell silent, as though no one knew what else to say. Nate gave her a nudge and cocked his head toward his bedroom. "Two seconds, Titch."

She frowned as he took her hand. He gestured for her to go inside, then closed the door behind them.

"I'm sorry."

Her eyes widened. "For what?"

His chin dropped to his chest, and he stuffed his hands deep into his pockets. "For yelling at you when you only had my best interests at heart. For storming out and leaving you here to deal with the fallout. For worrying you." He blew out a slow breath, his head gradually lifting. He met her gaze and then traced his fingertips over her cheek. "Do you forgive me?"

She caught his hand and pressed a kiss to his palm. "There's nothing to forgive."

His answering grin chased away the shadows beneath his eyes. "Then let's get out of here."

Excited, she mirrored his grin. "Dancing?"

He grazed his nose down hers. "Whatever my love wants."

CHAPTER 21

"Let's walk the rest of the way," Nate said after the traffic had been at a standstill for five minutes. He handed the cab driver a twenty, and they all climbed out of the car. Nate took hold of Dex's hand, and he and his brothers walked the last four blocks to the storage unit.

Jax keyed in the code and lifted the roller door. Inside was several boxes, all sealed and stacked three high. The unit was also filled with their dad's golf clubs, an old bike, a scratched mahogany sideboard that had been passed down from their maternal grandmother, and a piano that Nate remembered Mom buying because she'd thought it would be a good idea for them to play a musical instrument. Suffice to say none of them had either the aptitude or the patience to learn, and it had gathered dust in the dining room, but she'd refused to get rid of it, saying it added a touch of elegance to their home.

"Whose is the bike?" he asked Jax with a cocked eyebrow.

"Mine," Jax said with a grin. "I nagged Mom for weeks for a bike, but she thought the streets were too dangerous, so she refused. Dad talked her round in the end."

Nate's face twisted, and Cole laid a hand on his arm. "He was still your dad."

"I think he hated me."

Calum shook his head. "No, he didn't."

"He always treated me differently, and if you're being honest, you'll all agree."

Jax tugged on his bottom lip, his expression pensive. And then he sighed. "He was much harder on you than the rest of us. I figured he wanted to motivate you for some reason, like he thought you weren't pushing yourself hard enough or something."

"And instead, he must have gotten a kick to the gut every time he saw me because I reminded him of Mom's betrayal. I mean, I don't exactly look like the rest of you, do I?"

Before any of his brothers could answer, Dex beat them to it. "Actually you do. Apart from the color of your eyes, of course. But you have lots of physical traits in common with your *brothers*." She emphasized the last word, clearly to ram her point home. "Take a look in the mirror side by side and you'll see."

She turned her back on them and wandered over to the piano. She lifted the lid and ran her fingers over the keys. "I always wanted to learn to play, but we couldn't afford a piano," she said wistfully.

Nate's heart twisted for her. He mightn't have had it easy, but he'd never been short of *stuff*. Computer games, Lego sets, the latest sneakers that all the kids at school were wearing. Sure, he hadn't gotten the affection from his dad that his brothers had, but Mom more than made up for the shortfall, pouring all her love into him.

"I can ship it to you if you like," Jax said, causing Nate's eyebrows to shoot up into his hairline. Jeez, Dex must've made a good impression if Jax was willing to gift something of such sentimental value to someone he'd only met a few days ago.

"I'd love to take you up on that," Dex said. "But as Nate will no doubt attest to, I'd have to get rid of my furniture to accommodate it." She giggled. "I live in a very, very tiny apartment."

Nate made a mental note to speak to Jax privately and get the piano shipped to his place. He couldn't make Dex's apartment any bigger, but if he had his way, she'd be spending all her time at his house anyway.

Jax took down the first box. "Sorry, guys, but I can't remember which one the shoebox will be in, so we'll have to go through them all."

They all sat on the floor, each opening a box, and began the search. It took ages because they kept stopping and reminiscing about what they found inside, particularly when they came across some old photo albums of their school days. Dex paused her searching and watched as the brothers shared memories.

"You grew into your looks then?" she said, giving Nate a playful shoulder bump as he pointed out a formal school picture taken in seventh grade, about a year after the accident that killed his parents. He appeared happy enough, wearing a big, beaming smile, but his eyes held more than a tinge of sadness and knowledge that only someone who'd suffered would have.

"Lucky for you I did," he replied, flicking the end of her nose.

Cole held up a photograph and turned it over to check out the date on the back. "Hey, it's me. I must only be about six months old. Oh man, I've gotta take this back to show Millie. Aimee looks just like I did as a baby."

Calum snatched it off him. "Poor kid."

"Here's one of you, Calum about the same age," Jax said, waving the picture in the air.

Calum grimaced. "Well you ain't showing Laurella that one of me. Check out those chubby cheeks."

Dex laughed. "If she sees Cole's, she'll know what you looked like anyway. You're identical twins, in case you've forgotten."

"Oh shit, yeah."

Heat radiated through Nate's chest. *These guys are my family, and they always have been.* The realization caught him off guard, and he sucked in a breath.

"You okay?" Dex asked, squeezing his hand.

He nodded. "All good, Titch."

The fifth box Nate opened contained the shoebox. His breath snagged in his throat as the memories of the night that changed his life came flooding back. He went to remove the lid but found he couldn't.

"Here, you do it," he said, pushing the shoebox across the floor to Jax.

Jax lifted off the lid and peered inside. A smile curved his lips upward as he lifted out a stack of Christmas and birthday cards. He passed them around, and they all took their time to open the cards and read the greeting.

"That's it," Nate said when Jax picked up the right envelope.

Jax withdrew the card and then opened it out. The letter fluttered to the floor. He opened the paper as though it was the most precious piece of parchment. He unfolded it and scanned the first page, his eyes moving over the words. When he'd finished with the top sheet, he began reading the second one. From Nate's memory, that was Mom's original letter which his sperm donor had returned for some reason. Maybe it was too painful for him because he'd actually loved them both and was trying to cut ties as a way of coping. Or maybe he was an unfeeling bastard who found it easy to compartmentalize, and once he'd accepted his affair was over, had quickly moved on.

"Well," Calum said. "What's it say?"

Jax raised his head. Nate could only remember one other time when his eldest brother had looked so somber, and that was the morning after their parents' car crash. He'd sat them all down and given them the worst possible news in his calm, stoic manner that they'd all come to rely on.

Jax passed the letter to Calum, and he and Cole read it.

"Are there any other letters?" Jax asked Nate

"I don't know. I didn't get past that one."

"I need to see if I can find any more," Jax said, his face pinched as though in pain. "I totally get it if you don't want anything to do with this, but I have to try to understand what was going on with Mom. Why she risked her marriage to Dad, and her relationship with all of us. I'm guessing your birth father must have meant a lot to her. There's a huge amount of pain in her words when she wrote to break things off. If you want to go, I'll understand."

"I'm going nowhere," Nate said.

Jax took a breath. "Okay, then let's begin."

They spent the next several hours searching through every single box, but apart from that letter, there was no sign of any other communication between Mom and *him*. Jax closed the final box with a heavy sigh. He stiffly got to his feet and dusted down his jeans.

"That's it then."

"I guess so," Nate said, disappointment surging through him, despite his earlier insistence that he didn't want to know anything about his real father. There must have been a small piece of him that was desperate to learn where he came from, but hurt and pain had prevented him from acknowledging it. Now they'd arrived at a dead end, he really wanted to know.

Jax checked the time. "I'd better get back and relieve Indie. Some husband I've turned out to be."

"We'll come with you," Cole said. "Sorry, bro." He squeezed Nate's shoulder.

"Do you mind if I stay for a while?" Nate asked, and then with a quick look at Dex, "You can go back with them if you'd rather."

"I'm staying," she said, her jaw set in a determined fashion.

"No problem," Jax said. He removed his cell from his pocket and tapped at the screen. "I've texted you the code. Just make sure you lock up when you leave."

After they'd gone, Dex stood and wandered around the unit, touching various items as she passed by.

"You want to know, don't you?"

He met her gaze. "I thought I didn't, but yeah. Not that it matters. We don't even have a name. Only an initial. L. Probably stands for fucking Lothario."

"That'd be FL," Dex said with a grin.

Nate stood. He peered inside several boxes that they'd already searched, and then his attention fell on the sideboard. A spike of hope made his insides twist.

"We haven't checked this out," he said, striding over and opening the top drawer. Apart from a couple of pens and some scraps of paper, it was empty. The next one contained an elastic band and an empty plastic box. One by one, he opened the other drawers. Nothing. Incensed when the last one didn't have anything useful in it either, he slammed it shut.

"Goddammit."

He scraped a hand through his hair, annoyed at himself for daring to believe he might find some answers. He was too busy pacing and muttering himself to notice what Dex was up to. The sound of knuckles rapping on wood got his attention.

"What are you doing?"

She glanced over her shoulder with a frown. "When you slammed this drawer before, it sounded different to the others. At first I thought it might be because you shut it so forcefully, but now I'm not so sure."

Nate went to stand beside her. He removed the drawer from its runners and gave it a shake. Nothing seemed untoward. He set it on top of the sideboard and tapped the bottom. Sounded like a normal drawer to him. He removed another and repeated the action. Cocking his head to one side, he knocked on one and then the other. There was a definite difference in sound, although it could be something as simple as minute discrepancies in the raw material.

"See?" Dex said. "They sound different."

Nate glanced around but couldn't see any tools he might be able to use to prise the bottom of the drawer away.

"Here," Dex said, handing him a bobby pin she'd taken from her hair.

He guided it between the side of the drawer and the bottom. It took several attempts, but eventually, the bottom lifted. Nate got his fingernail beneath it and pulled it up. He drew in a sharp breath.

Hidden away from prying eyes were bundles of letters, each one tied with a navy-blue bow. Nate picked them up, immediately recognizing the writing. Every single letter was from *him*.

His knees gave way, and he sank to the floor. Dex joined him, her presence a comfort he couldn't find the words to express.

He dropped the letters in his lap, and then sat there, unmoving. Now he had potential answers within his grasp, he was finding it difficult to begin reading. It felt disrespectful to Mom to read intimate letters from her lover. No doubt she never expected them to be found, otherwise she wouldn't have gone to such lengths to hide them. And for more than twenty-eight years, her secret had remained just that.

"Do you want me to go through them?" Dex asked tentatively.

He found himself nodding.

She picked up a bundle, carefully removed the ribbon, and scanned through the letters. Finding nothing, she put them to one side and moved onto the second bundle and did the same. "From the dates, it looks like this is when he started writing to your mom."

She scanned each one, putting those she'd read to one side while she went on to the next one. By the time she started on the fourth, Nate's curiosity got the better of him.

"What do they say?"

Dex lifted her chin and met his gaze. "Whoever your dad was, Nate, he clearly loved your mom." She passed one over. "Here, see for yourself."

His fingers closed around the aged paper, yellowed around the edges and a little torn in places. The ink was faded, too, but the words were clearly visible.

My darling Rebecca,

As I sit here on my sofa all alone, my arms feel empty without being able to hold you. It's been a long three weeks, and I can't wait until you find a way to see me again. I know it's difficult, but I love and miss you.

I do understand and hear what you said in your last letter. I know it is impossible for us to be together. You have your children to think of, and I have mine. But you mean the world to me. My life is so much fuller since we first met. The longer we are apart, the more I yearn for you.

Please get in touch soon.

Love always,

Your Laurence.

Laurence. His dad's name was Laurence.

Nate picked up the next letter. As painful as it was to read such private and intimate thoughts, he had to carry on. He devoured the next few. All were in a similar theme to the first one, but then, toward the end of the second bundle, he found what he'd really been yearning for but hadn't dared to hope. He sucked in a breath and fixed his gaze on Dex.

"Listen to this."

My darling Rebecca,

Your news has stunned me. I've been sitting here for hours, reading and rereading your last letter. The light has faded, making your words harder to read, yet still I haven't moved.

It's clear to me now why you stopped coming to see me for all those months, but I do wish you'd been able to confide in me. It cuts me deep that you felt the need to deal with this on your own.

Oh, but my love, you've made me ecstatically happy and devastatingly sad. Happy because I now know there will always be a part of you and me in the world, an expression of our love, yet sad because I know I will never be able to tuck in my son at night, or soothe him when he's sick, or sing to him and make him laugh. I will never be able to do all the things a loving father should do, but I respect your decision. You have three other children to think of, and I know it would tear you apart to leave them behind. Jaxon would never let them, or you, go. And I know you love him, too. I don't begrudge you that.

But it hurts, Rebecca, so very much.

Try to include a photograph of Nathan next time you write. And please let me see him, at least once.

My love and adoration, as always,

Your Laurence.

DEX SQUEEZED his arm while he sat there in stunned silence. "Oh, Nate."

His eyes glistened over, and when he looked at Dex, she was all fuzzy. He blinked a few times to clear his vision. "He did love me."

He blindly reached for Dex. She didn't hesitate, flinging herself into his outstretched arms. "Of course he did. How could he not?"

He didn't know why it was so important that this stranger, this *sperm donor* had loved him, but it was. The fact he hadn't been the product of some one-night stand, but what seemed to be a true love affair validated him in a way he hadn't been prepared for. What if his dad was still alive? Would he want to meet him? He clung to Dex for several minutes before letting her go.

"There's still nothing to hint at who he was, though. Knowing his first name was Laurence isn't going to help very much." He got to his feet. "Come on, let's take the rest home. My brothers deserve to be a part of this."

CHAPTER 22

Nate poked his head inside the lounge area which, given it was the middle of the day, only had one or two guests relaxing and sipping coffee. He called over to the bartender, whose name escaped him.

"You seen Jax?"

She pointed to the ceiling. "He's on the top floor. A faucet in the penthouse is leaking."

"Okay, thanks." He looked down at Dex who was chewing her bottom lip, concerned. "Go grab a coffee, Titch. I'll be down shortly."

He jogged upstairs to the penthouse.

"Jax?" he called out.

"In here."

Nate wandered into the bathroom and spotted Jax lying underneath the sink.

"You were at the lockup a while," Jax said, but before Nate could answer, he added, "Pass me that wrench."

Nate did as he asked, repressing the urge to blurt out what he'd found. He perched on the edge of the bath. "You gonna be long?"

"Five minutes," came the reply. "Why?"

"I found some more letters at the lockup, after you'd gone."

The wrench hit the floor, and Jax wriggled out from under the sink. He wiped his hands on a cloth. "You did?"

"In the sideboard."

"That's impossible," Jax said. "Apart from a few miscellaneous items, the sideboard was empty."

Nate shook his head. "One of the drawers had a false bottom."

Jax's eyes widened. "What?"

Nate twisted his lips. "Mom really wanted to keep those letters secret. What I can't figure out is why, when she took so much care to keep them from prying eyes, she carelessly left that one in a shoebox."

Jax pulled a knee to his chest and rested his arm over it. "I doubt we'll ever know. Did you learn anything new from the letters?"

Nate nodded. "I know my dad's name was Laurence."

Jax frowned. "Laurence?"

"Yeah, why? Does the name sound familiar?"

Jax held out his hand. "Is there a surname?"

Nate shook his head. "Although we didn't get through them all. I thought I'd bring them back here so we can look together."

"Can I see the letters?" Jax asked.

Nate handed them over. "I already read these," he said, indicating the first few.

Jax scanned one after the other, passing each one to Nate after he'd finished. He'd almost got through them all when he gasped.

"Oh shit."

"What?" Nate asked, his skin prickling.

"I think I know who your father was."

Nate's eyes widened in shock. "You do?"

Jax passed over one of the letters and tapped the paper. "Laurence Monroe."

Nate frowned, confused. "Should that name mean something to me?"

"Laurence Monroe was the name of Indie's father."

Nate's head jerked back. "Fuck."

"My thoughts exactly."

Nate blew out a slow breath as the pieces of the puzzle fell into place. "That's why Dad went after him."

Jax nodded. "And why Indie's brother, your half brother, was so intent on getting revenge on this family."

Half brother and a half sister. Jesus. "Which is how you met Indie."

Jax briefly grinned. "We were destined to meet."

Nate swept a hand over his face. "What a fuck-up. How do we tell her?"

"Tactfully." Jax got to his feet with a heavy sigh. He put his hand on Nate's shoulder. "This must be a hell of a shock to you, too. You okay?"

Nate shook his head. "Honestly, I'm not sure. It's going to take some coming to terms with, but I reckon it'll be worse for Indie."

Jax and Nate walked downstairs, his stomach hurtling to the floor the second they entered the basement. His eyes locked on Dex's. She raised an eyebrow. He shook his head.

Indie was busy in the kitchen, making lunch. She glanced up and grinned. "I guessed you'd come running as soon as you smelled food."

Jax didn't return her smile. He looked as sick as Nate felt. None of them knew how Indie would react. Hell, he couldn't get his head around the fact that his half brother's wife was also his half sister.

"Babe, come and sit down for a minute."

"Let me just finish this," she said. "Two ticks."

"No." Jax's response came out short and sharp.

Indie frowned, her eyes darting between Jax, Nate, and Dex. "What's going on?"

Jax walked over to her, took her gently by the elbow, and propelled her toward the sofa. "We need to talk to you."

Her tongue dampened her lips. "Jax, you're scaring me. What's going on?"

He settled her on the sofa, taking her hand in his. "As you know, we went to the storage unit today, and, well, Nate found something that affects you."

She touched the base of her neck. Her fingers held a slight tremor. "What?"

Jax handed her the letter. "You'd better read this."

Nate gripped Dex's shoulder, and her hand came up and covered his as Indie scanned the letter that was about to blow her life apart. After she'd finished reading, she went very still.

"Indie?" Jax said when several seconds scraped by without her saying a word.

Indie folded the piece of paper over and leaned forward to set it on the coffee table in front of her. "Finally, I understand," she said quietly, lifting her eyes to Jax's. "Why your dad went after mine." She turned her eyes on Nate. "Ours."

Dex gasped as she caught on. She squeezed his hand even tighter.

"Indie—" Jax said.

"Can you give me a few minutes?" Indie said, cutting Jax off. "I need a moment to myself." She got to her feet and went to leave, but as she passed Nate from his position behind the sofa, she paused. "I won't be long. Then we'll talk." And with a quick sweep of her hand down his arm, she gracefully walked into her and Jax's room.

"Shit," Jax said, raking a hand through his hair.

Nate sank onto the sofa beside Dex. "I should have left those letters where they belong. In the past. I shouldn't have told you what I'd found."

"No," Jax said. "You did the right thing. We've had enough secrets in this family."

The three of them fell into silence. Dex propped up her head on Nate's shoulder, and he gently caressed her inner thigh while they waited for Indie to return.

Within five minutes, she was back, her spine erect, a determined set to her jaw that Nate couldn't read. He simply didn't know her well enough to second-guess her mindset. He hadn't bothered getting to know any of his brothers' significant others, being too wrapped up in his own misery. Except now, Indie meant a whole lot more to Nate than simply being Jax's wife.

Jax rose to greet her. She gave him a reassuring smile and pressed a kiss to his cheek. "I wonder if you wouldn't mind taking Dex upstairs. I'd like to talk to Nate alone."

Dex immediately got to her feet, leaving him feeling cold and exposed. He wasn't averse to holding his own if Indie's reaction became contentious, but it kinda felt like kicking someone when they were down.

Indie crossed over to the kitchen and returned with a bottle of beer for him and a glass of wine for herself. He took a swig and waited for her to say something. It seemed like the right thing to do.

"I don't normally drink before six, but today isn't exactly normal, right?"

"Definitely not."

Her eyes searched his face as though looking for some similarity. He guessed that because he found himself doing exactly the same.

"How do you feel?" she said, surprising the hell out of him. He hadn't expected that to be her first question. He gave it due consideration and then shrugged.

"I'm not sure. I've known I was the by-product of Mom's affair for years, yet I'd never given a shit about finding out who fathered me."

"And now you know, how do you feel?"

He tilted his head to one side, ignoring her comment. "How are *you* feeling?"

She pulled in her lips. "I'm not going to lie. It's a hell of a shock, but, you know, I'm a little bit excited, too. When Dad died, and then Phil, well…" She drifted off, her gaze focused on the wall behind him. She gave a brief head shake. "I thought I was alone in the world. I mean, I've got Jax, of course, but no blood relatives that I'm aware of." Her smile started out small, but soon she was beaming. "And now I have. I've got a brother."

"Half brother," he corrected, then immediately wanted to kick himself for being a dick.

Indie didn't break stride, though. She just smiled at him.

"Half brother… who's an ass." She threw back her head and laughed. It was impossible not to join in. "I know we've never been close, and I don't expect us to all of a sudden be texting or speaking on the phone every day, but maybe, over time, we could build some sort of a relationship that's about more than me being married to your brother."

"I'd like that," Nate found himself saying. "I never told you, but you made a really beautiful bride, Indie. I'm so glad I was there to share your special day."

She hugged him. "You're different, Nate, and I don't mean because of all this stuff with Dad. You've been different this whole visit. Your face isn't quite as hard and bitter."

Nate gave her a crooked grin. "You can probably thank Dex, although if you tell her I said that, I will disown you."

Indie made a cross against her heart. "Your secret is safe with me." She lifted her wineglass to her lips and took a sip. "You know, before Dad lost everything, he was such a wonderful father. The man in those letters, that's the man I prefer to remember. Loving, kind, funny. I'm not sure whether it was losing your mom that made him so angry and bitter, or whether it was your dad's revenge that took it's toll, but please don't think badly of him."

Nate wasn't sure whether he had it within him to be so magnanimous or forgiving, but one thing was certain: the pain and anger Laurence Monroe had carried around had, in the end, destroyed his family. Nate would *not* be that man.

"Nor of Phil," Indie continued. "He was your half brother, too. And despite what you might think, especially after what he tried to do to Jax, he wasn't a bad person, just misguided."

Nate nodded but remained silent. He wasn't sure he had it in him to be as charitable to the guy who'd almost got Jax killed.

"If you want to know anything about Dad or Phil at any time, please just ask me."

"Thanks. I will," Nate said.

She gave his hand a squeeze. "There's no rush."

"I'm sorry about what my dad did to your dad. Our dad." He chuckled. "Shit, this is gonna get real confusing."

She smiled with him. "I've always believed the real father is the one who brings up a child. Cares for them when they're sick, reads them stories at night. Cleans their scraped knees when they fall. That's what your dad did for you. And as for what went on between our fathers, well," she shrugged, "there's nothing to be done about the past. In a way, I'm relieved, because ever since Phil talked me into his stupid revenge plan, I've spent years desperately wanting to know the reason why your dad hated mine so much. Now I have the answer. I don't think Dad deserved what your father did to him. It takes two people to have an affair, but I'm guessing he loved your mom so much, he was consumed with hatred and jealousy."

"Yeah, and I was a permanent reminder of her betrayal."

"Yet he chose to stay with her and bring you up as his own. That shows the strength of his love. We all make mistakes, Nate. Christ knows I've made tons, not to mention one that almost got Jax killed and resulted in Phil's death. I'm just glad the bad shit stopped with our parents, and we can find a way to move into the future together."

Nate got to his feet and stuck out his elbow. "Come on, sis. Let's go put Jax out of his misery."

They found Jax and Dex in the lounge area, along with Calum and Cole who Jax must have called. Nate and Indie took a seat.

"You okay?" Jax asked them both, his hand reaching for Indie's.

Nate did the same with Dex, her warm skin grounding him. "Yeah, we're good." He turned to the twins. "Jax caught you up?"

"Yep," Calum said. "Do me a favor, bro. Don't ever ask me to draw your family tree."

"You are such an ass," Cole said, rolling his eyes at his twin.

"I'm sorry," Nate said, looking at each of his brothers in turn. "I wish I'd had the courage to tell you years ago, but I was so damned hurt, so angry at Dad and furious with Mom, so scared of losing you, even though I kept pushing you away."

"It's in the past, Nate," Jax said. "Don't keep beating yourself up over something that wasn't your fault."

He bit down on his lip. "I hope I haven't ruined your memory of Mom."

"Mom was human, Nate," Cole said. "That's all. You haven't ruined anything. She just happened to love two different men. She put all of us first, and that makes her pretty damned special in my book."

"Mine, too," Calum said.

"And mine," Jax said.

Dex moved closer. "You know what this is telling you?" she murmured.

Nate looked down at her. "No."

She grinned. "That I am *always* right."

DEX WAVED MADLY as Nate propelled her through security, his family eventually disappearing from view. When they got airside, she let out a deeply satisfied sigh.

"I've had the best time."

He curved an arm around her waist and kissed her temple as they set off for the first-class lounge. "We can come back soon."

She gave him a crooked smile. "What a difference a few days makes."

"Yeah, yeah," he said, rolling his eyes. "You've had your money's worth, Titch. Time to drop the smug attitude."

She tapped her forefinger against her bottom lip. "Hmm, I reckon I can get a few more days out of it yet."

They found a seat close to the window where they could watch the planes taxiing to the runway. Dex went to sit in a chair, but Nate caught her arm and tugged her down beside him. He tucked a lock of hair behind her ear, then caressed her lobe, which sent a shiver of delight creeping down her spine.

"I want to say thank you."

Her eyebrows almost disappeared into her hairline. "Apologies and thank you's." She glanced around theatrically. "Who are you, and what have you done with Nate Brook?"

A glimmer of a smile briefly danced on his lips, but it didn't break into a full-on grin at her teasing.

"I owe you everything. If it weren't for you, I'd still be all bitter and twisted inside, mourning the things I'd lost. But you pushed and pushed. You wouldn't give up, even when I said some pretty horrible things and treated you so very badly. Because of your tenacity, my little Dex, instead of losing it all, of destroying my family, I now have everything I ever wished for. I've rediscovered a closeness with my brothers that was smashed into smithereens seven years ago, and I've gained a sister, too." He bent his head and picked up her hand, his thumb rubbing gently across her knuckles. "And I have you."

She held her breath, her gaze fixed on watching him caress her skin. His head came up.

"I know we rushed into this thing so quickly, and I don't regret it for a moment, but after we get home, I want to take time to get to know you without the shadow of my secret looming over us.

Romantic walks along the beach at sunset, picnics in the park, bike rides—with cooter-safe saddles." He grinned, and so did she. "I want to know every single thing about you."

Bringing his hand to her face, she pressed it against her cheek. "Promise me something?"

"Anything."

"If you get lost inside your head again, talk to me. Don't keep things all bottled up inside. Let me help give you some perspective. We can fight and argue. Hell, I hope we do because I kinda like the making up part, but please don't keep things from me. Don't shut me out - that hurts most of all."

He blinked. "I promise."

EPILOGUE

Four Months Later

Dex closed the door to Bernard's office, unable to resist sticking up two fingers. Not that he'd see her, but still... she felt a shit load better. He'd been in a foul mood all week, and she couldn't wait for the clock to tick over to five p.m. so she could get the hell out of there. Nate had promised her a weekend to remember, and she hoped that started and ended in his bed.

She filed away some emails and marked a few for Bernard's attention when he'd gotten over his snit. With little to occupy the rest of her day, she flicked aimlessly through a celebrity magazine, pausing when she came across a picture of her and Nate. It still shocked her every time she spotted herself in the press, but it was something she'd had to get used to. In a way she found it comforting, because the only girl Nate was ever photographed with was herself. Despite what those two assholes had been gossiping about the night she'd gone to the set with Nate, he'd never once given her any cause for concern.

She was about to give the plants a quick watering to see them over the next two days when the elevator pinged to signal someone's arrival. She groaned. *Please don't let this be one of Bernard's clients hoping to see him without an appointment.*

Her head came up in time to see Nate strolling down the hallway. Her breath caught on an inhale. God, he totally did it for her. She never got sick of the sight of him. He was dressed in a pair of black fitted pants and a white shirt, open at the neck with the sleeves rolled up, revealing his strong, tanned forearms. Almost a year had passed since she'd first watched him come toward her a week after she'd started the job as Bernard's personal assistant. She'd spent six months drooling over him before that fateful day a few months earlier when his actions had caused Bernard to fire her, sending their relationship spiraling in a direction she couldn't have imagined in her wildest dreams.

He plunked a bag down at her feet and bent over to give her a kiss.

"Get changed, Titch. I'm taking you somewhere special."

She glanced at the clock. "I've still got thirty minutes to go."

"No, you haven't." He took her by the arm and pulled her upright. Pointing his chin at the bag he said, "Dressed. Now."

Excitement buzzed through her. As much as she was a feisty, independent woman, she secretly loved it when Nate went all alpha male. She unzipped the bag and frowned at the contents. She took out a gorgeous ivory dress that had somehow remained uncreased.

"This isn't mine."

"It is now, as is everything else in there."

She narrowed her eyes and then delved back inside the bag. She spotted a pair of ivory pumps, her makeup bag, a jade-green necklace with matching earrings—and a couple of straps of material that, she guessed, was supposed to pass for a bra and panties.

"Why do I need all this?"

He rolled his eyes. "I told you. I'm taking you somewhere special."

"Nate," she said in a tone meant to chastise. "You know I hate those pretentious places."

"Who said it was a pretentious place?"

"Well, if you were taking me to a diner, I'd hardly need this get-up, now would I?"

Nate made a frustrated noise. "Fuck's sake, Titch. Just get dressed."

She laid the dress over her arm, picked up the bag and, sticking her tongue out at him, swanned off to the restroom. She returned a half hour later to find Nate sitting in her chair, his feet up on her desk, and Bernard looming over him, his eyes bulging in response to something Nate had said. As she got closer, they both looked in her direction. Bernard, furious. Nate, mischievous. He unfolded his tall frame, got to his feet, and slid his gaze over her. She actually felt her body temperature increase.

"Bernard's given you a week of vacation time, Titch," Nate said with a wink that Bernard didn't see. "Isn't that good of him?"

Dex's eyes widened. "I haven't got a vacation planned."

"Sure you have," Nate said as he came toward her, snatching up her purse on the way. He took the bag from her hand and brushed a kiss against her temple. "Ready?"

Mute, she simply nodded.

"She'll see you in a week, Bernard," Nate said with more than a hint of glee in his tone. "Unless I manage to persuade her to jack in this shitty little job before then."

His hand clasped her elbow, and he steered her toward the elevator, leaving an apoplectic Bernard behind them.

"What have you done?" Dex asked, giggling as the elevator doors closed and Nate pressed the button for the lobby.

"Fuck him," Nate said. "And I meant what I said about trying to persuade you to leave."

She narrowed her eyes. "What would I do instead?"

He shrugged. "Me."

She giggled again. "You are a bad, bad man, Nate Brook."

"You love it."

"I love you."

He pressed closer, murmuring in her ear, "And I burn for you, Titch."

Nate helped her into his car and then tossed the bag in the trunk. He might not be the type to utter the usual three little words, but it didn't matter, because she was confident in his love.

He climbed in the driver's side and filtered into the traffic.

"Where are we going?"

"You'll see."

Dex pouted and folded her arms. "Spoilsport."

Nate didn't react, so she settled back in her seat and waited for his special place to be revealed. After what seemed like an age but, in reality, wasn't very long at all, Nate pulled off the highway and parked up in front of one of the best hotels in LA.

"What are we doing here?" she asked as they got out of the car and Nate tossed his keys to the valet.

Nate ignored her. He linked their fingers together and led her inside the hotel. He crossed the lobby and headed toward the conference rooms at the rear. He paused outside a set of double doors that had The Connaught Suite embossed in gold over the door.

"Do me a favor, Titch. Think before you speak."

She didn't get a chance to respond with "What the fuck does that mean?" because Nate opened the doors.

Dex's mouth fell into a perfect "O" shape as she was greeted by a roomful of people who all began clapping when they spotted her and Nate standing in the doorway. Nate's brothers and their partners were sitting inside, along with her high school friends from back home in Wisconsin that she hadn't seen since she'd moved to Los Angeles. Elva, her husband, and the kids were in the front row, their faces shining with happiness. Then her gaze fell on

Mom, sitting in a wheelchair at the end of a row of chairs, a bemused but excited expression on her face. There wasn't any recognition in her eyes, but for once, Dex's heart didn't clench in pain.

She turned around to question Nate about what the hell was going on, but instead of finding him standing beside her, he was bending down on one knee, holding out a diamond the size of her fist on the palm of his hand.

"I'm so sorry to spring this on you, Titch, but I was worried if I asked you in private, you might say no, and I couldn't risk that. So, selfish bastard that I am, I thought I'd put you in a difficult position." He cleared his throat while she continued to stare at him, her mouth flapping like a fish tossed on to the quayside. "You set me on fire from the moment you yelled at me across the street. Every night since, I've yearned for you, and only you. I don't deserve you, but if you let me, I will spend every single day of the rest of my life earning your love. I know I said I wasn't the marrying type, but you, Titch, my everything, you changed all that. So, in front of all these people, Dexter Nolan, will you marry me?"

Hot tears rushed to her eyes as she was drowned in a rush of emotion so strong it pushed all the air from her lungs. She sank to her knees, fisted her hands in his shirt, and pulled him to her.

"Where do I sign?"

* * *

Thanks so much for reading!

Have you discovered the Winning Ace series yet? Take one hot, rich, tennis ace, add a journalist ready for her big break, throw in a gigantic secret and kaboom! You have a series that'll keep you up long past bedtime.

Download Winning Ace, or binge-read the entire Boxset now.

FEEL LIKE A REAL TEARJERKER? Pick up your copy of My Gift To You, or read for FREE if you're a kindle unlimited subscriber

Like hot billionaires? Then the Irresistibly Mine duet is right up your street.

FROM ME TO YOU

Well, here we are, at the end of the Brook Brothers story. Thank you so much for reading. I really appreciate each and every one of you. I do hope you enjoyed getting to know the 'real' Nate - and with any luck, my beloved youngest Brook Brother can finally lay his demons to rest.

This isn't the last you've seen of Jax, Calum, Cole, and Nate though. I'm planning two spin-off novels. One will be Draven's story - the darkness is really going to come out in that one - and the other Zane's, Calum's best friend. I'm really looking forward to writing their stories. Draven constantly mutters at me. Who knows, he might even reveal his Christian name in that book… maybe LOL. He's resisting, but I'm going to try my best to persuade him.

To be kept up to date, and to share in exclusive excerpts and early cover reveals, be sure to sign up to my reader group (if you like email) or my facebook group, Tracie's Racy Aces (if you don't).

Would you consider helping other readers decide if this is the right book for them by leaving a short rating on Amazon? They really help readers discover new books.

Like an author - leave a review.

Reviews really help readers discover new books, as well as putting a great big smile on my face!

You can share your thoughts on Amazon, Goodreads, or on Bookbub, or feel free to contact me directly.

Why not follow me on Amazon to be alerted when I have a new release out. Alternatively, you can also follow me on Bookbub and those kind folks will also let you know there's a new book for you to discover.

BOOKS BY TRACIE DELANEY

The Winning Ace Series

Cash - A Winning Ace Short Story

Winning Ace

Losing Game

Grand Slam

Winning Ace Boxset

Mismatch

Break Point - A Winning Ace Novella

Stand-alone

My Gift To You

The Brook Brothers Series

The Blame Game

Against All Odds

His To Protect

Web of Lies

Irresistibly Mine Series

Tempting Christa

Avenging Christa

Full Velocity Series

Friction

Gridlock (coming soon)

Inside Track (coming soon)

ACKNOWLEDGMENTS

I know I'm starting to sound like a broken record, but as ever, I have so many people to thank. What a wonderful team I have. Each and every one of you are so important in getting me to the point where I hit publish. I love, respect, and adore you all.

In no particular order….

To my wonderful hubs for not complaining when I disappear for hours at a time, locked in my study while I bash away at my keyboard, and for the endless supply of coffee. You still make the best coffee I've ever tasted.

To Louise. My Rock. My friend and confidante. My amazing PA. The person I turn to for a giggle when I'm flailing about desperately, knowing that you'll pull an outrageous comment out of the hat that will have me doubled over laughing. You rock xxx

To my critique partner, Incy. When you sent the marked up MS of Web of Lies and there were three chapters where you barely made a note, I knew, I just *knew*, I had the story right and, even more importantly, I'd hit the right *emotional* level. Even so, you still made me work my balls off (not that I have balls, but if I did, they'd be worked to mush!) Thank you for pushing me so hard. Mwah.

To my alpha reader, Allison. I don't know how you do it, but your attention to detail, your ability to point out where something doesn't feel right, your skill in finding those consistency errors… so annoyingly brilliant! I'm so glad you loved Nate and Dex's story. And THANK YOU for one of the best lines I've ever had the pleasure to include in a book.

To Lexi - what can I say except NATE BELONGS TO YOU! I remember, months ago, sending you an excerpt from the first chapter and you were all "Mine!" and you've never wavered. I'd offer to help you fend off all those others who try to steal him from you, but you do such a good job of defending your corner that there's no point. Enjoy! PS, Send B and Jace now please…. and maybe Kylan (yes, I know I'm greedy!)

To Del. I can't thank you enough for everything you do. The hours and hours you selflessly put into my work, the painstaking line by line checks, and then, after all that, you have to put up with talking me through your suggestions for hours on end! I'm sorry Nate isn't as eco-friendly as you'd like him to be and that Dex doesn't like champagne - what a heathen she is LOL.

To Emmy. Thank you for fixing all my IBP's! Oh, and for reminding me of the many things eyes cannot do… Not to mention pointing out my danglers (no sexual pun intended). I can't help noticing only one 'crutch' mentioned in your edits this time - see, I am a learning computer. Just know that I adore working with you.

To my ARC readers. You guys are amazing! You're my final eyes and ears before my baby is released into the world and I appreciate each and every one of you for giving up your time to read— and point out the odd errors that slip through the net!

And last but most certainly not least, to you, the readers. Thank you for being on this journey with me. It still humbles me to think that my words are being read all over the world.

If you have a couple of minutes, would you consider leaving a short review on Amazon? Reviews really help readers discover new books, and they're particularly important for up and coming authors. You'd be helping more than you know

ABOUT THE AUTHOR

Tracie Delaney realized she was destined to write when, at aged five, she crafted little notes to her parents, each one finished with "The End."

Tracie loves to write steamy contemporary romance books that center around hot men, strong women, and then watch with glee as they battle through real life problems. Of course, there's always a perfect Happy Ever After ending (eventually).

When she isn't writing or sitting around with her head stuck in a book, she can often be found watching The Walking Dead, Game of Thrones or any tennis match involving Roger Federer. Coffee is a regular savior.

You can find Tracie on Facebook, Twitter and Instagram, or, for the latest news, exclusive excerpts and competitions, why not join her reader group.

Tracie currently resides in the North West of England with her amazingly supportive husband and her two crazy Westie puppies, Cooper and Murphy.

Tracie loves to hear from readers. She can be contacted through her website at
www.traciedelaneyauthor.com